Longboat Blues

by
H. Terrell Griffin

authorHOUSE™

1663 LIBERTY DRIVE, SUITE 200
BLOOMINGTON, INDIANA 47403
(800) 839-8640
WWW.AUTHORHOUSE.COM

First published by AuthorHouse 09/08/05

ISBN: 1-4208-8412-3 (sc)

Library of Congress Control Number: 2005908152

Printed in the United States of America
Bloomington, Indiana

This book is printed on acid-free paper.

Cover design attributed to Sandy Ingledue/Adman Graphics

Author photograph attributed to Jean Griffin

Dedication

This book is dedicated, with love, to my girls, Jean, Judy and Sarah, and of course, to my boys, Greg, Mike, Chris and Kyle. You are the ones who make my life sing.

Acknowledgments

A book is only as good as its author's story telling ability, with a little help from his friends. I would not have finished this book without the support and suggestions of my wife Jean, and of Vanessa Lee Brice, the world's greatest paralegal, who listened to me ramble about plot and structure, while trying to get me to focus occasionally on my law practice.

Invaluable editing advice came from my Longboat Key friends, Cotty Johnson, Deputy Fire Chief (Retired) Terry and Carol Conover, and Debbie Schroeder. I did not always listen to them, so any mistakes are clearly mine and mine alone.

My good friends Miles Leavitt and Ethna and Christine Lynch should receive some kind of medal for putting up with me all these years, and they are excused for thinking the book I've been talking about for a decade would never be completed. Austin Dwyer left us too soon. How I wish he were here to continue teaching us about courage and life and laughter.

I am indebted to Deb Stowell and Eric Lamboley for sharing their vast knowledge of the marketplace, and for their encouragement while I tried to find my muse.

Prologue

On the night Connie Sanborne died, I was crocked to the gills. There was no cause and effect relation between my drunkenness and her death; they were just random facts bouncing around the universe, and their confluence had no significance whatsoever. But that was the last night I got drunk, and the last night Connie enjoyed on this earth, so perhaps there was some connection after all.

While Connie was being strangled on the next island, I was sleeping off the several bottles of beer I had drunk the evening before. I had been doing that a lot lately, and I knew I had to make some changes. Connie's murder, and the ensuing upheavals on our island paradise, would fix that problem in ways I could not have imagined.

Her death would change a lot of lives, and open little boxes of secrets that we each thought locked for all time. For some, the ripple effect of those opened boxes would roar over us like an enraged tsunami, while for others it would be as a gentle wavelet, barely noticed. We all could have done without the disclosures, but in the end, it may have made us better people. On the eve of Connie's murder, life was good.

Chapter 1

The dying sun dipped into the Gulf of Mexico as I rode my boat south, just off the beach, heading for Longboat Pass and home. The lights in the houses and condos along Anna Maria Island were winking on, as the dark moved from the mainland over the bay, chasing the rapidly disappearing sun. The western sky was red and orange, with the dark smear of a cloud bisecting the face of the sun as it hung just above the horizon, as if testing the water before plunging in. The sea was dead calm, and the only noise was the roar of my outboards and the rush of the water under the hull of my fishing boat.

I had had a good afternoon, fishing about a mile offshore over a reef of used up highway, dumped by the county to attract fish; an artificial reef that on a Thursday afternoon was deserted. I had caught thirty or forty fish, none bigger than my hand, at the expense of as many live shrimp purchased earlier from Annie's bait and tackle, hard by the Cortez bridge.

It was April 15. The winter season was over, and I had deposited my tax return and a check for the IRS in the Longboat Key post office right after breakfast that morning. The bars and restaurants and other commercial establishments had had a successful season, thanks to all the snow birds who flock to these barrier islands just south of Tampa Bay during the winter months. Now the merchants would begin to relax, knowing they had survived another year. Things would slow down until the next northern onslaught began at Christmastime. The locals were able to get back onto the roads and beaches, and could take their boats out without worrying about being killed by a tourist on a rented jet ski. The hot and humid summer was approaching, a time of desultory living on the islands, a time of quiet. We were happy.

As I navigated the swash channel in close to the jetty at the south end of Anna Maria Island and headed under the old drawbridge spanning Longboat Pass, I glanced aft in time to see the sun disappear completely. Within seconds the sea turned black, capped for a moment by the splendor of bright colors, as if the sun had left part of itself spread upon the water. I flipped on my running lights as I slowed for the bridge. I made a hard right turn and ran a hundred yards south along the bridge, searching for the channel around the large shoal that lurked in the sound. I came left and then curving slowly to the right, ran between Jewfish Key and the northern tip of Longboat Key, staying just west of the sand bar, but not close enough to the island to rock the boats moored at the docks of the houses facing the little bay.

I cruised slowly toward Moore's Stonecrab Restaurant, and saw a familiar boat, thirty feet of dazzling go-fast fiberglass, tied to the dock in front. It was time for a beer, I decided, and a little conversation with people I liked. This time of the year there would be a number of locals at the bar, savoring the relative quiet of the off-season.

I idled to the dock, wrapped fore and aft lines around the pilings, cut the engine, the lights and the radio, and walked slowly toward the restaurant. Darkness had descended, and the soft spring night was interrupted by the colored lights strung along the edges of the piers. Dolly, the porpoise who lived under the dock, surfaced and blew quietly at me, wondering, I guess, why I didn't have a fish for her. The lights of the restaurant spilled over the porches of the building, reaching vainly for the black water along the dock. The high whine of an outboard out on the intracoastal competed with the chirping of insects on Jewfish Key which rested nearby, separating Moore's from the main waterway. The faint tinkle of laughter came from the bar overlooking the dock and merged with the rattling of halyards on the two sailboats anchored in the cove upon which the restaurant sat.

This is Florida at its best, I thought. The air was cool, not yet humid, and the little insects known as no-see-ums had not begun to bite. The northerners were all back home, shivering in their decaying cities, and scheming to return to Florida permanently. I hoped they didn't figure it out.

I went up the steps and into the lounge. There was the usual crowd clustered at one short leg of the U shaped bar, and a middle aged tourist couple seated directly across from them. There was a long mirror on one wall, and lighted signs with the logos of the Tampa Bay Buccaneers and Devil Rays on the wall opposite. A large tarpon was mounted on the wall behind the bar, with a fifth of Jack Daniels Black stuck in its mouth. The southern wall consisted of large plate glass windows looking down the bay to the city of Sarasota; one of the best views on the island. Debbie, the fortyish blonde bartender, a fugitive from Ohio winters, was tending bar. As I walked in she was resting her elbows on the bar, leaning over talking to the regulars. She glanced around when she heard the door open, gave me a wave and went quickly to the tourist couple to refresh their drinks.

The regulars consisted of Tom Bishop, who had recently retired after twenty-three years as our local police chief, Dick Bellenger, the dockmaster at a local marina where I had once lived on a boat, Connie Sanborne, the sales manager at one of the key's hotels, Dottie Johanson, a jolly seventy-something widow who ran the local library and knew everybody on the island, and my fishing buddy, Logan Hamilton, whose boat I had seen moored at the dock.

I was a little surprised to see Logan, since his work kept him traveling the country during the week. He would fly out of Sarasota on Monday morning and usually not return until Friday. He was some sort of financial manager, but I had never cared enough to understand exactly what he did for a living. Not that I didn't care about Logan; it was just that nobody on the island ever thought the other guy's line of work was very important. We were much more interested in how people spent their non-working time.

"Get fired, Logan?" I asked, as I pulled up a stool at the corner of the bar.

"Vacation," he said. "I get eight weeks a year now, so I have to spread it out. I called you earlier to see about a little fishing trip."

"Sorry I missed you," I said. "I got up early and went out all by myself. I could have used a hand catching all those fish."

"Miller Lite, Matt?" Debbie called from the vicinity of the beer cooler.

"Sure," I said. "Hey, Chief, you ready for another scotch?"

"Not yet, thanks. What did you catch?"

"Lots of fish," I said.

"Anything edible?" asked Dottie.

"Anything big enough to keep?" asked Deb as she put the cold beer bottle and mug in front of me.

"Not exactly," I said.

Connie, at the end of the bar, was quiet. "Hey Connie," I said, " how you doing?"

"Okay, Matt. Glad the snowbirds are gone." Connie was a tall slender woman in her mid- thirties, with close cropped red hair who laughed a lot. "Looks like you got a little sun today."

The conversation went on like that for an hour or so. Old friends enjoying each other's company, bantering back and forth. Buying each other drinks, knowing that some were keeping count, and would think you cheap if you didn't buy your share. A slow evening on the key. As I look back on it, I can find nothing that would indicate that anyone suspected that all our lives were about to change. If any one of us had known, I wonder what we would have said. How would our conversation have changed if somehow it had been revealed that one of us would never see another sunrise. How would we have handled that quiet cool evening overlooking Sarasota Bay?

At some point Debbie brought out enough hors d'oeuvres for all of us to make a rather unhealthy meal of. All kinds of fried sea food. We ate, and drank, and talked, and enjoyed the last tranquil evening any of us would know for awhile.

Connie left first, around nine o'clock, followed quickly by Dottie and Dick Bellinger. The Chief finished one more scotch and water and went out into the night. At some point earlier in the evening, the tourists had left the bar without anyone noticing. Debbie asked if Logan or I wanted anything else before she closed out the cash register. Taking the hint, we told her goodnight and walked out toward the docks.

I told Logan to call me later in the week if he decided to go fishing. We shook hands, and he clambered down into his boat. He cranked the twin three hundred horse power inboard/outboard engines, waved, and swung away from the dock. He rounded Jewfish Key and with engines roaring headed back north to the marina that stored his boat.

I stood for a minute on the dock, hoping to catch a glimpse of Dolly, but she had apparently gone looking for her supper in the bay. I got into my boat and cast off, heading south toward home. It was such a beautiful night I just idled along, barely making way, the engines softly turning over. There was no moon, but the sky seemed diaphanous, with the bright pinpoints of a billion stars shining through. Ten miles to the south, at the far end of the dark bay, sat the city of Sarasota, splendid in its multicolored lights, their glare fading upward into the emptiness of the night. The channel was marked on either side by slowly flashing red and green lights, providing a sense of gaiety to the black water and white stars. As I passed the Sister Keys on my left, I could hear an occasional cry from the nesting sea birds who live alone there.

About two miles down the bay, I turned into the channel leading to Sleepy Lagoon and my condo. I pulled the boat into my slip, secured it for the night and went home to bed. I was tired from the day on the water and sleepy from the beers I had drunk at Moore's. I brushed my teeth, dropped my clothes into the hamper, and crawled nude between the sheets. My last conscious thought was that the bed side clock read 10:00 o'clock.

Chapter 2

I was up at 6:00 the next morning. The beer from the night before made me a little sluggish, but a handful of cold water in the face and a quick brush of the teeth at least made me coherent. I slipped into a pair of shorts, socks and Reeboks, and walked across the street to the beach. I jogged south, just above the water line, occasionally dodging a wavelet coming bravely a little higher than its brothers. The Gulf on my right was its usual turquoise color, without a ripple to break its smooth face. There were no clouds that morning, and the sun's rays were slipping from behind the island, announcing the arrival of old sol, every Floridian's friend. A squadron of pelicans skimmed the Gulf, fishing for breakfast. A raucous band of gulls was fighting over a dead fish, left by last night's tide. As I neared them, they moved out of my path, squawking their displeasure at me for interrupting their meal. A mile or so out in the Gulf a small fishing boat headed north, its wake cutting through the green water like a surgeon's scalpel. Life was good.

I approached the condominium that marked two miles from my starting point, and turned back north, keeping a steady pace on the hard sand. I was working up a sweat even in the mild April morning. I felt good. The endorphins were kicking in. JAPDIP, I thought, just another perfect day in paradise.

When I got back to my condo the light on my answering machine was blinking. I wondered who would be calling me that early. I hit the button and listened to the message. It was Logan, asking me to call him immediately. The message had come in about fifteen minutes earlier.

I dialed his number, and a voice that wasn't Logan's answered.

"Is this the Hamilton residence?" I asked.

"Yes."

"Is Mr. Hamilton there?"

"He is, but he can't come to the phone right now."

"This is Matt Royal," I said. "He left a message for me a few minutes ago asking that I call."

"Oh hey, Matt. This is Bill Lester. Maybe you'd better come on over here."

Bill Lester was the island's current Chief of Police, and an old friend. "What's up, Bill?" I asked.

"Do Logan and me a favor, Matt, and get your ass over here right now." His voice was pitched low, urgent.

"Do I have time for a shower?" I asked.

"No." He hung up.

Logan lived in a beach front condominium complex of about 40 units, all facing the Gulf. The parking lot was on the north side of the building, crammed between Logan's building and the next complex down the line. There were three Longboat Key Police cars, two Manatee County Sheriff's cars, a Longboat Key Fire Department ambulance and the Manatee Sheriff's crime scene van parked haphazardly in the lot. A Longboat Key cop I knew was talking to a uniformed deputy at the entrance off Gulf of Mexico Drive. The cop recognized me and waved me into a parking place. I got out of my Explorer and walked back toward the building. I stopped and asked the cop what was going on.

"Let the Chief tell you, Matt. He's waiting in Logan's apartment."

"Logan?" I asked, dreading the answer.

"Logan is okay. He's with the Chief."

I let out a breath I did not know I'd been holding. I was relieved that Logan was okay, but still alarmed by the large police presence and the urgency in the Chief's voice over the telephone.

I took the elevator to the fourth floor. An outside walkway ran the length of the building with the apartment doors opening onto it. I'd been here many times, drunk and sober, but I had never seen the place crawling with cops before. There was a deputy at the elevator when I got off, who asked if I were Matt Royal. I assured him that I was, and he said to go on down to Logan's condo. At the door to Logan's home was another Longboat policeman who waved me in, murmuring softly, "Glad you're here, Matt."

Everything in Logan's condo was white. The walls and ceiling, the carpet, and the leather furniture. Even the tables and lamps were white wicker.

One end of the living room was all glass, with sliding doors leading to a balcony overlooking the Gulf. The effect of entering the white room and seeing the green Gulf through the wall of glass was startling to the uninitiated. Logan had once told me that he was not particularly enamored of all the white, but a decorator he once kept company with had talked him into it while he was trying to talk her into his bed. Each was ultimately successful, but Logan was disappointed in both results. He ended up with a white living room and a memory of what he cheerfully described as the world's worst piece of ass.

There was a yellow tape with black letters spelling out "Police Lines, Do No Cross" tacked across the front door of the condo. Two men wearing paper covers over their shoes were vacuuming the white rug. On the balcony, through the glass wall, overlooking the early morning placidity of the Gulf, lay a lump covered with a white bed sheet. A paramedic leaned against the balcony rail smoking a cigarette, his box of rescue equipment at his feet. I knew there was a body under that sheet, and for a moment I had the wild thought that maybe Logan's decorator had met a fitting end in this white sarcophagus.

Logan was sitting at a dining table just inside the door, facing Chief Lester who sat across the table. Logan was wearing a pair of shorts and a T shirt with the logo of the Suncoast Offshore Grand Prix, a boat race held every July in our waters. His hair had not seen a comb that morning, and his eyes were red rimmed. He looked tired and about ten years older that he had the night before at Moore's.

The chief was new to the job, having taken over from the retiring chief six months before. Bill Lester, thirty-seven years old, had spent three years in the Army Military Police Corps and sixteen years on the Longboat Key Police Department, rising through the ranks until he was second in command. When Tom Bishop retired, Bill was the logical and popular choice to succeed him. I had known Bill for years, and he had often joined Logan and me on snook fishing trips in Terra Ceia bay.

Bill had put on a little weight lately and, while he was not fat, he would have to be careful. His round face was punctuated by a small, neatly trimmed mustache that was as black as his hair. He was wearing a pair of beige dockers, a flowery shirt and boat shoes over a pair of argyle socks. On occasion I accused him of dressing the part of an island police chief as if he were waiting for the Hollywood writers to swoop down and make a movie about him. He always just grinned.

Leaning against the wall next to the chief was a large man of about fifty. He had a head full of hair, with the blonde of his youth losing to the gray of middle age. His face was ruddy, the face of a heavy drinker, with the little capillaries on the cheeks bursting into tiny veins of red. He was wearing a pair of brown slacks, a white short sleeve dress shirt and a solid brown knit tie. There was a tie tack of miniature handcuffs holding the tie ends together.

"Matt," the chief said, "Come on in. The techs have cleared this area. Just don't go any further. This is Detective John Banion of Manatee County."

Banion did not move to shake hands. I stood in place, looked at Banion and then at Logan. "What's going on Logan?"

"It's Connie, Matt. Under the sheet. She's dead," he said in a strained voice.

It was a blow to the stomach that took my breath away. Not possible, my mind screamed. Not Connie. "How?" I asked.

"We know how," Banion said, stepping closer to me. "We want to know who, but I think we've got that one answered, too." The stench of day old booze and cigarettes emanated from the detective, assailing my nose and churning my stomach. I stepped back.

"What's going on, Bill?" I asked.

"Logan called 911 at 6:05 this morning and said there was a body on his balcony. The call was routed to us because it's in our jurisdiction. Dave Beemer was the shift commander on the midnight and was heading back to the station to get ready to check out, when he got the call. He was only about two minutes from here and came right up. He knows Logan and recognized the dead woman as Connie and called me on my cell phone. I was on my way in to work and came right here. Manatee or Sarasota always works our homicides, so Banion was called in. Apparently, Logan called you just before I got here. He said he wouldn't talk to us until you were here."

"Logan?" I said, turning to him.

"I figured if there was a dead woman in my house I would be a logical suspect, and I didn't want to say anything without my lawyer being here."

"Logan," I said, "I'm not a lawyer anymore."

"You're still a member of the bar."

"A retired member of the bar," I said.

"I want you to represent me, Matt."

Chapter 3

The Longboat Key Police Department is small, and crime is almost unheard of on the island. There is the occasional theft from an unlocked car, but most of the calls to the police are about snakes in pools or cats in trees. Other than well heeled tourists, whom the town welcomes, strangers rarely visit the island.

In the 1950's Manatee County decided to put a public beach on Longboat Key. Longboaters, not wanting the hordes of people and traffic that strain the roads on neighboring islands, voted to incorporate a town that would include the entire island. Once the island had its own town government, the county government would have to have permission from the town to put in public facilities.

Longboat Key is about ten miles long and one-quarter mile wide at its widest. The county line runs across the island at its center, with Manatee County to the north and Sarasota County to the south. While not unheard of, it is unusual to have one city situated in two counties. The system, however, works pretty well.

The Longboat Key police have jurisdiction over the whole island, but because of its small size and inexperience with major crimes, from time to time the counties' Sheriff's offices are called upon to render assistance with their more sophisticated evidence gathering equipment and technicians as well as detectives. Longboat Key police, however, were in control, and the Sheriff's deputies reported to Bill Lester.

Logan's condo was about ten feet north of the county line, and was therefore within the jurisdiction of Manatee County as well as the Town of Longboat Key.

I had practiced law in Orlando and came to hate the mess that had once been an honorable profession. I had tried a lot of cases in my career,

11

and I did not think I had the energy to ever try another one. I found my-self dreading trial or anything else to do with the process. Then disaster. My wife left me. I resigned from the firm, sold the house in Orlando, and moved onto my boat moored at a Longboat Key marina. I became a drunk, or close to it, and my life was saved by a good man. I enjoyed the quieter life of the key, and had not once missed the practice of law. Life was one long vacation, and if I ever started thinking about getting back into the rat race, I knew all I had to do was go to the courthouse and sit in on a trial. So far I hadn't even had to do that. The thought of trying another case brought back all the dislike I had developed for the system. I sure as hell wasn't going to get involved in a murder trial defending a friend. But, I didn't think now was the time to tell that to Logan.

"Logan," I said, "Why don't you let me talk to these guys alone for a minute."

"Sure thing, Matt." Logan walked down to the bench by the elevator and sat down.

"What happened, Bill?" I asked the chief.

"The broad was strangled," Banion said.

"Connie, Detective," I said. "Her name was Connie Sanborne, and she was the sales manager at the Golden Beach Inn. She had a degree from Northwestern University, and an ex-husband who pounded on her regularly, until she screwed up the courage to run to a battered woman's shelter. She put her life back together, one piece at a time, and then she moved down here and started a new life. She was bright and pretty and a good friend. She was a lot of things Detective, but she sure as hell wasn't a broad. You keep that in mind."

"Fuck you, Counselor." Banion turned and walked away.

"Nice guy," I said.

"He's pretty rough," said the chief, "but he's a good detective and closes a lot of cases."

"I guess that's why the Sheriff puts up with him."

"You got it. Look, it appears that Connie was strangled. There's no blood and her throat is bruised. We'll know a lot more after the techs are done and the docs get the autopsy results in. Right now, we're going with strangulation as the cause of death."

"Are you going to arrest anybody?"

"If you mean Logan, the answer is no. At least not yet. But I'd like his word that he'll stick around town for the next few days."

"I'll talk to him. He looks kind of ragged. How about if I take him back to my place for now?"

"Sure, but he can't take anything out of the apartment. It's still a crime scene."

"We'll get by. Call me if you need us."

"What happened, Logan?" We were sitting in my living room overlooking Sarasota Bay. The sun was high and the water was smooth as a mirror. A small houseboat was chugging slowly southward, barely making a wake. The large white pelicans that came from the north to winter with us were floating near the channel, resting up, I suppose, for their journey home. I had made coffee and fed Logan a couple of half stale donuts. He seemed to be feeling better.

Logan was 5'10" and getting a little chubby. His belly hung over his belt like a small melon, not too big, but obvious. His hair was sparse now, and what was left was turning from brown to gray. A few strands were combed over the bald pate in a last ditch effort to halt the creeping erosion. He was from Massachusetts, and if you closed your eyes when he talked, you heard John Kennedy.

"I don't know, Matt. I got up to get a drink of water from the refrigerator, and it was just light enough to see Connie on the balcony. I thought at first that she was sleeping out there, but when I opened the door I knew she was dead. I saw a lot of dead people in Nam, so I knew. I shut the door and called 911."

"Do you have any idea what she was doing in your condo?"

"No, but you know we had a thing going, didn't you?"

"What kind of thing?"

"I guess we were what you might call fuck buddies. For the past year or so we'd get together now and then for sex. Just two single people taking the edge off. It wasn't love or anything, although you know I liked her a lot. We all did. Anyway, sometimes she'd just come over and surprise me. I didn't particularly like her doing that, but it didn't happen often, and I didn't want to hurt her feelings."

"Did she have a key to your place?"

"Yeah, but so do half the people on the island."

That was true. Logan was generous, and since he was gone a lot on business, he let friends use his place if they needed to sleep visiting relatives or for whatever reason. I had used his condo for a couple of nights the month before while mine was being painted. He had told me to keep the key in case I needed it again.

"Was she planning to come by last night?" I asked.

"Not to my knowledge."

"What time did you get home?"

"Late, around 2:00 this morning."

"Did you notice anything out of the ordinary when you came in?"

"I was drunker than a hoot owl, Matt. I went to Bridge Street after I left you last night."

Bridge Street was in Bradenton Beach on Anna Maria Island near the marina that stored Logan's boat. It had three or four rowdy bars frequented by tourists and commercial fishermen from Cortez across the bay. Logan would go down there sometimes to listen to the local rock bands that played the bars. He always had a first class hangover the next day.

"Could you have run into Connie and not remembered it?" I asked.

"My memory's a little spotty about last night, but I would remember if I had seen Connie. I spent most of the evening talking to an old army buddy I ran into. He left, and I had one more drink and drove home."

"I wonder if she was killed in your condo or brought there afterwards. Do you think you would have heard someone coming in after you went to bed?"

"I doubt it. I had a lot of scotch in me. I only got up because I was so thirsty. You know how booze does that to you."

"Maybe we'll know more after the techs and the docs do their things. What about her ex-husband?"

"You mean as the murderer?"

"Is it possible?"

"I guess it's possible, but I don't think she's seen or heard from him for several years. I doubt he even knows she's in Florida."

"Well, we'll let the police sort all that out."

"Do they think I did this, Matt?"

"I don't think Bill Lester does, but that creep Banion seems to think you're the bad guy."

"Will they arrest me?"

"Not on what they've got now. I think they would have to turn up some pretty good evidence that you did it before they could charge you. If the time of death was before you got home, I would guess you're in the clear. If it was somewhere between two and six in the morning you won't have an alibi, and it might be hard to convince them that Connie was murdered in your house and you slept through it. But what about a motive? You had no reason to kill her. I don't think you have to worry, but it'll be a few days before we know for sure."

"I'm real tired, Matt. If you don't mind, I think I'll go lie down for awhile."

"Help yourself. If you need anything, holler."

Chapter 4

The loneliest people in the world are the old folks, widows and widowers, who frequent the piano bars of the Gulf coast, looking for friendship. They must wax a little nostalgic at the sight of older couples who have escaped the grim reaper, having a good time in the same bars. They all sing along with the piano player, and she knows most of them because they are the regulars. Sometimes, one of the oldsters will get up and sing a solo. Some of them are surprisingly good; professional entertainers in their other lives in Chicago or Indianapolis or Cincinnati.

I was sitting alone at a table in a bar in a restaurant on Anna Maria Island. The chairs arranged around the piano bar were full of senior citizens, year round residents who were coming out now that the snowbirds had gone home. I knew some of them from previous encounters, and they would nod or wave in my direction as one left and another took the place at the piano bar. Most of them lived off their social security checks in the trailer parks that lined Cortez Road just across the bridge on the mainland. Pearl, the still sexy fifty year old piano player, who could belt out a tune equal to any chanteuse in the world, would call a name and gently tease the oldster who had just arrived, and then break into the favorite song of the new arrival. They ate it up. This was a connection, however tenuous, to other people. Someone knew their names, and cared enough to remember the songs they always requested. The song took them to a happier time, maybe to a young lover when they were all young and had a future.

I was feeling a little sorry for myself, as I do from time to time. For most of my life the present was the greatest time in which to live, but the future always held something better. I had recently come to realize that the best times in my life were past, and while the present is good, it will not change a whole lot. The future was the present, and it would slowly get worse, until I was one of these lonely seniors looking for companionship. Not a happy thought. Maybe this early retirement was not all it was cracked up to be. Can one actually get tired of fishing?

I was mostly concerned about Logan's future. I had been more positive with him than I actually felt. The very fact that Connie's body was found in his condo would make Logan a prime suspect. I didn't think Logan did it. He was by nature a gentle man who had seen all the killing he needed in Viet Nam.

Logan had slept all day, while I sat and read James Lee Burke's latest novel and rigged a new fishing rod. He awoke about six, and we went to Oma's on Anna Maria for pizza and beer. He was still tired and depressed and wanted to go back to bed. I dropped him at my condo and drove back across the Longboat bridge through Bradenton Beach and into Holmes Beach to a restaurant which seemed to change names every year. The food was spotty in quality, but the beer was cold and Pearl was always magnificent. Besides, she always played my favorite song when I walked in.

I was concerned about Logan's request that I represent him. I had vowed so many times never to get back into the rat race that was the practice of law. I had sat in too many deposition rooms, and listened to too many lawyers drone on incessantly with questions that even they didn't think were important. There had been too many sleepless nights worrying about this point or the other that might or might not come up in a case. Trial lawyers seldom sleep soundly.

On the other hand, if I handled only one case, it would not be like the old days of juggling more cases that one lawyer should. I was certainly capable of handling a first degree murder case. I had done it several times in my career and had never lost one. But Logan was a friend, and I was of the opinion that lawyers should no more represent friends and family than surgeons should operate on their friends and family. Yet, if Logan was charged, he would need someone who really believed in him. Did I? I thought so, but I had seen too many clients who first appeared to be something they weren't, and I was always surprised at my naivete when I learned the truth. Clients, like all people, wanted you to think the best of them, and they were not above lying to their lawyer if they thought that was in their best interest.

I really did not know a lot about Logan. He had come to the island about a year before I did. I was aware that he had been a helicopter pilot in Viet Nam, but he didn't talk about it much. I knew that he came from a wealthy Massachusetts family and that his parents were still alive. They had apparently despaired of him in his youth, but a tour in Viet Nam straightened him out, and he went back to college and earned a degree in business from the University of Florida. He had lived in various places in Florida since his graduation, finally settling on the key. He traveled extensively with his company, and it did not matter much where he lived.

I was not really surprised by his revelation that he and Connie had had an affair. Many of us on the key suspected it, and we had gossiped some about it, but never mentioned it to either Logan or Connie. That would have broken the code of the key; the one that tolerated every idiosyncracy, as long as it did not cause problems for anyone else. It was a live and let live philosophy.

The affair would be known to Banion by now. He would have heard the gossip, and he was probably already honing in on Logan as the chief suspect. But then, I had gotten the impression that morning that Banion had already decided that Logan was the guilty party.

"You don't like the entertainment?"

I looked up into the face and bosom of Pearl. She was tall, blonde, buxom and sheathed in a white sequined dress designed to accentuate her positive attributes. Bets had been taken on whether those magnificent mammaries were the result of good genes or a surgeon's skill.

"Hey kid. Sorry, I was about a thousand miles away. Sit down."

She sat. "Isn't it terrible about Connie? God, she must have gotten killed right after she left here. I may have been the last one to see her alive. Well, other than the killer."

"Connie was in here last night?" I asked, stupidly.

"Yeah, until about 11:00. She only stayed maybe an hour."

"Have you talked to the cops yet?"

"Sure. I called Bill Lester as soon as I heard about it. Told him she had been here last night. Some goofball from the county came by and took a recorded statement before I came to work this evening."

"Banion?"

"Yeah. That's his name. A real sourpuss."

"Was Connie with anybody last night?"

"No. She came in alone and sat up at the bar. Asked me to play a couple of old songs, had a couple of drinks and left. I don't think she even talked to anybody."

"Are you sure about the time she left?"

"Pretty sure. I take a break at 11:00, and she left just before that. I was surprised because we usually sit and talk during my breaks when she's in."

"Are you sure about the time she came in?"

"I play for fifty minutes and then take a ten minute break on the hour. I stick to the schedule, because you know what a hardass the owner is. I had already started back from my 10:00 break, so it had to be after 10:10. But not much. I think I was on my first song."

"You're sure she didn't talk to anyone at the bar?"

"Pretty sure. It was quiet last night, and there were only two or three other people here while she was at the bar. Some of the trailer park crowd, but I don't think Connie knew them. They were sitting on the bass end and Connie was all the way around at the treble end. She was real quiet, sorta depressed, if you know what I mean. She usually sings along and talks to everybody. But not last night."

"Did she say anything about where she was going when she left here?"

"No. She just waved and walked out. Unusual for Connie, you know? She's usually real friendly."

"Look, Pearl, if you hear anything about where Connie went after she left here or if anyone saw her, let me know, will you?"

"Sure, Matt, but what the hell is going on?"

"I don't know, but a friend of mine could be in trouble over this."

"Logan?"

"Yeah. Logan."

"That's ridiculous, Matt. Logan wouldn't hurt a flea. And he sure as hell wouldn't have hurt Connie. I think they had something going, you know?"

"What makes you think that?"

"I don't know. You could just tell. They would come in here together sometimes, and they, I don't know, just looked like they had something going. My ten minutes are up Matt. Time to get back. I'll call you if I hear anything."

"Play 'Misty' for me," I said.

"Right, cowboy. See you later."

She played "Y'all Come Back Saloon." My favorite song.

I was up early the next morning, sitting on my balcony drinking coffee. High clouds ambled slowly across the bay. Bright orange streaks splashed their puffy faces, a promise of the arrival of the sun. The air was cool, cooler than the water, and a mist hovered around the mangrove islands, giving them a surreal look, as if they were rising from the bay to meet the day. As the first bright arc of the morning sun crested the horizon, Logan belched. He was standing just inside the open doors to the living room, a cup of coffee in his hand.

"Beautiful, isn't it?" he asked.

"It was until you ruined the mood," I said.

"Sorry about that. Pizza always gives me gas."

"You want to go down to Izzy's for breakfast?"

"Nah. Half the people I know will be there, and I really don't want to face anybody yet."

"What's on the agenda today?" I asked.

"I don't know. I'd like to get back into my condo."

"My guess is that they're going to keep you out for another few days. They'll go over it with a fine tooth comb."

"We could go fishing."

"That we could, my friend, that we could."

We loaded the gear into my boat, stopped by Annie's for bait, and headed to Palma Sola Bay. We spent the whole day there, with a short trip to a waterfront restaurant for lunch, and more beer for the cooler. We didn't catch any fish, but Logan began to relax a little.

Two days later I heard from Chief Lester. He called to say that the medical examiner had finished with Connie, but there didn't seem to be any relatives to claim the body. They had found a small life insurance policy among her effects, and that would about pay for a funeral. The body was at Sand's Funeral Home on Manatee Avenue.

We buried her the next day in a small cemetery near the Manatee River, all the way out near I-75. There were no headstones, just those ground level plaques that the lawn mowers can clear when they cut the perpetual care grass. The cemetery promised to place one on her grave as soon as it came in. It had been ordered from their headquarters in Kansas City. A full service burial corporation, I guess.

There were about twenty people there to see Connie off. The sound of trucks traveling the interstate wafted toward us on the easterly breeze. I could hear the gentle shuffling of feet on the grass as the friends gathered near the open grave. Otherwise, there was quietness there on the flat land of the cemetery; the sun getting hotter now, as Florida's short Spring eased into Summer.

Death had come creeping into our little group on the sun swept island, and plucked one of us, seemingly without reason. None of us understood why it was Connie, but each of us was glad it was not he. I thought about a time, in winter, when I was on the Metroliner between Washington and New York, back in that other life when I was the quintessential lawyer. I was gazing out the window as the partially snow covered landscape rushed by under a low and cloudy sky. We came upon a cemetery, sitting on rolling ground, with large white tombstones marking the graves. Some were overturned, lying flat on the ground as if years of guarding the dead had finally tired them. We were probably somewhere in Maryland or maybe Delaware. The graveyard was empty, except for a solitary couple in overcoats, arm in arm, standing at a grave. I wondered then if the grave was perhaps that of their child, or a parent, and what tragedy brought them there on that day. I knew I would always remember them, and they did not even know I existed. They were gone in an instant, as the train hurried north carrying me on some long forgotten errand. But that image came to me now, and I wondered if there were people on the interstate, rushing by, wondering at our grief, and we didn't even know they existed.

The minister from the chapel on the island had agreed to say a few words, even though he did not know Connie. He was a quiet and gentle man who cared for his flock and their friends. I knew that old Chief Bishop was a longtime member of the church, and I guessed that he had asked the preacher to come. It was a dignified end for a lady who had regained her dignity on Longboat Key.

We drove back in on highway 64, turning south on highway 41, to Cortez Road and drove straight out past the Coast Guard station and onto Anna Maria Island. Logan and Dick Bellenger were in the Explorer with me. We stopped at a bar overlooking Anna Maria Sound and spent the afternoon holding our own little wake, getting drunk and remembering Connie.

The dead haunt me. I'm not so freaked by death itself, but by my thoughts of the last day of those who die. The accident cases never know when they get out of bed in the morning and eat their oatmeal that it will be their last sunrise, their last bowl of mush. Is there any vision of what lies in store that day? Do they have any inkling, even a twinge?

Once, a long time ago, I was walking down a jungle path, through an area that had seen a firefight at daybreak. The dead lay where they had fallen: American boys and Vietnamese boys, so different in life, so alike in death. As I rounded a bend in the path I saw a man in the uniform of a North Vietnamese regular, bending over the body of his comrade. He must have heard me a moment before I came into view, because he was already turning and raising his AK-47. I was holding my M-16 at an easy combat ready position, barrel pointing down at a 45 degree angle, finger on the trigger. Before the soldier could get his rifle pointed at me I had a bead on him and was pulling the trigger. It only took a second, from the time I saw him until I killed him. But, in that small space of time I saw it register in his eyes, or perhaps his face. He new that death had come calling, and that he was looking at his killer. I saw resignation, and despair, and regret, and, I think, acceptance.

My shot caught him in the middle of the chest. He was dead before he hit the ground. I kept moving, ever watchful for his buddies, scared as an eighteen year old gets, wondering if this was my day to die. They say that youth is bullet proof, that the young think they will live forever. But I knew better. I had seen too many of my teenage contemporaries die a violent death in that fetid country. I tasted my mortality every day, and on that day, I had killed a man, not for the first time, but close up, like never before. I only had that fleeting glance of my prey, but I have never forgotten him. I wondered often about his life, and about the strings of chance that brought us together on a fine morning in a jungle far from our homes.

Death is random. We never know when or whom it will strike. The healthy young mother who discovers a lump in her breast, the teenager on his way to school who happens to share the road with a drunk driver, a soldier on a jungle path who was a millisecond slower than another soldier on the same path.

But while death is finality for the deceased, it is perhaps only a small memory for the soldier who lived, or the doctor who told the mother she was past hope. And death is grief for those left behind.

So, on a bright spring day, we sat in a bar overlooking the water, and remembered Connie. We told funny stories about her, some larger than the reality, and mourned her in our way. We said goodbye to a woman we all liked, knowing that soon she would begin to fade into the evermore dimming recesses of our memories.

Chapter 5

Summer comes quickly in Southwest Florida. One day the humidity drops in like an unwelcome guest, bringing wet air that causes people to sweat as soon as they leave the air conditioning. The sea breezes cross the coasts on both sides of the peninsula driving the thunderstorms that bring the daily rain that, for a time, cools the afternoons.

That year, Summer arrived in mid-May. There had been no rain, and over in the middle of the state forest fires raged. There was turmoil in the middle east, the Democrats and Republicans were fighting over tax cuts in Washington, and a young Midwestern governor named George Wentworth, the son of a former United States Senator, was making his run for the Republican presidential nomination, even though the nominating convention was more than a year away.

It had been a month since Connie's death, and the island had hardly burped over it. Life moved on. The world does not intrude loudly on Longboat Key, and in a place with as many old people as these islands, death was familiar. I missed Connie, but every day she receded further into my memory. Once in a while, I would walk into a bar, knowing the local crowd would be there on that particular day, and be momentarily surprised at Connie's absence. We didn't talk about her much, except to occasionally wonder who could have murdered her.

There had been a flurry of articles in the daily newspapers over on the mainland in the first week after her murder. I read that the police had found Connie's apartment undisturbed. Her car was parked in her reserved space in the apartment parking lot. There was no sign of a struggle in the car. There were no leads on the perpetrators. It was a real life mystery that caused a lot of gossip on the key. The island weekly ran an article about her death, and the next week a follow up personality profile in which I was quoted. A columnist in Sarasota, who seemed to hate policemen in general and Longboat Key policemen especially, ran a couple of columns castigating law enforcement for not finding the murderer. Logan was never mentioned.

Logan had stayed at my condo for a couple more days until he got a call from Chief Lester telling him he could move back to his own place. On Monday Logan left Sarasota-Bradenton airport on his next business trip and returned to the island on Friday. He and everyone else settled back into their routines.

On a bright morning, the third Saturday in May, Chief Lester called me at home. He didn't waste any words. "Matt, late yesterday the Manatee County grand jury indicted Logan for the murder of Connie Sanborne. Banion and I are heading to his place to arrest him. I thought you would want to be there."

"What? You can't be serious." I said, stunned.

"Dead serious, Matt. We're leaving the station now."

I was wearing shorts, boat shoes and a tee shirt from the key's most recent annual St. Jude's festival. I headed for Logan's, thinking that this was a chickenshit thing for the State Attorney to do. Logan could not possibly get before a judge for a bail hearing before Monday. He would have to spend at least two nights in the lockup. Then it occurred to me that if the State Attorney took the case to a grand jury rather than filing an information, it would be a first degree murder indictment. It was almost impossible to get a judge in Florida to set bail on a murder one case. Logan would probably have to stay in jail until the trial.

I arrived at Logan's place just as the chief and Banion drove up in an unmarked car. I shook hands with both and asked, "What the hell is this all about, Bill? I thought everyone was convinced that Logan had nothing to do with Connie's murder."

"I was, Matt," said the chief. "But new evidence came up, and the State Attorney went for the indictment."

"What new evidence?" I asked.

"You'll have to get that from the State Attorney, Matt. I just thought you'd like to be here."

"Damn, Bill, I wish I weren't here. Can I go talk to him before you arrest him?"

"Fuck no, counselor," said Banion. He still smelled of old whiskey and stale cigarette smoke. His eyes were the red of a first rate hangover. "We're taking that fucker to jail. Now."

24

"Bill?" I implored.

"Go on up, Matt. We'll give you five minutes."

"What the fuck, chief? You shouldn't even have called this fuckhead. Let's get the bastard in the car and take him to the stockade."

"Go on, Matt. We'll wait," the chief said.

I took the elevator to the fourth floor, dreading this message more than any I had ever delivered. I knocked on the door. No answer. I knocked again, and then peered over the walkway railing to the parking lot. Logan's car was gone. I felt a great sense of relief, and immediate guilt at my relief. It would be better for me to break this to Logan than to have Banion arrest him and haul him off to jail.

I went back downstairs and told the cops that Logan was not at home. "Bullshit," said Banion.

"Go see for yourself asshole," I said. "You're such a genius you didn't check the parking lot for his car."

"Fuck you, Counselor," said Banion.

"He always says that," I said to the chief.

"Calm down, both of you," said Lester. "You sound like a couple of schoolyard bullies trying to outdo each other. Do you know where he is, Matt?"

"No, I don't," I said honestly and, I hoped, earnestly. "It's Saturday morning. Maybe he's playing golf. He doesn't check in with me everyday. He might be out of town for the weekend. Sometimes his trips keep him out for more than a week. What made the state decide to indict him?"

"DNA," said the chief. He had apparently changed his mind about telling me about the evidence.

"What?"

"Connie had been raped. We never mentioned it to the public, but the medical examiner found it when he did the autopsy. He was able to get a sample of semen from her vagina and sent if off for DNA testing. We also tested some hair the techs found in Logan' comb in his bathroom. There was a match. It's like a billion to one chance that the semen isn't Logan's. The results were faxed to us Thursday and the State Attorney took it to the grand jury late yesterday."

"Something's wrong here, Bill. You know Logan wouldn't do something like this."

"I wouldn't think so, Matt. But you never really know what people are capable of. The DNA evidence is hard to refute."

"What now?" I asked.

25

"We find the mother," growled Banion, "and we put his ass in jail, and then we try him and put it in the electric chair." A real hardass.

"Fuck you, Banion. You'll have to go over me to convict him," I said. Hardass is a two way street.

"Bring it on, fuckhead," he said.

"Jesus," said Bill Lester. "Both of you are nuts. Let's go Banion. If you hear anything Matt, let me know."

"Sure, Bill. Listen, if you find Logan, go easy. There's probably an explanation for all this."

"I hope so, Matt, but I don't really think so."

The two cops loaded into the unmarked and headed back south on Gulf of Mexico Drive, leaving me standing in the hot sun, roasting like a pig on a spit. I was stunned. Logan couldn't have done this. On the other hand, after O.J., everybody in the country knew that DNA evidence was as solid as you ever get. Including me.

I went back to my condo, and popped a cold Miller Lite. I was restless, not sure what to do. In a fit of little boy pique at that idiot Banion, I had announced that I would take Logan's case. I guess I could back down, but I hated to lose face in front of Banion. As if it really mattered. I'd probably go the rest of my life and never see him again, and Bill Lester would certainly understand that I was retired and the reasons why I didn't want to represent Logan. And yet, the juices were flowing. They hadn't done that in a long time. I was starting to plot trial strategy, thinking about how to get bail set, whose depositions to take, where to hire a DNA expert for the defense. I didn't want to do this. Should I move for a change of venue? No, I wasn't his lawyer. A lot of people on the mainland do not like Longboaters, thinking we are all as snobbish as some of the denizens of the high rises on the south end of the key. Would Logan be better off with say, an Orlando jury? Not my call. I was retired. I'd better bone up on the Florida Rules of Criminal Procedure. Why? I wasn't taking the damn case. The phone rang.

"Hey, Matt." It was Logan, his voice strained.

"Logan. Have they arrested you yet?"

"You know, then. How?"

"Bill Lester called about an hour ago and asked me to go to your condo with them. Where are you?"

"That's not important, Matt. I need to know if you are going to represent me."

"What's going on Logan? Talk to me."

"If you're my lawyer I can tell you anything and it will be privileged, right? You can't tell anybody."

"That's right, Logan, unless you tell me you're going to commit a crime. In that case the privilege goes out the door."

"Tell me you're my lawyer, Matt, and I'll talk to you."

"Okay. I'll be your lawyer. But only for now. As soon as we can get things sorted out, we'll hire you a lawyer."

"Good enough, for now. I'm in Boston. I called my answering machine this morning, and there was a message on it telling me I had been indicted. I think it was Mary White, but I can't be sure."

Mary White was a long time friend of almost everyone on the key. She had come down from Tennessee more than forty years ago, and had been married to a Manatee County cop all that time. He was near retirement, and did not go on patrol anymore. He had some sort of desk job, maybe warrants. He must have mentioned it to Mary, and she felt it was her duty to alert Logan.

"What's going on, Matt?"

"I don't know much. Bill Lester said that the medical examiner found that Connie had been raped, and the DNA in the semen matched the DNA from some hair taken from your comb. They just got the test results back. When are you coming in?"

"I'm not, Matt."

"You've got to Logan." I was alarmed. The worst thing Logan could do was become a fugitive.

"There's no bail for first degree murder, is there Matt?"

"No, but maybe we can talk the judge into making an exception."

"I'm not willing to bet on that, Matt. I'll keep in touch. I didn't do this, Matt."

"Logan, I want to believe you, but the DNA is a killer."

"The semen was mine. We had sex that evening, rough sex. She liked it like that sometimes. But it wasn't rape, and I didn't kill her."

"You told me you hadn't seen Connie that night after she left Moore's.

"I know," he said. "That was a stupid thing to do, but once it was out of my mouth I was embarrassed to tell you I had lied. I'm sorry, Matt."

"Alright. I accept that, Logan. Give me the name of your Army buddy, the one you were with that night, and I'll see about getting a statement that will give you a ready alibi. If we can show that the state's case is weak, we'll have a better chance at bail."

"I don't know his name, Matt."

"Come on, Logan. An army buddy you spent an evening with and you don't know his name?"

"I'll be in touch, Matt. Soon. I'll call your cell phone at eight A.M. sharp, when I call. If you're not there, I'll call back every other hour on the hour until I get you. If you need me, call Fred." He gave me his brother Fred's number and hung up.

Anybody with a lick of sense would see that Logan had put me in a tough position. I knew he wasn't coming back to be arrested, but if I told the cops that, they would get real antsy and issue all kinds of bulletins. The police would know that Logan was from Boston and would alert the department there. They would find his brother, and maybe Logan. But I was a lawyer, and my duties went only to my client. I had no duty to tell the cops anything, and would probably violate my oath as an attorney if I did say anything. It was a no-brainer. Let the cops find him.

I locked up and headed to mid-key for lunch at a bar and restaurant called O'Sullivans'. It was a pleasant Irish country inn sort of place owned by two sisters from County Cork, Molly and Irene O'Sullivan. They were about a year apart in age, both in their early forties. They had worked as barmaids and waitresses in several places on the island for ten years, often working two jobs each and saving their money. About ten years before, they were able to make a down payment on a place that had housed several different restaurants over the years, all unsuccessful. An Irish country inn setting on a beach may seem a little incongruous, but it worked. Because they were well known to the locals, and because the locals appreciated their spunk, O'Sullivans' was well patronized. The girls, as they were universally called on the island, were doing well, but they were working sixteen hour days to make it go. I had gotten to know the sisters when I was living part-time on the island, and ate at their place as often as possible.

I arrived about two o'clock, still early enough for lunch, but late for the crowd. Glenda, the elegant blond hostess, was behind the bar. I was the only customer. I took a seat at the bar, and ordered the cottage pie, which is beef stew without the vegetables, cooked in a deep dish with a thick crust of mashed potatoes, browned on the top, covering the beef. I ordered a Harp, an Irish beer on tap.

Molly saw me and came over. "Hey, Matt. How are you? I heard they indicted Logan." Her years in Florida had robbed her of most of her Irish brogue, and all those hours working were taking their toll on what was left of her youth.

"Sit down and have a beer with me," I said.

"Well, I'll sit for a minute, but I've still got to take care of the book work for last night and lunch."

Molly asked Glenda to pour her a Coke, and asked, "So, Matt. What about Logan?"

"You heard right, Molly. A grand jury indicted him yesterday for first degree murder."

"Logan didn't kill her Matt. He doesn't have it in him to hurt anybody."

"I know, Molly. But he doesn't have much of an alibi. He was drinking with an old Army buddy, but I don't have a clue as to where to find the buddy."

"Are you going to represent Logan?"

"For now. I don't think it's a good idea for me to try this case. I'm too close to Logan. And to Connie for that matter."

"You know, there was a guy in here one night at the bar asking about Logan. Said he and Logan had been in the Army together. Wanted to know if I knew Logan."

"When was this?"

"About a month ago. Probably just before Connie's murder."

"Do you remember anything about the guy?"

"Not really. I only talked to him for a couple of minutes. He wanted to know if I knew where Logan lived. I lied and told him no, and he left."

"Have you ever seen the guy again?" I asked.

"Not that I remember, Matt. Is it important?"

"Probably not, but if you see him again, ask him to call me."

"Sure Matt. Gotta get back to the books. See you later."

I finished my meal amid small talk with Glenda, and headed home.

Monday arrived, hot and humid. I did my four miles on the beach, and was glad to return to my air conditioned condo. There was no lounging on the balcony this time of the year. It was just too hot.

I made myself a bowl of cereal and a pot of coffee and settled down with the morning Sarasota paper. The headline shouted that a local man had been indicted for murder. The story was about Logan and Connie and had information that I didn't think would have been given to the press in the normal course of things.

I picked up the phone and called Chief Lester. "Bill," I said when he came on the line, "How did Logan end up on the front page?"

"I don't know, Matt. But it didn't come from here."

"I'll bet Banion knows somebody at the paper. What is his problem, Bill?"

"Banion is maybe the best detective I've ever seen. He hates lawyers because he's seen too many bad guys get off because they had good legal counsel. His wife died two years ago, and I think the stress of the job and of losing her turned him into a real problem drinker. But I promise you, Matt, he's a better detective drunk than most of them are sober."

"Why would he leak something like this to the press? What does he gain by it?"

"He probably thinks a bad press will make it tougher for a jury to give Logan a break when he's tried. Have you heard from him, Matt?"

"Banion?"

"You know who I mean, Matt."

"Bill, you're my friend, and I hope when this thing is over you'll still be my friend. But I'm Logan's lawyer, and I can't discuss this with you."

"I understand, Matt. No sweat. But you know it's going to go a lot easier if he turns himself in. If he's caught, it's going to be bad."

"Have they decided who the prosecutor is going to be yet?"

"Elizabeth Ferguson. Know her?"

"I've seen her name in the paper. She does only capital felonies, right?"

"Yeah. And she's beautiful and a real ball buster. Every cop and lawyer in the twelfth circuit has hit on her. Nobody gets anywhere. They call her the ice queen. And her name is Elizabeth; never Beth or Liz or Betty. You'll do well to remember that."

"Thanks, Bill. I'll be talking to you."

I had met Logan's brother Fred on one of his visits to our key. I called him in Boston. He did not know where Logan was but told me that Logan had called. He would be checking in regularly with Fred, but wanted to keep Fred ignorant of his whereabouts.

"Logan says you're going to represent him," said Fred.

"For now. Until we can get a real lawyer for him."

"Logan doesn't have any money. He's afraid he'll end up with a public defender."

"Come on, Fred. Logan has been doing good. He's probably got more money stashed away than most of us."

"Not really. He lost a bunch in a bad investment that he doesn't like to talk about, and he spent a lot sending our dead brother's daughter through college. I think he's about broke. I know he took out a large second mortgage on his condo last year."

"What about your folks? They've got money."

"No they don't. My father was a commercial fisherman. Worked the boats out of Gloucester and barely made enough to keep us in food and clothes. Logan just made up all that malarkey about having wealthy parents."

"I'll be damned."

"Yeah."

That afternoon I cranked up my computer and went onto the internet to find Elizabeth Ferguson. One of the first things a trial lawyer learns is to know the opposition. In the internet version of the national legal directory I found the bare bones information on the prosecutor. She was born in Statesboro, Georgia, graduated from Georgia Southern University with a bachelors degree and three years later from Mercer University School of Law in Macon, Georgia. She had been admitted to the Florida Bar ten years before, and she was thirty-five years old.

I searched the archives of the Sarasota newspaper and found several articles about Ms. Ferguson. She had tried a number of high profile death penalty cases in the last three years, and had lost none. Before that she would occasionally show up in the paper while prosecuting other felons. One article was a personality piece about her that was published soon after she won her first death penalty case.

I learned that she had been born into a large family and had had to work her way through college in her hometown. She excelled academically and was awarded a full scholarship to study law at Mercer. When she graduated she married a fellow student from Sarasota, and the couple set up housekeeping in a condo on Siesta Key. He went to work for a prestigious firm in Sarasota, and she followed her instincts and applied for a job at the State Attorney's office. Elizabeth had graduated near the top of her class and edited the Law Review, a job held only by the most academically gifted students each year. With those credentials she had no trouble getting the job.

Over the years she had worked hard, tried a lot of cases and honed her courtroom skills. She hardly ever lost. After seven years of marriage she had divorced her husband and moved to a small house near the waterfront in Sarasota. She did not appear to have much of a social life.

While I was on the computer, I figured I might as well bone up on the Florida Rules of Criminal Procedure. I surfed into the Florida Supreme Court's web site and read for an hour or so. Nothing much had changed.

About six that evening there was a knock on my door. It was the delivery guy from Oma's Pizza on Anna Maria Island. I had gotten to know him casually over the years, given my penchant for ordering pizza rather than cooking.

"Got your pizza, Mr. Royal."

"I didn't order a pizza."

"Mr. Hamilton ordered it."

"I don't understand."

"He called the order in, paid with his credit card and said to tell you to enjoy."

"Did he order anchovies on it?"

"No, sir. Everything but anchovies."

God, I hate anchovies. I took the pizza, tipped the boy, and dug in. I wasn't sure what Logan was up to, but I enjoyed the pizza.

Chapter 6

After my jog and a cup of coffee the next morning, I showered, shaved and put on the only suit I had left from a rather extensive wardrobe from my former life. It was navy blue with a subtle chalk pinstripe. I added a blue and yellow striped tie, the colors of the Seventh Cavalry, according to the salesman, and a light blue oxford button down shirt. All this finery sat atop a pair of highly shined wingtip loafers with tassels, wrapped around a six foot body, still lean and with most of its dark hair intact. I thought I looked pretty spiffy in the full length mirror, and God help me, I looked like a lawyer.

The Twelfth Judicial Circuit of Florida covers Sarasota, Manatee and Desoto counties. The State Attorney and Public Defender are housed in a nine story modern building adjacent to the old courthouse in Sarasota. From there they fan out over the three county area to do justice. It was to this building that I went on that bright hot late May morning.

I took the elevator to the seventh floor and announced to the receptionist that I was Matt Royal and that I had a 9:00 o'clock appointment with Ms. Ferguson. I was told to have a seat.

I had barely touched my rump to the battered sofa that took up one wall of the small reception room, when a woman entered, her hand out, saying, "Mr. Royal? I'm Elizabeth Ferguson. Come on back."

She was dressed in a gray suit, a navy blouse open at the neck and dark shoes with medium heels. Her blonde hair was cut above her shoulders, and set off lovely face, punctuated by large sky-blue eyes. She was tanned, but not leathery as so many of the Florida sun worshipers become. She had a trim body, small waisted with breasts that could not quite hide behind the suit jacket. Her legs were long, and I guessed her to be about five seven.

"Can I get you a cup of coffee?" she asked.

"I would love one."

"Lets stop by the kitchen and you can fix it like you want it."

We turned into a small room with a sink, a refrigerator, a microwave and a commercial drip coffee pot. She got two Styrofoam cups from the overhead cabinet and poured them both full. "There's cream and sugar on the counter," she said.

"Thanks. Black will be fine."

She reached into her coat side pocket, extracted two quarters and dropped them into a mason jar with a coin slot in the lid. "My treat," she said.

"Thank you."

"My office is this way."

We went down a corridor with offices opening off either side. At the end we turned right into a secretarial area in which sat a black woman working on a computer.

"Mavis, this is Matt Royal," Elizabeth said. "Mr. Royal, my secretary, Mavis Jackson."

"How do you do, Ms. Jackson."

"I understand we'll be working together soon, Mr. Royal."

"How's that, Ms. Jackson."

"The Hamilton case."

"I'm not sure for how long. Pretty soon, he's going to need a real lawyer."

"I hear you, Counselor. I hear you." Mavis said, chuckling.

Elizabeth Ferguson's office was small and crowded with a scarred old mahogany desk, two legal size file cabinets and two chairs for guests. Hanging on the wall behind her desk were her diplomas from Georgia Southern and Mercer. Her executive chair looked new and expensive. Her windows looked out over downtown Sarasota, the bay and out to the Gulf.

"It took me ten years of hard work to get that view," she said. "I had to buy my own chair. The state is not a generous employer."

The vestige of a Southern accent wrapped her words in a softness that attested to her heritage. The Southern background and education would explain her easy charm that at first seemed to be at odds with her reputation as a hard nosed prosecutor who gave no quarter in the courtroom.

"Why don't you leave? Go into private practice," I asked.

"I like to put the bad guys in jail. I think I'd get bored doing whatever civil lawyers do."

"I see you went to Mercer. So did I."

"You must have been before my time," she said, with a wry smile.

"By several years."

"Why is the beachbum lawyer coming out of retirement to take a loser of a case like this?"

"Beachbum?"

"We have mutual friends."

"Oh?"

"The girls."

"Ah."

"They speak highly of you."

"I live on the bay. I hardly ever go to the beach."

"Well, you know what I mean."

"For now," I said.

"What does that mean?"

"I'm representing him for now. He has no money, and I'm afraid a public defender would not give his defense the time it deserves."

"I thought he came from money."

"Apparently not. I understand from his brother that he's broke. He can't get a lawyer without money, and he's afraid that the public defender wouldn't get too serious about defending him. He's in kind of a bad situation."

"Bad situation? Matt, may I call you Matt?"

"Certainly."

"Matt, he's been indicted for first degree murder. That's more than a bad situation."

"He didn't do it, and I don't think you'll be able to prove a case."

"He's not helping himself by remaining a fugitive. Are you going to bring him in?" The mood had shifted in a hurry. We were down to business.

"I don't have that kind of control."

"Have you actually been retained to represent Logan?"

"Yes."

"If he's broke, how has he paid you?"

"He bought me a pizza."

"A pizza? For a capital murder case? That's not much."

"It was a supreme. Had everything on it."

"How can we get this thing moving, Matt? I want him in custody."

"Let me see your evidence."

"You know I can't do that."

"You'll have to give it to me sooner or later."

"I don't have to do anything until he's arraigned, and we can't arraign him until we arrest him."

"Look, Elizabeth. You've had more than a month to investigate this thing. You're not likely to get any more evidence than you have now. Why not give me what you've got, and let's see if I can talk you into dropping the case."

She looked at me with incredulity. She started to say something, thought better of it, and closed her mouth. Then, "No can do, Matt. Bring him in, and I'll show you my cards."

The Sarasota Memorial Hospital takes up a lot of space on the Tamiami Trail south of town. It has grown over the years and has developed a reputation as a first class institution. Tucked away on the back side of the campus is a small two story office building that seems out of place among the gleaming white buildings of the hospital. The building houses some of the junior executives of the hospital and Bert Hawkins, the Chief Medical Examiner for the Twelfth Judicial Circuit.

I had met Dr. Hawkins on several occasions. He was a golfing buddy of Tom Bishop, the former Longboat Key police chief. and had once joined us on a fishing trip on a large boat owned by one of the winter visitors who had more money that God. I hoped that he would remember me.

I went into the office and told the receptionist that I didn't have an appointment, but that I had been in the neighborhood and thought I would take the chance that Dr. Hawkins was free for lunch. She took my name, asked me to wait a minute and disappeared behind a closed door. Within a couple of minutes Bert Hawkins came striding through the same door.

"Matt, good to see you. I was asking Tom Bishop about you just the other day." He was a large man, about my height but built like a linebacker. He probably weighed 250 pounds, but there was no fat. He had a full head of iron gray hair that he wore over his ears. You got the impression that he was not being fashionable, but just didn't get to a barber shop regularly.

"Hi, Bert. Glad to see you. I just dropped in to see if you had time for lunch."

"Sure do. I'm buried under paper work back there and was looking for an excuse for a break."

"How's Marina Jack suit you?"

"Great. I like their grouper fritters."

We took my Explorer and headed back north on Tamiami Trail, making small talk about fishing and the doctor's golf game. We pulled into the parking lot of the restaurant overlooking the municipal marina and the bay. The sun was high and hot, and by the time we parked and walked to the restaurant we were both sweating.

We were taken to a small table overlooking the bay. There was a little wind and the bay rippled slightly as the breeze crossed its face. A small schooner, sails furled, motored under the Ringling Causeway bridge. A couple of jet skies cut across its bow, and I could see the captain give the finger to the drivers.

We both ordered iced tea and grouper fritters. When the tea came, Bert looked at me and smiled. "Okay, what do you want to know?"

"About what?" I asked, all genuine surprise.

"Deductive reasoning, Matt," he laughed. "You're Logan's buddy, you're a lawyer, and I'm the state's witness to the rape of a dead girl."

"Well, I've been meaning to call you for lunch anyway. I figured I might as well kill two birds with one stone."

"Are you representing Logan?"

"Yes." There. It was done. I was now back in harness. I would have to see this thing through. Logan was my client, like it or not.

"Have you talked to the SA's office?"

"Yes. I met with Elizabeth Ferguson this morning. She won't give me anything."

"I can't tell you a lot, Matt, and it'll probably piss Elizabeth off if I tell you anything. But you'll have a right to know what I know sooner or later, so why not sooner."

"I won't be telling anyone we talked Bert, if that bothers you."

"Hell, no. I'm going to tell you everything I know, and then I'm going to call Elizabeth and tell her what I told you. You lawyers play too many games for me. Let's throw up the evidence and let the chips fall where they may, is what I say in mixed metaphors."

"Was strangulation the cause of death?"

"Yes, without question."

"Was she raped?"

"I don't know. There was bruising around the opening of the vagina, but there was no tearing of the tissue inside. Usually in rapes we see both. The woman is scared out of her mind and is certainly not secreting the fluids that lubricate the vagina for intercourse. When she is penetrated there is tearing of the fragile tissue just inside the opening. I didn't find that in this case, but I did find semen in the vagina, and DNA tells us that it belonged to Logan."

"What led you to conclude that she had been raped?"

"Nothing. I didn't conclude that. I gave my report to Banion, and he took it from there."

"Do you think the bruising is enough evidence to make a rape charge stick?"

"If I were asked to assume that a woman of Connie Sanborne's age had said she had been raped, and the examination findings were what I found here, I would have to say that in all likelihood a rape did occur. But here, we have a dead woman. She can't tell us what happened. I would testify to the facts as I found them without reaching any conclusions."

"Would rough sex cause the kind of bruising you saw?"

"I guess it could, but it would have to be pretty rough."

"Did you find anything else?"

"Nothing of any real significance. She had had a lot of broken bones at some time in her life, but that was years ago."

"How could you tell?"

"When I opened her up I noticed that several of her ribs on either side had been broken and healed back together. There was also a thin scar behind her right ear, as if a plastic surgeon had done a face lift. Only, when a face lift is done, the scars are on both sides. I decided to x-ray the face and found that her right cheek bone had been shattered. It looked as if a pretty good plastic man went in and put her back together. I also found a bruise on her brain, indicating that she had had a bad concussion at some point in her life. All this was years old though, and really of no consequence in terms of her murder. It just piqued my scientific curiosity."

"She was married to a guy who used to beat the hell out of her on a regular basis."

"That would explain the fractures."

"Were you able to determine a time of death?"

"Not exactly. But based on the temperature of the body when my tech got to the scene and the amount of rigor, I'd estimate that she was killed between eleven p.m. and one a.m. We wouldn't be off more than an hour either way."

"Anything else?"

"No, that was about it. I can get you a copy of the report when we get back to the office."

"I'd appreciate that."

We ate our meal and chatted about mutual friends and the plight of the Buccaneers, deciding that they would probably end the season at the bottom of the heap again. I drove the ME back to his office, got a copy of his report, and went home to Longboat.

Chapter 7

After graduating from law school at the top of my class, I joined an old and very established law firm in Orlando, going to work in its litigation section. I did all the expected things. I joined the Jaycees, the Young Republicans, the Chamber of Commerce, the Kiwanis Club, and worked for the firm like a son of a bitch. I tried a lot of cases and won more than I lost. I rose in the ranks of the various organizations I had joined and became well known in the community. I was active in politics and counted among my closest friends two Congressmen, a United States Senator, the Governor of Florida, and many lesser local office holders. I was representing large corporations and making a lot of money. I had the obligatory foreign car, the large house and a thirty-six foot boat that I kept on Longboat Key and spent as much time on as possible.

While in law school I had made the best investment in my life. I married Laura. She was beautiful and warm and loving. She didn't really care about all the material things I provided, but simply wanted children and more of me. I kept putting off the children, and not giving her enough of my very valuable time, and finally blew the investment.

Four years before, I had come home late one night after a political meeting and several drinks with the boys. She told me to sit down as she had something important to tell me. She told me that her biological clock was ticking, and that she did not have much more time to have the family she had always wanted. She said that she did not really know me anymore, and although she loved me, she had to do what was right for her. While visiting her brother in Atlanta the year before, she had met a widower, a doctor, who was raising his three year old child alone. They had seen a lot of each other since then, and he had asked her to marry him. He wanted more children, and she had decided to take him up on his offer. She was in love, and thought she could make a better life in Atlanta with him. She was leaving. She wanted no alimony, and nothing of our property other than her automobile. She would appreciate it if I would quietly get us divorced as soon as possible.

My world fell apart. I guess I had been self destructing for quite some time, but Laura's decision was the terminal event. Laura had been the only real anchor in my life, and as I thought about it, the only person who really mattered. Or at least, without her nothing else mattered much at all.

I was depressed, feeling sorry for my rotten self, and drinking too much. I dropped out of the organizations that had been such a part of my life. I spent less and less time in the office and more and more time on my boat, wondering what had gone so very wrong in my carefully constructed and successful life.

My partners at the law firm were understanding and tried to help. I was unresponsive, and finally the executive committee of the firm decided that it would be in the best interest of all of us if I left. They bought out my share, and I sold the house. With the money in hand, I moved aboard the boat. For six months I hung around the marina and did nothing but drink beer and feel sorry for myself.

By that time I was beginning to run out of money, and I was not too concerned about what I would do when that happened. One day I was sitting on the bridge of the boat drinking my fifth or sixth beer of the morning, wondering what to do about a job, when I heard a man call, "Ahoy, the Miss Laura." An archaic greeting, more fitted for a fine yacht than my relatively small craft. I turned to see a well dressed man of about fifty coming down the dock. He was wearing a pair of white duck pants, a solid blue polo shirt, and blue Sperry topsiders without socks. He had a gold President Rolex watch on his left wrist and a large class ring from the University of Georgia on his left ring finger. His hair was solid white, cut fairly short, and combed back from a razor part.

"Are you Matt Royal?" he asked.

"Sure am. Come aboard."

He climbed into the cockpit and up the ladder to the bridge. "I'm Jason Clark. I'm a friend of Laura and Jeff Simmons. I believe she's your former wife."

"Yes, she is. How about a beer?"

"A little early for me, thanks."

I opened the cooler and took out my last Miller Lite. "How is Laura?" I asked, opening the beer can.

"She's worried about you. She told me that you've had a bad time since the divorce, that you're wasting your life, and that you're probably the best lawyer in the state of Florida, if not the entire country."

"Well, I'm not a lawyer anymore. I'm what is known as a boat bum, and very happy about it. Besides, Laura is prejudiced."

"There are several other people whose judgment I respect, who back up Laura's assessment. I want you to handle a case for me."

"Wonderful. I don't have an office or secretary, and I'm probably not even current with the Florida Bar. Go see my old partners in Orlando."

"Did you ever hear of Jasonics Corporation?"

"Sure, the medical equipment manufacturer. The biggest in the country. You want them sued?"

"I own Jasonics. I'm a physician and a tinkerer. More tinkerer than physician, I guess. Twenty years ago I invented an artificial heart valve and got rich on it. Since then I've patented twenty-seven medical devices that are the heart of Jasonics. I've got more money than I'll ever spend, and I've earned every dime of it by hard work and honest dealings."

The rest of his story was similar to many I'd heard over the years. Five years before, at the age of 46, he got out of the day to day business end of Jasonics. "Then I got sick. My wife was killed in an automobile accident, and I wasn't too much good for anything. Two years ago, while recuperating, at the suggestion of a friend, I began tinkering again. I came up with an idea for a new laser tool for microsurgery. I fabricated the equipment and took it to a friend of mine, a surgeon, to see what he thought. He tried it out, and told me that it was inadequate for the purpose intended. I gave up on the idea and didn't think too much more about it."

Then, two months before, he had discovered that the identical piece of equipment was being manufactured and marketed by Jasonics biggest competitor, and his friend, the surgeon, was on their board of directors.

"Did you confront the surgeon?" I asked.

"Yes. He just laughed and told me to go to hell. He said there was no way to prove he hadn't invented the tool, and he had gotten the patent on it."

"Why didn't you take the idea to Jasonics in the first place?"

"I'm not sure. Although I own the whole company, it was being run by a very competent staff, and I had been sick and out of it for three years at the time. I guess I wanted a proven item to take to the company. Maybe I just wanted to show them that I was still a worthwhile individual."

"Sounds to me as if you need a good lawyer. How much money is involved in something like this?"

"I don't know. The money isn't really important to me. I'll probably give it all to charity. It's just that this snake of a surgeon should not be able to get away with this. If there's any justice in the world he should not profit from his theft."

"Look, Doc," I said, "I learned a long time ago that there is a lot of justice in this world, but it usually has absolutely nothing to do with right and wrong. The system screws people every day and calls it justice. The big devour the small, the powerful the weak, and its all called justice. I was a trial lawyer for a long time, and I took advantage of a lot of people. It was a big game. See if you can out-think and out-talk the opposing lawyer. Never stop to think about abstract things, like right and wrong. The system works and will ensure a just outcome. That's what we used to tell the civilians. Bullshit! The guys with the most money and the best lawyers win. Justice? Crap. It's all crap. In all those years of trying lawsuits I never tried one that advanced mankind in any way. I won cases that I should not have, and I lost cases I should have won. Right and wrong had nothing to do with it. It was money, and power, and sleight of hand. You would spend thousands and thousands of dollars getting a case to trial. You would have the very best lawyers money could buy on both sides of the case. You would pay five hundred dollars an hour for expert witnesses on a given subject, and of course they would come to exactly opposite conclusions. Interestingly enough, their conclusions would always fit the theory of the case of the lawyer who had hired them. Did you ever notice in criminal cases where insanity is a defense that there are psychiatrists on both sides who examine the same poor son of a bitch of a defendant, and come to diametrically opposite conclusions? The prosecution's shrink always says the guy was sane at the time of the crime, and the shrink hired by the defense always says he was insane. And they get all this high powered expensive talent into the courtroom where the judge presiding is some low paid clown who has worked his whole life for one state agency or another, who can't or won't make it in private practice, and for whom the law is a great mystery. And then the lawyers strive mightily to pick the dumbest people on the drivers' license rolls to serve on the jury. Christ, the average juror is dumber that the average judge, and that takes some doing. Justice? Bullshit! It's a term used in the legal business to buffalo the civilians. It's all bullshit, and I'm glad I'm out of it." I was running out of breath.

"Will you represent me?"

"Man, I told you. I'm not a lawyer anymore. Get yourself a real lawyer. Hell, I'm probably an alcoholic anyway, and if you know anything about the breed, you know we can't be trusted to stay sober long enough to find the courthouse, let alone take on major litigation."

"I checked with the Florida Bar. You are only a year behind on your dues. Two hundred fifty dollars will reinstate you, and you'll be in good standing. I talked to Vanessa Brice, and she'll quit her job and go back to work for you with two weeks notice.

"I don't know whether you're an alcoholic or not. I know that I am. My sickness came from the bottle. I got drunk and caused the wreck that killed my wife. Jeff Simmons was my doctor, and after he patched me up physically from the accident, he and Laura pulled me together emotionally. Laura said that you are an idealist who got caught up in the legal business as opposed to the learned profession that you thought you were dedicating your life to. She said that you always wanted to mount your charger and tilt at windmills, but were so caught up in being somebody, the ageless hero perhaps, that you forgot why you had gone into the law. I know a lot about Matt Royal, and I'm betting that he can win this case and feel a lot better about himself in the process."

"It's intriguing, Doctor, but given my present circumstances, not very practical."

"I'll pay all your office expenses plus four thousand dollars per month to you for as long as it takes to finish the case. If you win, I'll pay you one-third of the gross recovery, less expenses advanced. If you lose, I'll eat the expenses and you won't owe me anything. All I ask is that you give me your very best effort."

"I need to think it over."

"No. I want an irrevocable decision from you now. If you don't think you can handle it, we're wasting each other's time. I think you can do it."

I bought the deal.

I went back to Orlando, rented a two room office and some furniture, and got to work. Vanessa, who had been my secretary the whole time I had been with the firm, came back to work, and we dug into the case. I got off the booze and didn't even miss it. I started working out at a health club and got the old body back in shape, and worked harder than I ever had in my life. Jason Clarke stopped by from time to time, and became a good friend. He really meant what he had said. He wanted to win because he had been wronged. We worked on that crazy case for over a year, and last summer the defendant company settled with us for twelve million dollars. The surgeon was indicted for fraud, and the state revoked his license to practice medicine. Jason paid me three million dollars, less the money he had advanced, and used the rest of the money to endow an alcoholic treatment center outside Atlanta. I paid Uncle Sam his share of my earnings, gave Vanessa a bonus large enough to ensure that she would not have to work again if she didn't want to, bought the condo, and invested the rest of the money in stocks that gave me a small but safe return. I would be able to live comfortably for the rest of my life.

Chapter 8

My cell phone rang at eight o'clock the next morning. It was Logan. "Did you get the pizza?" He asked. He sounded weak.

"Yes. Are you okay? You don't sound so good."

"Just tired, Counselor. I'm fine."

"Where are you?'

"Can't tell you yet, Matt. You might have to tell the cops at some point."

There was a small chance he was right. "Okay, for now, Logan. I met with the prosecutor yesterday. She wants you to give yourself up."

"No way. I'll rot in jail waiting for the trial. The only way I'm going to get out of this is to find out who killed Connie."

"I also met with the medical examiner. It may not be as bad as it looks."

"What did he say?"

"He can't conclusively say Connie was raped, but he can conclusively say the semen was yours."

"I told you we had sex that night. When I left you at Moore's I took my boat back to Bradenton Beach Marina, and Connie was waiting. As soon as I tied up, she jumped in the boat. The place was deserted, and Connie started grabbing at me, telling me she wanted me bad. She didn't have anything on under her skirt, and she lay back over the engine cover and told me to get on. I tell you Matt, it was erotic. Here this woman is with her skirt up at her waste, no panties, her legs spread, and ordering me to perform. I about lost it right there in my pants. She kept screaming at me to do it."

"Logan, Doc Hawkins says there was a lot of bruising around her vagina. How could that happen?"

46

"Matt, she was crazy that night. Every time I got near her she would push her body at mine. I know this sounds terrible, but she liked to have broke my dick a couple of times. It hurt like hell. I would get close, and she would lunge. Finally, it went in, and I came immediately. She did too."

"Was this unusual behavior, or did you two go at it like this regularly?"

"It was unusual, Matt. Sometimes she liked it rough, but that never turned me on. She wanted me to slap her once, and I refused. Another time she asked me to squeeze her nipple hard enough to hurt. I did and it seemed to turn her on. I think there was something dark down in her mind; something left over from the husband. But she had never been like this before."

"What time did this happen?"

"As soon as I got to the marina. I left Moore's about 9:30, and its only a ten minute run up to Bradenton Beach."

"Did you stay there long?"

"No. It was really weird. The whole sex thing didn't take more than ten minutes, and she left. She was strange that night. I asked her if she wanted to come to my place, and she just laughed. She didn't say anything else; just left."

"What did you do then?"

"I went to Dewey's." Dewey's was a bar on Bridge Street on Anna Maria Island.

"How long were you there?"

"About time for one beer. I ran into my Army buddy, and we left and walked down to Frisco's where it was quieter and we could talk."

"The buddy with no name. Why didn't you tell the cops you had been with Connie that night?"

"Gotta go, Matt. Call you later."

The phone went dead. I sat at my desk, thinking again about trial strategy. If the state couldn't prove rape, and I didn't see how they could after what Bert Hawkins had said, all they had was that Logan had hd sex with Connie on the night of her death and that she was found in his condo. That wasn't much to hang a murder case on, and I figured Elizabeth Ferguson knew that as well as I did. She must have something that I didn't know about.

Elizabeth probably didn't know about the alibi and the nameless army buddy. Given the time of death, I was pretty sure that Logan's army friend could clear him. If Logan's times were correct, he would have gotten to the marina about 9:40, had sex and left by 10:00. Dewey's was only about two blocks from the marina, so he would have been there a few minutes after 10:00. That also fit with Pearl's memory that Connie showed up at her piano bar a few minutes after 10:00. It would be about a ten minute drive from the marina to Pearl's bar.

The ME said that Connie was killed between 11:00 and 1:00 with maybe an hour's grace on either side. Pearl would testify that Connie could not have been killed before 11:00, because she was sitting at the piano bar. If Logan had been with his friend from shortly after 10:00 until 2:00, he was in the bar when Connie was killed.

Logan's alibi would probably take him out of the picture. He said that he'd been with his army buddy for several hours. If we could place him in the bar drinking from about 10:30 until closing at 2:00 a.m., it would have been impossible for Logan to have killed Connie.

If I could establish the alibi, Logan would be home free. While Elizabeth would have the statement that Pearl gave to Banion, she would not have any way to know about the alibi witness. Elizabeth would know that Connie was alive at 11:00 and dead no later than 2:00. Those were the three critical hours. What did Elizabeth know that I didn't? She had to have had more evidence than what I had seen in order to even think about charging Logan with first degree murder. She was too good a lawyer to hang herself out on such a thin reed.

The other question that kept nagging at me was that if Logan didn't kill Connie, who did. I would need to work on that theory a little. One of the oldest defense lawyer tricks in the book is to try somebody else for the crime your client is accused of. I thought the alibi would handle things, but a good lawyer always has plan B. I would have to try to develop another murder suspect.

I knew I wouldn't know anymore until Logan called again. It was frustrating, and I couldn't figure out what kind of games Logan was playing. Why not just tell me everything? What was he trying to do by giving me small pieces of the puzzle with each phone call? It didn't make sense, and I figured it was about time to tell him to defecate or decommode, as they used to say in the Army.

Since I knew I wasn't going to solve the problem that day, I called my old friend Denny, known for some long forgotten reason as K-Dawg, and we went fishing. Didn't catch a thing.

Chapter 9

"How's it going, buddy?" It was eight o'clock and Logan was on the other end of the phone line.

"Tell me about this army buddy, Logan," I said.

"What do you want to know?"

"Look," I said, getting angry, "I didn't want this case in the first place, and I promise you I will drop it today if you don't start leveling with me."

"Sorry, Matt. I don't know what to tell you. I walked into Dewey's, and this guy sitting in the corner called me by name. I didn't recognize him, but he told me we were in flight training at Rucker together. He introduced himself to me as Bill Smith. I didn't remember him, but he knew a bunch of the guys I knew and the places we used to hang out in around Ozark. I didn't want to hurt his feelings by telling him I didn't remember him, and besides it was fun talking about the old guys. A lot of them didn't make it back from Nam."

"Why didn't you tell me you didn't know his name?"

"After Connie's death," Logan said, "I went looking for him. He told me he was staying at the Tiki Beach Resort up on Anna Maria, but they never heard of a Bill Smith there. I called a couple of my old flight school buddies, and neither of them remembered him either. There wasn't a Bill Smith in school with us that anybody can remember."

"Didn't you find that strange?" I asked.

"Of course I found it strange. But what could I do?"

"You could have mentioned it to me." I said.

"It didn't seem important until I was charged with the murder."

"You know, Logan," I said, "This complicates things a lot. The alibi I was counting on to get you out of this mess just disappeared."

49

"I know", he said. "I'll get back to you." He hung up.

I rooted around in the box into which I throw my occasional snapshot and found one of Logan and K-Dawg standing on the back of my boat during a fishing trip the past summer. I also found one of Connie and three other locals that I had taken by the pool of my condo complex on the July 4th weekend the year before. Connie was smiling. A lump jumped into my throat and left as quickly. I felt a tiny pressure around my eyes, the beginning of wetness. I was surprised at my reaction. I thought I had grieved all I was going to for Connie. Perhaps we never really get over the death of someone we care about. I had never lost anyone close other than friends who died in Viet Nam, but somehow that was expected. My parents were both dead, but they had died in their time. Connie went way too early and without warning, and I guessed that was the reason for my reaction.

I took the pictures down to Eckerd's on the Avenue of Flowers, where they have one of those computer developers. You can put your photo in, use the monitor to crop it, and then print as many as you want for about a buck a piece. I made ten of Connie smiling and ten of Logan, cropping out K-Dawg and the others.

I headed for Dewey's at 4:00 that afternoon. Summer had settled on the islands, and the heat shimmered on the asphalt of Gulf of Mexico Drive as I headed toward the Longboat Pass Bridge. The span was rising as I approached, and the barricade was down. I came to a stop, the air conditioning compressor in the Explorer going full blast. The water in the pass was green and cool looking, lapping on the pure white sand of Beer Can Island just west of the bridge. A small boat with an outboard was beached there, and a couple and two small children were playing in the water. A large party fishing boat from Cortez was heading in from the Gulf, full of tourists who were coming back after a couple of hours fishing, with a lot of fish and very red skin. Dark clouds were moving in from the mainland, the scouts of the daily thunder storm that was fast approaching. The tourists would probably get wet. Pavarotti was singing "Nessum Dora" on the tape deck, and I was singing along. My Italian left as much to be desired as my voice, but then nobody was listening.

The boat cleared the bridge, full of laughing people waving at the poor sods in the cars. I drove onto Anna Maria Island, watching the speed limit. It drops as you come onto Anna Maria, and the Bradenton Beach cops made a large part of the city's revenue each year hanging out behind the shrubs lining the entrance to the parking lot at Coquina Beach. I navigated the traffic circle at Bridge street a quarter turn and headed two blocks east to Dewey's Five Points Bar.

The building squated in the sun, hunkered down on a slab of terrazzo, sheltering its customers from the Florida heat. A five pointed star, swathed in neon, hung over the door. No one knew what it meant or why it was there. The bar had changed little in the sixty years that it had stood on the street that once was the approach to the bridge to the mainland. It drew from the working people who could still afford to live on Anna Maria and from the nearby trailer parks housing the poorer retirees. Occasionally, just for kicks, some of the gilded residents of the south end of Longboat would stop by to observe the natives. I often had a beer there with the owner, an ancient lady who had been running the place since it opened.

Inside it was cool in the air conditioning provided by the ancient Carrier standing in the corner. The customers were mostly men and women who worked hard for their livings and enjoyed their off-hours with a few beers and a little conversation with their friends. A battered pool table covered in chalk stained green felt graced the center of the small room that was the lounge. Along the wall opposite the bar sat a scarred shuffleboard table, awaiting the next game. It wouldn't be long in coming. A game seemed to be constantly in progress. There was a juke box with mostly country music, or what passes for country these days, a cigarette machine, and a large inflated green frog hanging from the rafters over the pool table. Next to the cash register at the end of the bar hung a large picture frame with a melange of snapshots of various customers having fun in Dewey's. On the wall behind the bar hung an old cardboard plaque announcing that the four most important things a woman does is look like a girl, act like a lady, think like a man, and work like a dog. The women at Dewey's understood that kind of aphorism.

Dewey was one of those women. In 1930, Dewey Clanton had left the hill country of South Carolina and landed on this island. She had paid $1500 for the property near the bridge and built herself a bar. She had been there ever since, serving up beer and pretzels, pickled pig feet and slim jims. She had never told anyone how she came into the $1500, a large sum in those days. She was eighty-five now, and a little stooped with age. There was nothing stooped about her mind though, and her spirit was as full and winsome as it must have been when she had started behind the bar on that first day so many years ago. She was thin, and her hair was a soft red. Her face was wrinkled, the result, no doubt, of so much laughing. She was a happy lady, quick with a joke and a chuckle.

If you asked, Miss Dewey, as she was known to her customers, would tell you about the old days, when the road in front of her place was a one lane approach to the only bridge connecting the island to the mainland. She remembered the problems she had encountered when the county or state or somebody had widened it to two lanes. It was not until the 1950's that the bridge was torn down, after the new Cortez Bridge had been completed and the approach from Cortez Road was in place.

I had gotten to know Dewey when I first started coming to the islands some years before. I would sit and drink beer and talk to her through the long summer afternoons, listening to her stories about the old days, when few people lived on these islands. I had brought my friends from Longboat here occasionally, and some, like Logan, had made it a regular stop.

"Look what the cat dragged in," said Dewey, as I walked into the bar. "Where you been hidin', boy?"

"I've missed you, Dewey," I said.

"Likely story, boy. I bet you been chasing around after them younger women and ain't even thought about me." She gave a large whoop of laughter and leaned over the bar to kiss me on the cheek.

She put a Miller Lite on the bar with a cold glass. I poured it, held it up and said in my best Bogart, "Here's looking at you, Kid."

"You need to work on that some."

"I guess you heard about Logan," I said.

"Yeah, but I don't believe it. I used to see him and Connie in here together some. Logan ain't the type to be killin' nobody."

"That's what I think. Look, Logan tells me that he was in here the night of the murder. Do you remember seeing him?"

"As a matter of fact, I do," Dewey said. "And the reason I remember is that I heard the next day about Connie, and I thought then that Logan was in here the night before, his usual self you know, and now he would have to grieve over Connie. I thought maybe that would be his last happy night."

"Why do you say that, Dewey?"

"Well, it was obvious that they was in love, or at least had something going. They'd sit here alone and hold hands and talk. You know how quiet it gets in here on week nights after everybody's finished with happy hour."

"I never guessed they were a pair," I said. "Logan told me after Connie's death, but I got the impression they were just two people who met in the night occasionally."

"I don't think so, Matt. There seemed to be more to it than that."

"Was Logan in here alone the night of the murder?"

"Well, Connie wasn't with him, but there was a man sitting with him for a little while. I don't think they had but one drink a piece, and then they left."

"Did you know the man he was with?"

"No, but he'd been in here a few times. I guess he was a tourist. I never saw him again after that night."

"Do you remember what time they left?"

"It was before closing. You know, if I don't have entertainment, I have to close at midnight. Some kinda stupid liquor law. And they was gone sometime before I closed. The place was busy that night, and noisy. After Logan left, everybody seemed to head home. I remember a couple of the fishermen from Cortez came in and got into an argument over their first drink. They had been somewhere else first I guess, 'cause they was flying low when they got here. You know I don't put up with that kinda crap, so I sent 'em packing, and closed early. Logan probably left here around eleven."

"Did Logan and the man come in together?" I asked.

"No, the other guy had been here for a couple of hours, sipping beer. He called Logan by name and they seemed to know each other. They were laughin' and cuttin' up, and then they left."

"Logan may have gone down to Frisco's after he left here. Do you know anybody over there?" I asked.

"You'll want to talk to Slim Jim Martin. He owns the place and tends bar. He's tall and skinny and mean as hell, and nobody messes with him much. He keeps a baseball bat under the bar in case he needs to quiet things down."

"You're sure Logan left around eleven?" I asked.

"Pretty sure. What's this all about Matt?"

"I'm trying to trace Logan's route that night. I need to find the man he was drinking with, and maybe establish an alibi."

"I heard you was comin' out of retirement. Are you sure you want to do this?"

"No. But I don't seem to have much choice right now. Maybe when things settle down, Logan can get a real lawyer."

"I wasn't suggestin' you weren't no real lawyer, Matt. I hear things, and I heard you used to have a pretty big reputation."

"Well, I quit, Dewey. Maybe I won't have to take this case all the way in. We'll see. I gotta go. If you happen to see the guy Logan was with that night, give me a call, OK?"

"Bet your ass, boy. I hope you can save Logan's bacon."

I had never been to Frisco's, and did not know anybody there. It was nearing five o'clock, so I decided to walk the block down Bridge Street and see if Slim Jim could be of any help. It had already been a long time since the murder, and I knew that the more time that went by, the dimmer memories would get.

Frisco's was dark and small. There was a bar along one end of the room, with seven or eight stools taking up the space. A few tables were crowded into the rest of the space. This was a place for drinking. Nothing else. No pool, no music, no ambience.

A man who probably stood six feet five and weighed 150 pounds was behind the bar. Two old guys in tee shirts huddled over glasses filled with dark whiskey at a table in the corner, not talking or reacting to anything. They reminded me of two cats sitting in a yard, side by side, seemingly oblivious to each other. I had always wondered if the cats had some sort of extra sensory perception that allowed them to communicate without words or gestures. I doubted that the old timers in the corner had that faculty.

"Are you Jim?" I asked, as I slid onto a bar stool.

"Yep, what'll you have."

"Got a Miller Lite?"

"Yep."

He put the bottle in front of me, and was turning away, when I said, "Got a minute, Jim?"

"Yep."

A man of few words, I thought. "I'm Matt Royal. Dewey Clanton told me you might be willing to help me out with a problem."

"I doubt it, but if you're a friend of Dewey's, I'll do what I can. She just called. Said you were coming in."

"Do you know Logan Hamilton?

"Nope."

"I showed him the picture of Logan."

"Yeah, I know him. Didn't know his name was Logan. Didn't he just get indicted for killing that chick a month or so back?"

"That's the one."

"Man. I never made the connection between this dude and Logan. I knew the chick too."

"You did?" I was surprised.

"Knew her to see her. She came in a couple of times with your buddy there," he said, pointing to the picture.

I showed him the picture of Connie. "Is this the woman?"

"Yep. I recognized her picture in the paper when she got killed."

I remembered that both the Bradenton and Sarasota papers had run pictures of Connie with the story about murder on Longboat Key. I never figured out where they got the picture, but it was the same one in both papers.

"Do you remember the last time you saw Logan in here?"

"Yep."

"When?" This was getting to be a difficult fact finding mission.

"Are you a cop?"

"No. I'm a just a friend of Logan's trying to help him out of this jam."

"The night the chick was murdered."

"What do you mean?"

He looked at me, exasperated. "That was the last time I saw your buddy."

"How is it that you remember that?"

"Well, he was drinking double scotches with a buddy, and getting drunk as hell. The buddy left, and he had a couple more and left. A couple days later I saw the picture in the paper and remembered that this guy and the chick would come in together some. It just stuck in my mind that he was here on the same night the chick got killed."

"Do you know who he was with that night?" I asked.

"Nope. Never saw him before or since. And I got a good memory for faces."

"Do you remember what time he left?"

"Nope. Is it important?"

"Real important."

"When was she killed?"

"The night of April 15."

"Hang on a minute," he said, and disappeared through a door behind the bar.

I sat, nursing my beer. The old timers hadn't said a word since I came in, and I don't think they'd moved either.

Jim came back through the door, holding what appeared to be a receipt. "I remember that your buddy was the last guy out that night, and I locked the door as soon as he left. I always go to the bank next door and deposit the money in the ATM. Here's the receipt for that deposit."

I looked at the receipt. It was time stamped for 1:44 A.M., April 16.

"How long was Logan here that night?" I asked.

"Couple of hours, maybe a little longer."

"Thanks. Can you hold on to this receipt for me? It might be important."

"I've got every receipt I ever got," he said. "You know, banks will screw you every chance they get."

I thanked him and left. The old codgers in the corner were as still as stone.

I drove back across the bridge onto Longboat Key, and about four miles further to the Golden Beach Inn. It was not quite 6:00, and I knew the general manager would be having his after-work drink in the bar near the indoor pool. I parked, walked through the lobby and out onto the covered pool deck. The pool bar was suspended above the pool, accessible only by a circular wrought iron staircase. There were two visitors sitting at one end smoking cigars, and a boy of about ten eating a pizza at a table in the corner. One of the men would occasionally look over at the child and say something.

My quarry was at the opposite end of the bar, hunched over a tall glass of amber liquid. He was a big man in a rumpled suit and a five o'clock shadow. He wore a large class ring on his left ring finger, advertising that he had graduated from some Midwestern university known mostly for its football team. He glanced at me as I took the stool next to him.

"Hello, Matt," he said.

"How you doing, Keith," I said.

"Not bad. We've got the summertime blues around here, but we're doing better than last year."

"Good. Did you ever find a replacement for Connie?"

"Yeah. She's not as good as Connie, but she's okay. I was surprised to see that Logan killed her."

"He didn't Keith," I said. "He's been accused, but I don't think they'll be able to bring him to trial."

"Well, all I know is what I read in the paper."

"That's not always the best source," I said. "I want to find Connie's ex-husband, Keith. Can I have a look at Connie's personnel file?"

"I don't see why not. She won't mind." Keith Hastings was a dour man who had come to the key a couple of years before to manage the Golden Beach Inn. He did not live on Longboat and had never been friendly with the locals. He had hit on Connie a few times, and once, when Connie ran into him on the mainland in a bar, he had become abusive. He told Connie that she was a goddam tease, and that he was going to have her one way or another. He apologized the next morning, and Connie had let it slide. She said he was a good boss who let her do what she was supposed to do without interfering. That, according to Connie, overcame his occasionally hitting on her.

I had met him a number of times in this very bar, where he came every day that he worked. He would have one drink on the house, drop a two dollar tip for the bartender, and leave. No one knew if he had a social life, but it was rumored that he had left a wife and family somewhere up north.

"It might help me to get a lead on who killed her," I said. "I think she would have wanted us to do everything we could to clear Logan."

"Sure," he said, and finished off his drink in one swallow.

In his office Keith pulled Connie's personnel file from a large filing cabinet setting against one wall. "You can look through this, and I'll make you copies of anything you want," he said.

It was a thin file, containing an application, a letter from the registrar at Northwestern University, attesting that Connie had received a Bachelor's degree in social work twelve years before. She had gone to work at the Golden Beach four years before, and made $30,000 per year at the time of her death. She received job performance reviews every six months, and both Keith Hastings and his predecessor had given her top marks for a job well done.

"I'd like a copy of her application and the letter from Northwestern," I said. Do you have anymore information on her in another file, maybe?"

"No, that's it. We've tightened up some on our personnel policies since I took over, but I didn't bother the employees who were doing a good job. Our later hires have a much more extensive background check."

"I appreciate this, Keith. Can I buy you a drink?" I asked.

"No thanks. I've got to get home. Some other time."

"Any time, Keith. Thanks again," I said.

I went back to the bar for another beer, and a little conversation with the bartender whom I had known casually over the years. "Darlene," I said, "Does Keith ever have more that the one beer here?"

"I've seen him drink himself silly on two or three occasions. He was always in a foul mood when he did. Usually, though, he just has the one beer. I think he's one of those mean drunks who knows it, and usually controls his drinking."

"When was the last time he got drunk here?"

"Several weeks ago. I don't remember just when."

"Anyway to find out? It might be important on a case I'm involved in."

"Every drink I serve is put into the computer attached to my register. If my computer doesn't jibe with the number of drinks sold the night before, I'll hear about it from the food and beverage guys. I can probably figure out the date, because I always put Keith's drinks under a management category. Let those guys figure out how to charge it."

She went to her computer terminal and worked the keys. "April 15," she said. "I remember now, because I thought he was probably pissed about his taxes."

I sat in my living room, reviewing the application. The sun was setting in the west, casting a burnt orange reflection off the white clouds hanging above the bay. The tide was out, and through the glass doors I could see an egret wading in the shallows looking for a meal. He would stand very still for a long time, and then in the blink of an eye, drop his head into the water, and come up with a small fish in his beak. He would tilt his head, and the fish would slide down his throat. He would be there for hours, I knew. A bird of great patience.

The information on the application was slim. Connie had been born 34 years before in Rockford, Illinois, and graduated from high school there. She had finished Northwestern in four years, and worked for two years for a foundation that ran a homeless shelter in Chicago. She had apparently married then, because for the next six years she listed her occupation as housewife. The Golden Beach manager had not written to the foundation for a recommendation, probably because of the passage of so much time.

In the block for emergency contact, she had written "none" and then explained that her parents were dead and that she had been an only child. She had no known relatives.

I had the feeling that the only person who would have wanted Connie dead was her ex-husband. I knew a little about spouse abusers from past cases, and I knew they were an unwholesome bunch. They were usually on some sort of power trip, and felt that their wives should be under their thumbs at all times. It was not that unusual for a man with a history of abusing his wife to go off the deep end when she screwed up the courage to leave him. A lot of homicides were committed by these men, who felt betrayed by the object of their abuse. This was the reason why most abuse shelters were hidden. The people who ran them were aware of the husband's propensity for lethal violence and wanted to protect the poor woman.

If Connie's ex-husband had found out where she was living, he might have come looking for her. It was the only scenario that made sense. Unless Keith was in the picture somehow. He had made a few runs at Connie, and was threatening when drunk. I wondered if there was mere coincidence in his getting drunk on the key on the very night Connie was killed. I didn't think Connie had any enemies, and I didn't think Logan killed her, not even by accident during rough sex.

I took off my thinking cap and headed for O'Sullivan's for a dinner of wings and beer. I know, its not a nutritionally balanced meal.

Chapter 10

By the time I finished my jog on the beach and read the paper the next morning, it was almost ten o'clock , nine in Evanston, Illinois. I called the Chicago area information operator. A computer gave me the number of the Alumni office at Northwestern University and informed me that for 85 cents more, it would dial the number. Bad deal. I hung up and dialed the number myself. When you're retired you have to be careful of these extra little expenses.

When the phone was answered I explained that I was trying to find an address of an alumna and wondered whom I needed to talk to. The young lady on the other end of the phone explained that they did not give out that information, and I asked to talk to whomever was in charge. "That would be Mrs. Cooper," the voice said, and sent me into the nether world of modern communications. I listened to a Puccini opera coming over the wire until it was abruptly cut off by another voice, "This is Mrs. Cooper."

"Mrs. Cooper, my name is Matt Royal. I'm a lawyer down in Longboat Key, Florida, and I'm investigating the death of one of your graduates. I was hoping I could get the last address you had for her."

"Oh my goodness. I'm always sorry to hear that one of our people has passed on. What was his name?"

"Actually, it was a woman named Connie Sanborne. She graduated there about twelve years ago."

"She was young, then. How did she die, if I might ask?"

"She was murdered, Mrs. Cooper."

"Oh, I'm sorry to hear that. But I'm afraid we have rules against giving out the kind of information you're looking for."

"I guess that rule is to keep solicitors from bothering alumni, but that won't be a problem for Connie," I said.

"Well, Mr. Royal, a rule is a rule, you know. If I broke it for you, I would have to break it for everyone."

Ah, I thought, the last refuge of the bureaucratic mind. "Would you let me speak to whoever is in charge up there?"

"Why, I'm in charge, sir. I'm the alumni director."

"Would it help if our chief of police told you about Connie's murder and vouched for me?"

"I guess it wouldn't hurt," she said.

"Would you call him at the station and then call me back?"

"Alright, Mr. Royal. I guess I can do that much."

I gave her the police department's number and hung up. She called me back in about twenty minutes.

"I talked to Chief Lester," she said. "He was very nice and told me I could trust you."

"Thank you for your effort."

"I pulled Connie's file. This is the second time her death was reported, but it was a mistake the first time."

"That's odd," I said. "What was that all about?"

"About four years ago we got a letter from her husband telling us that Connie had died and we should remove her name from our mailing list. A few days later we got a letter from Connie telling us that she had divorced her husband and taken her maiden name back. She also said that if we heard from him that she was dead, not to believe it. She gave us a new address."

"What was the new address?"

"A post office box in Sarasota, Florida," Mrs. Cooper said.

"Was Sanborne her maiden name or her married name?"

"Maiden. Her married name was Jarski."

"Do you have an address for her prior to her divorce?" I asked.

"Yes. Mrs. David Jarski, 418 Linder Street, Des Moines, Iowa."

"Thank you very much, Mrs. Cooper. You've been a great help."

"You're welcome, Mr. Royal." She hung up.

I then put in a call to the reference librarian at the Des Moines public library. These people provide a wealth of information if you simply ask. I asked the lady who answered the phone to check the criss-cross directory for me and tell me who lived at 418 Linder St. She put me on hold for a minute and then told me that David and Lisa Jarksi occupied the home in question.

I called Delta and made reservations for a flight from Tampa to Des Moines, with a change of planes in Cincinnati. I would leave the next morning. early. Then I called K-Dawg and told him I would be out of town for a few days. On the island, you never leave without letting someone know. Otherwise, they'd worry.

Years before, a very bright lawyer named Fred Peed, had told me that whether you were a first class lawyer or not, your clients thought you were, and first class lawyers always fly first class. I still subscribed to that bit of philosophy, even though it made no economic sense. In this day of frequent flier mileage everybody flies first class. It is not the luxury it once was, but the seats are bigger and the drinks are free.

I took the airport shuttle van up to Tampa, taking the Sunshine Skyway Bridge across the mouth of Tampa Bay, through St. Petersburg and back across the bay on the Howard Frankland Bridge. Pelicans were diving into the bay for their meals, and I smiled, remembering the story a friend told, of explaining to some Midwesterner that the Pelicans were committing suicide when they dove headfirst into the water.

The Tampa airport is a marvel of passenger amenities, and you never have to walk more than a few feet from parking to plane. We made it in plenty of time, and I boarded after a minimal hassle with the security measures.

The flight was uneventful. I was wearing my lawyerly navy blue pinstriped suit, with a powder blue button-down shirt and a maroon and white striped tie. I always got better service on planes if I dressed the part and rode first class. I know, I'm a little preppie sometimes.

I wasn't sure exactly how I was going to approach David Jarski. I couldn't just knock on his door and accuse him of killing his ex-wife. But, he was the best bet I had for the murderer. No one else would have had any motive to kill Connie, and I didn't think her murder was random. Not with the body showing up at Logan's apartment.

The only thing I could figure was that Jarski had somehow found Connie on Longboat and had followed her the night of her death. If he had sat outside Moore's while we had drinks, it would have been no problem to follow her down to the marina. He must have waited there when he saw Logan's boat come in. Maybe he was just stalking her and had become enraged when he saw Logan having sex with Connie. This would be the kind of thing that could send a batterer into a murderous rage.

I thought that I should use some subterfuge to meet Jarski and get some idea of his movements during the third week of April. If I could put him on Longboat Key during that time, I could make a pretty good case that he murdered Connie. I didn't have to prove he did it, just prove enough circumstances to put a reasonable doubt in the mind of the jury that tried Logan.

I got to Des Moines shortly after noon and rented a Chevy Cavalier from Hertz. I got directions to the Merle Hays shopping mall from the counter girl at the rental car terminal and headed there. I found what I was looking for in the middle of one of the side concourses of the mall; a machine I had seen in every mall I had ever been in. I put a dollar in and manipulated the touch pad and in a minute had four very professional looking business cards that identified me as Matthew Royal, General Agent of Princeton Insurance Group, with offices on Michigan Avenue in Chicago.

I found Linder Avenue on the city map I purchased at the first gas station I came to after leaving the mall. It was on the north side of town, near Interstate 35, part of a neighborhood probably built before World War II. The houses were mostly bungalows, lining streets shaded by large overhanging Elm trees. The sidewalks were swept clean, except for an occasional tricycle or small metal wagon. It looked like a neighborhood that was being recycled; older people moving on or dying and the younger folks with their kids moving in. It was not a wealthy neighborhood, but it was pleasant in the Spring sun, reflecting low level prosperity and neighborliness.

The Jarski home at 418 was typical of the other houses on Linder Avenue. It had a fresh coat of white paint, and the dark shingle roof seemed fairly new. A long porch ran along the entire front of the house. At one end was an old fashioned porch swing suspended from the ceiling by light chain. There were large flower pots on either side of the front door, filled with a flowering green shrub of some sort. A small bicycle with training wheels sat at the other end of the porch, seemingly unafraid of being stolen. A driveway ran up the side of the house to a single car detached garage at the back of the house. The door was closed, and I could not tell if a car was there.

I parked in front of the house at the curb, and sat for a moment thinking of how to approach a wife killer. It was hard to imagine violence in this quiet neighborhood, and I didn't think Jarski would kill me on sight. I decided that I looked like an insurance agent, and would just feel him out to start with.

A knock on the driver's side window startled me. I turned quickly to see an aging lady in a floppy hat, holding a rake and showing a large smile. I rolled the window down. "Sorry," she said. "Didn't mean to scare you. But Dr. Jarski's not home."

"Dr. Jarski?"

"The man who lives here. That's who you're looking for isn't it?"

"I didn't know he was a doctor."

"He's a Ph.D. Teaches history out at the community college. That is who you were looking for, isn't it?"

"Yes, but I don't know him. I was hoping to catch him at home."

"Well, he usually gets in about 3:30. He picks Lisa up at school and comes home."

"Lisa?" I asked.

"His daughter. She goes to the elementary school over on Redmond St."

"What time does his wife get home? I'd really like to talk to both of them."

"Oh, she's dead, poor thing. About four years now."

"Did you know her?"

"Connie? Sure, they lived here for a couple of years before she died. She was real sweet. Took good care of her family."

"I don't mean to pry. Its none of my business, and I planned to meet with Dr. Jarski about some insurance," I said. "But, I had the impression that he was married."

"Nope. I've lived right across the street for fifty years. Raised three sons and two daughters in that house. Knew the Popes who lived in the Jarski house for most of those years. He died, and Millie ended up in a nursing home. The Jarskies bought the house when Dr. Jarski got the job out at the college. Came here from Chicago with little Lisa. Then Connie got sick, and it took her two years to die. Breast cancer. What a waste."

A late model Ford Taurus passed by slowly and turned into the driveway of the Jarski house, stopping just past the sidewalk. A girl of about eight got out of the passenger door and ran toward us.

"Hi Mrs. Gibbs," she said. "I made an A on my spelling test today."

"Good for you Lisa," the elderly lady said. "You're real smart, just like your daddy."

A small man in a rumpled suit had got out of the car. He was about five eight and was balding on top. He made up for this with a thick pony tail hanging to his shoulder blades. He wore gold rimmed spectacles and did not look at all like a man who could have beat up Connie Sanborne on a regular basis. She could have taken him with one hand.

I got out of the car, and as he approached, stuck out my hand. "Dr. Jarski? I'm Matt Royal."

"How do you do Mr. Royal?"

"He came to see you David," Mrs. Gibbs said. "I was just trying to get out of yard work and was passing the time of day."

"I enjoyed chatting Mrs. Gibbs. May I have a minute of your time Dr. Jarski?"

"Go ahead," said Mrs. Gibbs. "I've got some fresh lemonade that I'll bet Lisa would like."

"Come up on the porch, Mr. Royal," Jarski said.

Lisa and Mrs. Gibbs crossed to street toward her house, with Lisa talking loud and fast about her school day. We mounted the porch, and Jarski gestured me into the swing. He pulled up a chair facing me, and said, "What can I do for you, Mr. Royal?"

I handed him my card. "I'm with Princeton Insurance Group, and we're investigating the death of a woman in Florida."

"How does that concern me?"

"He name was Connie Sanborne. She graduated from Northwestern University twelve years ago, and according to the alumni records, was married to you."

"I don't understand," he said. "My wife's maiden name was Connie Sanborne, and she graduated from Northwestern twelve years ago, but she died of breast cancer four years ago. There must be some kind of mixup."

"Do you have a picture of her?" I asked.

"Sure. Come on in the house."

We went through the front door into the 1930s. The room was decorated much like my grandmother's house in Waycross, Georgia was when I was a child. The dark hardwood floor had two hooked throw rugs in big circular patterns. The sofa was humpbacked and bordered on either end by tables with cloths hanging over the sides. There was an upright Philco radio in one corner and a small writing desk against the wall next to it. On the long wall opposite the front windows sat an upright piano.

"Nice room," I said.

"I have made a specialty of the study of the years leading up to World War II," he said. "I often think I was born about fifty years too late. Connie and I liked the 30's ambience."

He walked over to the writing desk and picked up an 8 X 10 picture resting in a sterling silver frame. "This was our wedding picture," he said. "Who would have thought it would have lasted such a short time."

The picture was in color and had been taken in front of a church alter. Jarvis had a head full of hair, hanging just below his ears. The bride was looking up at him with a large smile. Her dark hair hung to her shoulders, black under the white lace of the cap and veil. She wasn't the Connie Sanborne I knew.

"Let me show you a picture of the woman whose death I'm investigating," I said, pulling the picture of Connie taken by my pool that hot summer day. "Do you recognize her?"

"No," he said. "Can't say that I do. Are you sure this woman graduated from Northwestern at the same time as my Connie? There couldn't have been two people with the same name without Connie knowing about it."

I put the picture back in the inside pocket of my suit coat. "That 's the information I was given, Dr. Jarski. I'm sorry to have bothered you." We shook hands, and he showed me to the door.

I settled into my rental car, turned the ignition, placed the seatbelt in the prescribed position, and was about to leave, when I heard Jarski call to me. He was coming down the sidewalk at a fast pace, and came around to the driver's side of the car. I hit the power button to lower the window.

"May I see that picture again?" he asked.

I dug it out of the pocket of my coat laying on the passenger seat, and handed it to him. He studied the picture intently for a minute or so.

"You know," he said, so low I could hardly hear him. "I may know this woman. If it's who I think it is, she had long black hair, and worked with my wife for awhile in Chicago."

"What's her name?"

"If I'm right, this is a woman named Vivian Pickens. I only met her once, and that was before we left Chicago. But she and Connie were pretty close for awhile. Connie gave me a list of people to notify of her death, and Vivian was one of them. I dropped her a card a few weeks after the funeral."

"What kind of work did Connie do in Chicago?" I asked.

"She was a social worker, but after Lisa was born she stayed home."

"Do you still have Vivian's address?"

"I think so. Come on back inside."

We climbed the steps to the porch and went into the living room. He went to the writing desk, opened the middle drawer and came back with a sheet of paper with typewritten names and addresses.

"This is the list of people Connie wanted notified," he said as he handed me the paper.

Vivian's name was next to a street address in Chicago. I noticed several other names that did not mean anything to me, and the Office of Alumni Affairs at Northwestern University.

"Did you notify the Alumni Office at Northwestern too?" I asked.

"Yeah. I made sure I let everyone on the list know. I guess Connie wanted to have her death listed in the Alumni magazine so that people she had known in college would know."

"This is strange," I said. "I got your address from the Alumni Office and was told that Connie's death had been reported about four years ago, and then a few days later, they got a call from Connie telling them that she had divorced you, and that you must have sent the death notice out of spite."

"That's absurd," he said, his voice rising. "Why in the world would anyone want to do something like that?"

"I don't know, but maybe I can find out. Did you meet Connie in college?"

"No, I went to the University of Chicago to graduate school. Connie had finished Northwestern and was working at a half-way house for women near the UC campus. I actually met her while waiting for a bus one day."

"What kind of place was the half-way house?"

"It was a place for women who had been released from prison but hadn't completed their sentences yet. The state would send them to this half-way house, where they could go to work during the day and have a structured environment in which to live. They got job training and help in finding a job. It was really quite successful, but Connie seemed to burn out after a few years. She was glad not to have to go back to work, I think."

"Was it run by the state?"

"No. It was run by a private foundation. I think someone had given the foundation a lot of money at some point, and it ran this place as a non-profit. It was called the Grant Settlement House."

"Is it still there?" I asked.

"As far as I know. It had been in business for thirty or so years when Connie worked there. They're on East 63rd Street, almost right under I-94. In fact, the address for Vivian is the same as for the Grant."

"You've been a big help, Dr. Jarski. I'm sorry I had to bother you."

"Look, Mr. Royal, I don't know what this is all about, but if you find out that someone is impersonating my wife, I'd like to know about it."

"I'll let you know what I find out Dr. Jarski."

Chapter 11

My airline guide book told me that the first flight I could get out to Midway Airport in Chicago was at six o'clock the next morning. I found a motel off the interstate near the airport and checked in. I ate a greasy country fried steak dinner in the motel coffee shop, and headed for my room. I read a few chapters of Dennis Lehane's latest novel and went to sleep.

I got up early, dressed and drove to the airport, turned in my car and took the shuttle to the terminal. I boarded an American Trans Air flight, a small passenger jet, and was offered a cup of coffee and a sweet roll for breakfast. I arrived at Midway at 7:30, rented a car at the Hertz desk, got into a new Chevrolet and left. I took 63rd street out of the airport and drove the few blocks to the Grant Settlement House.

Just as I was parking the car, my cell phone rang. It was Logan.

"How are you, buddy?" he asked.

"Great. Look Logan, was Connie a real red head?"

"What do you mean?"

"You know what I mean. You saw her naked."

"Oh. Nah. She was red on top and black on bottom. Like a Georgia football player. Why?"

"Not funny, Logan. I was just wondering. How are you doing?"

"About the same. Still moving around. Where are you?"

"In Chicago."

"Chicago. What the hell are you doing there?"

"I'll tell you later. Call me in a couple of days. Gotta go now." I clicked the off button on the phone and got out of the car.

The Grant Settlement House was a four story nondescript building, set in a block of buildings that looked much the same. A glass double door had its name painted at about eye level. I pushed through the door and found myself in a small reception area that was furnished with two straight back chairs and a sofa that looked a little more comfortable. There was a green metal desk in front and to the side of a door that I assumed led to the rest of the building. A woman in some kind of uniform sat at the desk. She was about forty with close cropped brown hair going to gray. She was trim, wearing glasses and a smile. Her uniform shirt, open at the neck, had a badge and a shoulder patch with a private security firms logo.

"May I help you, sir?" she asked, smiling.

"Yes. I'm trying to find out some information about a woman who worked here several years ago. Is there someone I can see who might help me?"

"I'm sure our Ms. Turner would be the one to see. She's the director. Have a seat and let me see if she can see you now." She picked up a phone and turned her back to me, speaking softly. She hung up and said, "Ms. Turner will be right out."

I took a seat on the sofa. I was still wearing my lawyer suit and tie, and felt like a professional. I wondered what kind of woman Ms. Turner would be. Probably some matronly type, I guessed. I was right. A woman of about sixty came through the door and approached me. She was a few pounds overweight with gray hair hanging almost to her shoulders. She wore a green dress, a gold wedding band on her ring finger, and no other jewelry. She was smiling and holding out her hand. "I'm Cynthia Turner," she said. "Can I help you?"

"I'm Matt Royal, Ms. Turner. I'm interested in a woman who used to work here. I wonder if I could have a few minutes of your time."

"Certainly. Come on back. I'm not sure how much help I can be, given confidentiality restraints. Who are you interested in?"

We went through the door behind the receptionist and down a corridor with offices on either side. We turned into the fourth office, which was furnished with a metal desk like the one in front, and a couple of old side chairs.

"Connie Sanborne," I said.

"Forgive the offices, Mr. Royal. We operate on a tight budget and take a lot of government cast-offs for our furniture. May I ask what your interest in Connie Sanborne is?"

"Did you know her?"

"I've been here since the beginning, Mr. Royal, more than forty years. I know everyone who ever worked here."

I gave her one of my cards, one of the real ones that identified me as Matthew Royal, Attorney at Law, Longboat Key, Florida. "I'm looking into the murder of a woman whose name was Connie Sanborne, and I have been told that she worked here some years ago."

"Yes, Connie worked here after she graduated from Northwestern. But she married a boy from U of C and moved to Iowa, I think. But I don't understand. Her husband wrote me a note a few years back saying that Connie had died of breast cancer."

"I just left her husband in Des Moines. I don't think I'm dealing with the same Connie Sanborne, but the murdered woman claimed to have graduated from Northwestern the same year that your Connie did. Yet, the alumni office only has a record of one Connie Sanborne."

"What is your interest in this, Mr. Royal, if I may ask?"

"I'm representing the man who is accused of killing Connie."

I pulled out the picture of Connie taken by my pool, and handed it to Ms. Turner. "Is that Connie Sanborne?"

"Oh, no. This doesn't look anything like Connie."

"Do you recognize this woman?"

"No. She doesn't look familiar."

"Does the name Vivian Pickens mean anything to you?"

"Why, yes. She was one of our clients."

She looked at the picture again, studying it intently.

"If you imagine long black hair on the woman in the picture..."

"Of course," she interrupted. "This is Vivian. Was she murdered?"

"The woman in that picture was murdered in Longboat Key about six weeks ago. She used the name Connie Sanborne, though. I'd never heard Vivian's name until yesterday. You said she was one of your clients. What does that mean? It was my understanding that she worked here."

"Mr. Royal, what I'm about to tell you is mostly a matter of public record, and some of it is gossip. But I guess it can't hurt Vivian now."

She told me this story. Vivian Pickens was from somewhere down south. She had come to Chicago when she was sixteen, running from an abusive parent. She waitressed for a while in coffee shops and fast food joints, and began to experiment with drugs. Her salary and meager tips could not keep pace with the drug bills, and one night she had sex with a dealer for a vial of crack. It was easy. She tried this a few more times, and then started sleeping with men for money to feed her growing habit. Within two years of coming to Chicago she was working as a call girl in a ring run by a pimp known as Golden Joe. She sold her body and provided her johns with cocaine. When she was twenty-five, she was arrested and charged with prostitution and the sale of cocaine. She was tried, convicted and sentenced to eight years in prison. She had spent four years at the Illinois women's prison and was released to the Grant Settlement House.

It was at Grant that Vivian had met Connie, who was the social worker assigned to her. Vivian was an innately intelligent woman and had taken some business and secretarial courses while in prison. She had used those skills at Grant and became sort of an assistant business manager for the foundation. Vivian had been good at it, and was considered a great success. She and Connie were the same age and had become close. Connie once told Ms. Turner that she, Connie, might have ended up the same way Vivian had if she had come from the same background.

Vivian had spent one year at the Grant, as it was called, and was ready to venture out on her own. She was put on probation and found a job at an accountant's office a few blocks north of the University. She would stop in periodically, but eventually the visits stopped. Some time after the visits had ended, Vivian's probation officer called the Grant looking for her. She had missed two mandatory meetings, and a warrant would be issued for her arrest if she missed another.

A few weeks later Ms. Turner called the probation officer to inquire about Vivian. She was told that Vivian never showed up again, and that a warrant had been issued for her arrest. This was about the same time that Ms. Turner had gotten the note from Dr. Jarski telling her about Connie's death. She'd had never heard anything about Vivian again.

"We have a lot of success stories here, Mr. Royal, but we can't save them all. Some of these women never get their lives straightened out. I thought Vivian would be one who did."

"Perhaps she did, Ms. Turner. If the woman in that picture is really Vivian Pickens, she came to Longboat Key as Connie Sanborne and started a new life. She was the sales manager for one of the beach hotels, and she had a lot of friends."

Mrs. Turner expressed her regrets about Vivian's death, and gave me the name and address of Vivian's probation officer. I thanked her and left the building.

I sat in my car at the curb and called Bill Lester on my cell phone. After identifying myself to the police department operator, I was put through.

"Where the hell are you, Matt?" Bill asked.

"In Chicago. Look, Bill, don't you routinely fingerprint murder victims?"

"Sure. Why?"

"I'll tell you in a minute. But first, tell me if you ran Connie Sanborne's fingerprints."

"I'm sure the medical examiner printed her, but there was no need to run the prints. We all new who she was."

"Maybe not, Bill. Do me a favor and run Connie's prints through the FBI computer."

"I guess I can do that, but why?"

"I don't think the person we thought was Connie was really named Connie Sanborne."

The chief let out a slow exclamation of breath. "Wow," he said. "Then who the hell was she?"

"I have an idea, but I'd like you to run those prints for me and let me know what comes up."

"Okay. If she was ever printed anywhere, I should have the information in a couple of hours. Where can I reach you?"

I gave him my cell phone number.

I suddenly remembered that I had not had breakfast. It was almost mid-morning, and the day was getting hot; an unusually warm Spring in Chicago. I spotted a coffee shop at the corner and left the car and walked down the street. The neighborhood was decaying. The signs were everywhere. Graffiti were on the walls of many of the building, and no attempt had been made to clean it off or paint over it. Some of the buildings were empty, with large slabs of plywood covering the windows. I guessed that thirty years before this had been a neighborhood shopping district with small shops and grocery and hardware stores. Down a side street I saw what must have been a trucking terminal of some kind. There were about a dozen semi trucks backed into a loading dock, but otherwise the street was deserted.

I opened the door to the coffee shop, which bore a computer printed sign that said, "Home of the bottomless cup of coffee." A blast of air came shooting down from some kind of overhead contraption, startling me. I shut the door and the air stopped. A waitress standing by the door chuckled. "It keeps the bugs out," she said. The small restaurant was awash in air conditioning, the cups of coffee before the diners steaming in the cool air. A television set perched on a shelf high up in a corner, placed so the patrons could see it. CNN was running a newscast about Governor Wentworth and his chances of getting his party's nomination for President.

There was a counter along the length of the shop and booths against the window. The counter seats were taken by burly men and two hard looking women. I assumed these to be the drivers of the rigs parked down the block. I was definitely out of place with the lawyer look. They probably thought I was a pimp.

I took a seat in a booth and ordered eggs over easy with grits and white toast. The waitress, a small boned middle aged woman in a pink uniform and hair net, informed me that she did not have grits, but that I could have hash browns. I told her that was okay. I asked for coffee, no cream. She said, "You can't get it here without cream. You can get it without milk, though." She hooted at her joke and walked off.

I sat and reviewed what I knew. I was feeling a little out of sorts. How could Connie or Vivian or whatever her name was have fooled all her friends so badly? I was a little angry at Connie/Vivian because she had made a fool out of me and the others. Then I mentally kicked myself, thinking, "You idiot. Think what that poor woman must have gone through." I wondered how Vivian could have turned herself into Connie so easily, but as I thought about it, I knew it wasn't that hard.

They were close to the same age, and Vivian knew enough about Connie to handle any idle questions. She knew where Connie was born, so it would have been easy for her to go to Connie's hometown and get a certified copy of her birth certificate. She probably had access to Connie's social security number from her work at the Grant, and could adopt it as her own. She would have gone to a driver's license bureau in Des Moines, identified herself as Connie Sanborne and told them that she had lost her driver's license. With the birth certificate and proper social security number, she would have had no trouble getting a duplicate license issued. When she got to Florida she would only have had to turn that license in at any Florida Driver's license office and gotten a Florida license issued. It was simple. With the license and birth certificate, she had a new identity. She also now owned a degree from Northwestern University, and assuming that a prospective employer did not check too far back, she would have no trouble getting a job. Unless you were trying to find employment in a classified government agency, there was not much of a check done on anyone. The human resources manager of the typical employer might send a routine inquiry to the college to make sure that the employee had the degree she said she did, but that would be the end of it. That is about what happened to Connie, I thought. She had made herself into a different person by taking a dead woman's identity. But why?

I paid the bill, left the hard joking waitress a three dollar tip, and went outside, again getting a blast of air from above the door. The streets were heating up, with the sun moving almost directly overhead. I took my jacket off and held it over my shoulder. Sweat was beginning to dampen my white dress shirt. I was irritable and the harsh coffee was settling uncomfortably in my stomach. I reached the rental, got in and cranked the engine, turning the AC to high. I sat there for a minute with the door open, letting the car cool down. My phone rang. I reached over to the passenger seat and wrestled the phone out of my inside coat pocket. It was Bill Lester.

"Shit, Matt. That wasn't Connie Sanborne we buried."

"What did you get, Bill?"

"Her name was Vivian Pickens. She was busted in Chicago nine years ago and charged with prostitution and possession of cocaine with intent to sell. She was tried, found guilty and sentenced to eight years in prison. There is a warrant out on her for violation of probation. What the hell is going on?"

I told him what I had found out. "What I don't understand," I said, "is why she ran. According to the people at the half-way house, she was doing fine. Her probation period was about up, and with her skills she could have gotten a good job. She probably could have stayed right there at the Grant."

"Who knows," he said. "Still, Matt, this doesn't change anything as far as Logan is concerned. It's no big deal to change the name of the victim on the indictment."

"I know, Bill, but this sure makes me curious about Vivian. Do you have anything else on her?"

"No, that's it. Name, place of arrest, charges and warrants. That's about all you get out of the feds. I remember when you couldn't get that much without weeks of waiting and begging. Ain't computers grand?"

"Yeah. Thanks Chief. I'll be in touch."

"Wait a minute. When're you coming home, and what about Logan?"

"I'll be there in a couple of days. We'll see about Logan."

"Take it easy, Matt." The line went dead.

The Illinois Probation and Parole office was housed in a nondescript mid-rise building, called the State Office Center, on Michigan Avenue. I found a parking place and walked the two blocks back to the building in a glaring noon day sun. By the time I entered the musty smelling building, I had saturated my shirt with sweat, and my mood was darker than my navy blue suit. I climbed two flights of stairs and entered a large room full of disreputable looking people lounging in the molded plastic chairs. Some were sprawled across several chairs, sound asleep. There was a counter at one end of the room behind which perched several clerks on high stools staring at computer terminals. I approached one, and said politely, "I wonder if you could help me."

"Take a number and be seated," she said, without looking up from her monitor.

"I need to speak with Will Ledbetter, please. Is he still in this office?"

"You'll have to take a number and wait your turn," she said, still staring at the monitor.

"What is your name, please?" I inquired, smiling.

"What do you need to know that for?" she asked, finally looking at me.

"Because," I said, "When the director of this department asks me who was rude to the gentleman who chairs the Senate Committee responsible for this office's budget, I want to be able to give him a name."

Her eyebrows went up. Her mouth opened and then closed, then opened again. "Just a moment, Sir. I'll tell Mr. Ledbetter you're here. Your name?"

"Royal," I said. "Matthew Royal."

She picked up the phone, punched in three numbers, and said, "Senator Royal is here to see you, Mr. Ledbetter." She paused a moment, said, "Yes, sir," and hung up the phone. "He'll be right with you Senator," she said, a pained smile briefly crossing her face.

A moment later a large black man, wearing a short sleeve white shirt, a paisley tie and a plastic pocket guard in his shirt pocket came lumbering through a side door. He looked at me and asked, "Senator Royal?"

"I'm Matt Royal," I said, sticking out my hand. We shook and he asked me to come back to his office. We walked through a maze of cubicles partitioned off by those cloth covered screens that you see in offices everywhere. His office was small and cramped, with a beat up wooden desk covered in papers. There was a vinyl and metal desk chair situated under a grime caked window, and two fold up metal chairs for visitors.

He motioned me to a seat, and said, "What can I do for you, Senator?"

"I'm not a senator," I said. "I'm a lawyer from Florida, and I think I have some information about one of your probationers."

"I thought Carol said you were a senator," he mumbled.

"I might have led her to believe that in order to get her attention."

"Oh, well, what the hell. Carol is probably having one of her bad days. Come to think of it, I don't remember her ever having a good day. Who do you have information on?"

"Does the name Vivian Pickens ring a bell?" I asked.

"Oh, yeah. I remember Vivian. She was one of the smart ones. I thought she'd make it, but one day she disappeared. I never could figure out if she's hiding or if she's dead. What do you know about her?"

"She's dead," I said. "You should be getting notification through your normal channels in a few days."

"I'm sorry to hear that. I always liked Vivian, and thought she would make it through the program and turn her life around. What happened?"

"She was murdered about six weeks ago in Longboat Key, Florida. She had been living there for about four years under an assumed name. You were right about her. She did make it. She was the sales manager for one of the beach hotels."

"What is your interest in this?" he asked.

"I'm representing the man accused of murdering her."

"Golden Joe?"

"The pimp? No. Why would you think that?"

"Joe's the only one who would have any reason to kill her," he said.

"Why would Joe want to kill her?"

"She testified against him in a murder case. That's the reason her sentence was reduced and she got the halfway house. Joe was sentenced to life for the murder, but I heard that he got out of prison about four months ago when the Supreme Court said that the prisoners were entitled to early release if they had a clean prison record. Joe only served about nine years."

"What can you tell me about Vivian's involvement in a murder case?"

"This goes back to about ten years," Ledbetter said. "Vivian and a woman named Paulette Massilon were working the convention circuit for Golden Joe. He had bellmen and other hotel people on his payroll, and they would steer out of town johns to him. One night Vivian and Paulette worked a deal together. Apparently some high roller liked two girls at a time, and Joe sent Vivian and Paulette to the Lakeview Hotel to meet him. When they got to the room Joe was there with a shitpot load of cocaine he was selling to the john. Apparently everybody snorted a line and Joe left. There was plenty of booze and coke and everybody used some of it all. At some point Vivian passed out, and when she came to, the john was standing over Paulette beating her with the base of a lamp. Vivian passed out again, and when she woke up Paulette was on the floor with her head bashed in. Vivian had been badly beaten as well and was lying on the floor trying to get to the phone when hotel security came busting through the door. Someone had called to complain about the noise.

"Luckily, when Vivian got to the hospital that night there was a young plastic surgeon on duty who took over her care. Her face was all busted up on one side, and she had some other broken bones. He did a good job on her at the county's expense.

"No one ever figured out who the john was, but with Vivian's testimony Joe was convicted of felony murder because he was involved in the felony of drug sale that resulted in a murder. Vivian pled guilty to prostitution and drug sale and got an eight year sentence reduced to four years incarceration and four of probation."

"So," I said, "You think Joe may have killed Vivian for revenge."

"I really don't know. But, he got out of prison shortly before you say Vivian was murdered. I guess he wasn't real happy about her testimony at the trial."

"Do you know where Joe is now?" I asked.

"No. I wasn't his probation officer, but I heard through the grapevine that he never showed up for his first probation conference. I don't think anybody knows where he is, but I heard he's back in the drug trade."

"Do you know where Vivian was originally from? Did she have any family left?"

"Let me get her file. I keep the skips right here."

He crossed to room to an old brown metal filing cabinet setting in the corner. He pulled out the bottom draw and retrieved a file. Sitting back at the desk, he opened the file and started pawing through all the loose pages. He pulled a piece of note paper from his middle drawer and wrote on it. He stopped and pulled one page from the file, leaned back in his chair and read the paper.

"This is interesting," he said. "I had forgotten about this. My notes say that the last time she came in she was concerned that somebody was following her. She had seen the same car parked in front of her apartment house two days in a row, and the morning she came in she saw the same car parked in front of her office. She could never get a good look at the driver, but she could tell he was a white man. That's all the note says, and that's the last time I saw her."

"How long ago was that?" I asked.

"A little over four years ago."

Interesting. She had first shown up on Longboat during the Spring months four years before, shortly after the tourist season had ended. "What about her family?" I asked.

He pushed the paper he had written on across the desk. "As far as we know, she only had a father left. Here's his address."

I thanked the man, shook his hand, and left the office, finding my own way out. As I passed the front counter I smiled at the clerk and said, "Hope to see you again soon, Carol." What the hell, let her have something to worry about for pissing off a senator.

Chapter 12

Pahokee, Florida sits on the southeastern shore of Lake Okeechobee, and if I had not known better, I would have thought I was in a third world village. Highway 441, coming up from LaBelle, is a narrow two lane road of crumbling macadam bordered on each side by deep ditches that keep the flow of water from the Everglades from submerging the road. The town perches hard by the levee protecting it from the lake that sits like a large hole in the south central peninsula of Florida. It is a hardscrabble town, peopled by migrant farm workers from Mexico and the Carribean and a few Americans, black and white. The store fronts were unpainted, and many were boarded up. A crowd of sullen young men had gathered in front of the only thriving business, a liquor store. A high hard sun beat down on them as they stood around in the still air. The humidity was already high at mid morning, and the smell of body odor permeated the air. It was the kind of town that you drive through fast, with your windows up and your doors locked. I had come to visit Howard Pickens.

The address written on the piece of paper handed me by Vivian's probation officer listed an address in Pahokee. I had flown out of Chicago's O'Hare Airport shortly after leaving Ledbetter's office, and I landed at Ft. Lauderdale-Hollywood International Airport reasonably on time. I found the Hertz counter and rented another Chevrolet. I never have to worry with the baggage area, for the simple reason that I never trust my bags to the airlines. If I can't carry it on the plane with me I leave it at home. When I get where I'm going, I need clean underwear and my shaving kit. If I were to check it through, chances are that I would never see it again. I had recently read that the flight attendants were lobbying the Federal Aviation Administration to require that most bags be checked. I thought they should have been lobbying their baggage handlers to take better care of people's luggage. If you could trust the airlines to deliver your checked bags to the proper place at the proper time, there wouldn't be any need to carry all that stuff on the plane.

The heat hangs heavy in South Florida in late May. It is filled with moisture, the humidity high. It permeates every cranny; even the shade is hot. Except on the water, there is no breeze to stir the heavy air. People begin to sweat moments after stepping from their air conditioned sanctuaries. The natives have always known this, and remembered the time before air conditioning came to Florida, followed soon after by hordes of Northerners seeking the sun. The natives will tell you that air conditioning ruined the state.

I boarded the bus that would take me to the rental car company's off airport lot to pick up my Chevrolet. It was half filled with men in suits, wilting in the afternoon heat. As we left the terminal the sky darkened, and within seconds, we were driving through a hard rain punctuated by lightning flashes and thunder. The regularly scheduled afternoon thunderstorm had arrived. It would only last a few minutes, and it would cool the air for a little while. Before dark came, though, the sun would again heat up the peninsula.

The jets sat on the runway, hunkered down against the storm, too cautious to take off into the windshears and lightning of the tropical storm. Their engines idled, the turbines turning slowly to keep the air conditioning churning through the cabin to cool the passengers, while the attendants served little bottles of booze to the businessmen headed out to their next meeting somewhere in the country. The young people hustling cars on the rental lot had donned yellow rain slickers, and they ran crab like, dodging puddles and oncoming cars.

The bus driver dropped me off right behind the car assigned me by the computer and told me to have a good day. The rain had slowed to a drizzle, and steam was beginning to rise from the asphalt that surrounded us for miles. The jets began to roar their take-off ditty as they lumbered down the runway, reaching for their natural element, the sky.

I threw my overnight bag into the trunk and drove out the exit, stopping briefly to show the guard that my rental papers were in order. I eased out of the airport property onto US highway 1, known in Broward County as Dixie Highway. I found and old mom and pop style motel nearby, ate something unremarkable at the Denny's next door, and went to bed.

I awoke early, checked out of the motel, ordered a cup of coffee and an Egg McMuffin at the McDonald's down the street, and ate breakfast as I drove out toward the turnpike. I drove west on I 575, and then north on highway 441, up through the Everglades and into Pahokee.

The lushness of the landscape of the interior southern part of Florida never fails to move me. At first glance the River of Grass seems to be endless and barren, but it is teeming with birds and reptiles, mammals and fish. As I moved north I came into the rich bottom land that is so conducive to growing cane for the sugar industry. On the horizon I could see the smoke flowing upward from a sugar cane processing plant. The fields were full of cane, six or seven feet high, with white flowers topping each bunch. The road was built up, so that I could see over the cane, which gave the impression of a sea of white plumes, undulating quietly in the little breeze that blew across the landscape. The road was filled with large trucks going toward the plant full of cane, or returning empty to the fields.

The address I had been given for Howard Pickens was four or five years old, and I didn't know if he still lived there, or was even alive. I tried to call him, but there was no listing in the phone directory. I decided to come anyway, on the chance of finding him.

I stopped at a convenience store and asked the clerk for directions. She told me that the address was in a worker's camp out in the cane fields. I drove about five miles north of town on 441, and found the dirt road shooting off to the east through the cane fields, straight as a ruler, all the way to the horizon. After about three miles on the hard dirt road I came to a cluster of houses built into a clearing on the side of the road. There were about twenty houses sitting in a semi-circle, old and tired looking, squatting on their concrete block pilings. The paint was fading and a few had plywood nailed over windows. There was no grass, and about a dozen black and Hispanic children were playing in the dirt in front of the houses. I stopped and asked a girl of about ten if she knew Mr. Howard Pickens. She didn't answer, but pointed to a house about mid-way in the semi-circle. I parked my car in front of the house and walked up the wooden steps to the little porch. A screen door separated me from the inside, but there did not seem to be a wooden door at all. A sour smell emanated from the house, and I could hear a radio in the background tuned to a talk show. I knocked on the door and waited. In a moment, a white man appeared in the front room. He was wearing a pair of tattered shorts and a tee shirt that didn't quite cover his large protruding belly. He hadn't shaved in several days, and the gray hair surrounding his bald cranium hadn't been combed in a year. He had a can of Budweiser in his hand. As he got closer to the door, I realized where the sour smell came from. He hadn't been near a shower in a week.

"Yeah?" he snarled.

"Mr. Pickens?" I asked.

"Yeah. Who're you?"

"My name is Royal. I'm a friend of Vivian's."

"Big fuckin' deal," he said. "Whadda you want?"

"Can I come in? I'd like to talk to you for a minute."

"What the hell. Come on in."

The house was small. I was in a living room, and a hall ran back toward what appeared to be the kitchen. There was a door on either side of the hall, and I guessed one went to the bedroom and the other to the bathroom. The living room furniture consisted of an old recliner chair and a brown sofa with the cotton stuffing coming out at odd places. On one wall was a table with old magazines stacked on it. There were no pictures or any other evidence of life in the room. "Sit down," he said, motioning to the sofa. He took the recliner.

"What kinda trouble is the girl in now?" he asked.

"I'm sorry to have to tell you this, Mr. Pickens, but Vivian is dead."

A look of momentary pain crossed his face, but was gone so quickly I couldn't be sure if what I said had registered with him. "Shit! I mighta knowed," he said. "When the money stopped coming I figured she either died or got arrested again. What happened to her?"

"She was murdered," I said. "I'm sorry."

"Who killed her?"

"We don't know. I'm trying to find out. A friend of mine has been charged with her murder, but I don't think he did it. We don't have much to go on. You said she was sending you money?"

"Yeah, she sent me a money order every other week. Wasn't much, but it helped me pay the rent and buy a little beer and food."

"Did you ever see her or talk to her?" I asked.

"Nah. She came around here about four years ago and said she was moving back to Florida and had a good job. I had just been shown the door by the sugar company. They said I was too old. I'd been cooking for these migrant workers for thirty years, but suddenly I'm too old. The pension they give me wasn't enough to live on, and I wasn't old enough for Social Security yet. They let me live in this house though, even if I do have to pay rent."

"You haven't seen her in four years?" I asked.

"No, but a few weeks after she left she started sending me the money orders."

"Did you ever talk to her after she left?"

"Nah. She sent me the name of some woman in Sarasota with an address and told me if I really needed her to get in touch that way."

"Who was the woman in Sarasota?"

"Hold on a minute," he said, and lumbered up from the chair. He went down the hall and through the door on the left. He came back a moment later with a typed letter, dated in the spring, four years before. The letter read,

> "Dad,
>
> I'm enclosing a money order for $50. I will send you one every two weeks. If you need anything else you can contact me through Ms. Connie Sanborne, P. O. Box 2871, Sarasota, Florida.
>
> > Vivian"

"Did you ever try to contact her?" I asked.

"Nah. We weren't ever close. After her ma took off she pretty much lived with a colored family in town. I didn't see much of her. Then I heard she went to Chicago and got sent to prison. When she showed up here fours year ago, she was just passing through. She didn't stay more'n an hour. Other than that letter, and the money orders, I never heard from her again."

"Didn't you want to know why the money orders stopped coming?"

"No. I figured if she wanted to stop sending them that was her business. I kinda thought she was in trouble again, on account of the time the police came by asking about her."

"Wait a minute," I said. "When did the money orders stop coming?"

"I guess I got the last one back in April or so."

"When did the police come by asking about her?"

"That would have been in early March. I remember because it was the same week of my birthday. I turned 62, and could start getting my social security. Since I had that, I didn't really miss the money orders much."

"Were these local police?" I asked.

"Nope. They was some kinda feds. There was two of them. Came in a big black car, a new one."

"What federal agency were they with?" I asked.

"I don't know that they said. Just said they was federal agents. I asked what it was about, but they wouldn't tell me."

"Did you tell them where to find Vivian?" I asked.

"Sure, they was federal agents. I did send Vivian a letter telling her that they was looking for her. I figured she'd know what was going on and could do what she liked about it. I wonder if they ever found her?"

I thought they probably had, and I didn't think they were federal agents.

Chapter 13

I left that disreputable old man more puzzled than when I had arrived. I couldn't figure any reason why someone would want to hurt Connie/Vivian. I knew I would have to get used to thinking of her as Vivian. Truth to tell, I was a little hurt by the subterfuge she had pulled on me and all the other island people. It was hard to think of this bumptious redhead as a crack driven prostitute and ex-convict. Do they call them ex-cons now? Perhaps ex-inmate would be more politically correct.

I drove north along the eastern rim of the lake and then turned west across its northern shore until I reached U. S. Highway 27. Heading north on 27, one slowly moves away from Lake Okeechobee, through cattle country, where the legendary cattle catchers of Florida history once roamed, and into the southern end of the citrus belt. It is a pretty drive, but like all of Florida, it is becoming overcrowded. I read that Florida has a net gain of a thousand people a day. When you think about all the old folks who die on a given day and the numbers of Floridians retiring and moving to North Carolina, the number of new residents each day must reach toward fifteen hundred. It is a staggering amount of people, and it is taking its toll on the Florida I knew and loved. Still, I wouldn't want to live anywhere else.

When I got to Wauchula I turned west onto highway 64, and chased the setting sun home to Longboat Key. I always get a lift when I cross the Manatee Avenue bridge to Anna Maria Island. Tampa Bay spreads out majestically to the north, crowned by the Sunshine Skyway Bridge, its golden towers marking the shipping channel. A phosphate carrier was steaming slowly under the bridge, putting out to sea from the Port of Tampa. A tendril of smoke curled lazily upward from the funnel just aft of ship's bridge structure. I wondered briefly what exotic port it might be steaming toward, and decided it was probably headed for Baltimore. Anna Maria Sound and Sarasota Bay lie to the South. You can see the Sarasota skyline from the old drawbridge, and I always know I'm home. I drove south on Anna Maria island, crossed the Longboat Pass Bridge and a couple of miles further turned left into my condo complex and pulled into a guest parking spot. I would get someone to follow me down to the Colony Beach Resort the next day and turn in my rental car.

I stood under the shower, thinking about what I had learned over the past few days. I was at a loss as to what to do about Logan and Vivian. Things were becoming a little clearer, but I could not put the pieces of the puzzle together. Too many pieces were missing, and the picture was still fuzzy.

The facts of a case come to you just as they are. They don't always fit your theories, and so you have to alter your strategy to fit those immutable facts. Sometimes the facts are unpleasant, and they begin to change your perceptions. You find that truths you never questioned are not truths at all. Connie was the perfect example. She was not who I thought she was. Yet, she was. She wasn't the Northwestern graduate with an abusive husband, but she was the perky, sincere person we islanders had come to love. From a personal standpoint Connie's background was not important, and there would be no reason for me to blow her carefully constructed cover. On the other hand, I was sure I would have to use Connie's truths in some manner to defend Logan. Both truths.

I got dressed and headed for O'Sullivan's for dinner.

The place was almost empty. It always is at the end of May. The winter crowd is gone and the summer people are waiting for their children to get out of school to come down. The girls were in Ireland visiting family. My old friend Dallas Mahoney was sitting at his usual place at the end of the bar. He was in his mid-seventies, and had owned a successful business before selling out and moving permanently to his vacation condo on the Key. His wife was in a nursing home on the mainland, where a creeping Alzheimer's disease had finally robbed her of any semblance of sentience. She did not know him any more, and that hurt his heart. But it was a huge heart, and he maintained a quiet good humor. His three grown sons were spread about the country, all successful, and all doted on their dad, visiting him regularly. I admired and respected Dallas, and liked him more than almost anyone I'd ever met. Logan Hamilton was his best friend.

"Hey, you old coot," I said, as I sat on the stool next to him.

"Well, well, well," he grinned. "The famous attorney slips back into town. I heard you were up north doing the lord's work."

"You talk to Logan?" I asked.

"Yeah. He told me you were all over the Midwest looking into his case."

"What else did he tell you?"

"Nothing. Said he couldn't talk about what you and he discussed."

Good for Logan, I thought. At least he's got enough sense not to pass on information, even to Dallas. "How are things going?" he asked.

"I'm not sure, Dallas. Logan is not the most cooperative client I've ever had. He seems to be holding a lot back, and I don't know why. I know you guys are real close. Has he said anything that might help me?"

"Not really. He did say that he thought Connie must have been nervous about her ex-husband just before she died, but that you had found out that wasn't true. That's about all he said."

"What do you mean Connie was nervous? Logan hasn't said anything about that to me."

"I'm not sure exactly. I know that Connie was a little concerned about a week before her death. She said that she thought she was being stalked by someone. She wouldn't say anything else about it. We thought she had maybe seen her ex-husband and was concerned that he might be looking for her. She didn't want to talk about it anymore, and we didn't pay a whole lot of attention to it. After she died, we thought maybe the husband had shown up and murdered her."

"Well," I said. "It wasn't the husband." I didn't need to tell Dallas anything else about Connie's background. It would come out soon enough, and the people who had been her friends would be hurt by her lies. I hoped they would be able to get beyond her past and remember the lady she had become.

The next day, I parked in the visitor's space at the Longboat Key Police station on Bay Isles Parkway. It was hot at eleven in the morning. A few cumulus clouds floated lazily through the cerulean sky. The hedges around the building cowered in the heat, their partially brown foliage a quiet rebuke of the watering restrictions imposed by the Southwest Florida Water Management District. The air smelled of newly mown grass, tinged with the exhaust of a police cruiser idling in the space next to the heavy glass entry door. I opened the door and walked into the lobby, grateful for the cool air that circulated in the room.

The reception area was small, befitting a small force. A Formica covered counter graced one side of the room. A gray haired woman in her sixties sat behind it typing into a computer. She smiled as I walked in and said, "Hello, Matt. Or is Counselor more appropriate these days?"

"Morning Iva," I said. "You get any younger looking, I'm going to make a run at you."

"You silver tongued devil. You make me wish I were twenty years younger and single."

"Right," I said. Iva had been happily married to the town maintenance supervisor for 35 years. "How's our young captain getting along?" Her son David was an island standout. He had been a high school football star, graduated from West Point, and was serving as a company commander in the 82d Airborne Division at Ft. Bragg, North Carolina. The entire island was proud of him.

"Oh, he's doing great, Matt. I'll tell him you asked about him. We'll never forget your help in getting him the appointment to the Academy. He always asks about you. You here to see the chief?"

"Yeah, if he's in. I don't have an appointment."

"He's here. Hang on a minute."

She picked up the phone and punched in a couple of numbers. "Chief, Matt Royal is here to see you." She paused, and then said, "Yes sir."

"Go on back," she said to me as she hung up the phone and buzzed me through the gate next to the counter. I followed the hallway that led to the offices in the back of the station.

Like every thing else about the headquarters, the chief's office was small, his desk covered in paper. He looked up as I walked in, a fleeting expression of despair on his face. "I'm a cop, Matt. What the hell is a cop doing with all this paper work? I've become a bureaucrat with a badge. How you been?"

"Been good, Bill. Got back yesterday, late."

"Find out anything?"

"Nothing I can talk about yet. I wonder if you've found out anything else about Vivian Pickens."

"No, but then I haven't been looking, either. Manatee is handling all that now."

"You don't really think Logan did this, do you Bill?"

"No, I don't, Matt. But its out of my hands now. If you come up with something I'll be glad to help in any way I can."

"Thanks, Bill," I said, getting out of my chair and heading for the door.

"Matt, you know it would be better on Logan if he turned himself in."

"I know, Bill. I know. See you soon."

On my way out I promised Iva I'd come to dinner at her house soon.

Chapter 14

A few days later, I called Elizabeth Ferguson at her office and asked if she would meet me for a drink at O'Sullivan's after work. Strictly business, I told her. She agreed, but said she had to go home first and feed and walk her dog. We agreed to meet at 8:00 o'clock.

I stopped by the Holiday Inn and ate a small pizza in the snack bar by the indoor pool and got to O'Sullivan's just as Elizabeth was pulling into the parking lot in her small Chrysler convertible. She was wearing a pink sleeveless blouse, white shorts and white sandals. I waited outside the door for her and we walked in together.

"Do you want a table or the bar?" I asked.

"Bar's fine."

I ordered a Miller Lite and she asked for a glass of Harp. I was mildly surprised, as I had figured her for a white wine kind of girl. When I told her that, she laughed.

"Nobody in Statesboro, Georgia drinks white wine," she said. "It's either whiskey or beer."

"How have you been?" I asked.

"Busy, Matt. And I've got to be in court at 8:30 tomorrow, so we're going to have to make this quick." So much for a friendly drink, I thought.

"I'd like to discuss the Hamilton case with you," I said. "I thought this might be a better place than your office."

"Bring him in, Matt, and then we'll talk."

"Look," I said, "I'll make you a deal. I'll bring Logan in, if you'll agree to start the trial the day after he shows up."

"I don't know if I can do that, Matt," Elizabeth said. "There's a lot of heat on my boss to get an arrest and conviction on this one."

"Elizabeth, you're not going to get a conviction," I said without much conviction, "but I can guarantee the arrest. Logan doesn't want to spend months in jail waiting for his trial to start. He'll present himself to the Sheriff on a Sunday afternoon, we'll waive arraignment and start the trial the next morning. Who would lose in that proposition?"

"What about discovery?"

"We could do that informally. You give me everything you're required to disclose, give me thirty days to follow up on it, and Logan will appear. If you get a conviction he's going to jail for a long time. All I'm asking for here, is that he not have to sit in jail waiting for trial."

"I doubt my boss will go for it. We could start a whole new trend here. Every defense lawyer in the circuit will be asking for the same kind of deal."

"Maybe if your boss is convinced that this is the only way he's going to get Logan into a courtroom, he'll agree to the deal."

"I'll run it by him, Matt. But don't hold your breath."

"Want another beer?"

"No, thanks. I've got to run. I'll call you after I talk to the boss."

"Thanks, Elizabeth. See you soon," I said, as she climbed off the stool and headed for the door.

I sat for a while, nursing my beer and watching the cars flash by on Gulf of Mexico Drive. The Gulf was a dark backdrop, with only the lights of an anchored shrimper winking on the horizon. There were two tourist couples at the other end of the bar, talking quietly with Jill, the night bartender. Otherwise, I was alone with my thoughts. The Key is a sleepy place in May.

There is a phenomenon that occurs with some frequency on the island. People find paradise when they come here, and for the first couple of years they revel in their freedom from the worlds of theirs pasts, and they congratulate each other for having the good sense to move to our small corner of the world. Then that other world starts to intrude. Some find they do not have enough money to last a lifetime; others tire of the essential sameness of island living. Ours is a lush island, and it is also an island of lushes. We drink too much, too often and begin to wonder if we made a mistake coming here. We call it the Longboat Blues, and I was feeling a little of that as I sipped my beer. Not because I was on Longboat, but because the world had intruded with a vengeance on my little slice of paradise. Logan's life depended on decisions I would make over the next month or so. I had been there before, but never with a friend for a client, and particularly not with a friend whom I was beginning to think might be guilty.

Logan was in the wind, and he might never be found. Was I doing him any favors by talking him into giving himself up and standing trial? I didn't know. On the other hand I didn't want him to be a fugitive, always looking over his shoulder; waiting for the inevitable day when he was arrested. If he had to go to trial, and I was convinced that he would have to do that sooner or later, then sooner was better.

I paid my tab and walked out into the night. The air was heavy with humidity, and the smell of burning trees drifted on the wind from the middle of the state. The rumble of thunder, slight as a whisper, teased my ears. On the horizon, far out in the Gulf, I could see the streaks of lightning. There was a storm out there somewhere, and I wondered briefly about the seaman on the ships that regularly ply the sea lanes. I climbed into the Explorer and headed home, feeling inexplicably sad. I had a case of the Longboat Blues.

A hard clap of thunder woke me in the wee hours. Lightening danced over the bay outside my window, with the thunder following close behind. The storm had moved over the island, and I was glad for the shelter provided by my bed. There is some atavistic fear of storms, but when snuggled in a warm bed, there is a feeling of safety, of relief for the calm found in any structure.

The storm was moving fast, and the sound of the thunder receded quickly across the bay. I drifted back to sleep, only to wake an hour later from a troubling dream. I was rummaging around down deep in my soul, being chased by dragons through close tunnels, my nascent claustrophobia screaming at me to wake up. The anemic light of a sunless dawn was creeping over the mainland. The sky was overcast, the bay gray and rippled with whitecaps where the wind caught the tops of the small swells; the way it is in winter when the cold fronts tumble out of Canada. Only it was hot out there, the air conditioning working overtime to keep the heat at bay. A hard rain was falling, the drops hitting the aluminum railings of my balcony with a staccato rattle. My sleep was finished.

There would be no jogging on the beach today. I showered, fixed a bowl of cereal, retrieved my St. Petersburg *Times* from the front door and settled in for a quiet morning. I was on my third cup of coffee when the phone rang. It was Molly O'Sullivan.

"I hope I'm not calling too early," she said.

"No, been up for hours. I thought you were in Ireland."

"We got back yesterday. Had a great time. Matt, do you remember me mentioning that a guy came by the restaurant one night last spring looking for Logan?"

"Sure. You thought it was a little suspicious."

"Yeah, well, I think I saw him yesterday going into the police station."

"Are you sure?"

"Not positive. I was in my car coming back from the post office picking up my mail. I saw him going into the station, and thought he looked familiar, but I couldn't place him. It came to me in the middle of the night that this was probably the guy looking for Logan. I haven't been able to get back to sleep thinking about it. I thought you'd like to know."

"I sure would, Molly. Can you describe him?"

"Sort of a tall guy. Probably in his fifties. About six feet, graying black hair, around 200 pounds."

"What time did you see him?"

"It must have been about four. We landed at Tampa about two and caught the shuttle down. I dropped my bags and went to the post office."

"I appreciate this Molly. Don't mention this to anyone else. It may be very important. I'll see if I can find out who this guy is." We exchanged a few pleasantries and hung up, with me promising to stop by and hear about her vacation.

It was a few minutes after eight, so Iva would be at work at the police department. I called her.

"Iva, it's Matt Royal."

"Nice to hear from you on such a dreary day, Matt."

"Thanks, beautiful. I wonder if you can help me with something."

"Sure."

" I saw somebody going into the station yesterday that I should know, but for the life of me I can't place him." I repeated Molly's description. "He came in around four o'clock." I hated lying to Iva, but she'd probably forgive me.

"That was probably Mr. Cox. He came to see the chief."

"The name doesn't ring a bell. Is he a lawyer?"

"No, I don't think so. Hold on. He gave me his card when he came in. Here it is. Sam Cox, Vice President for Security of Rundel Enterprises, Incorporated."

"Well, I guess he just looked like someone I know. I hope he isn't planning to open an industrial plant on our island," I said, chuckling.

"I think he might have some problems with zoning." Longboat Key is the tightest zoned community on the planet, and the thought of something industrial on the island was laughable. "He said something about his company planning an event on the Key and he wanted to meet the chief in case any security matters came up."

"Thanks anyway, Iva. See you later."

"Bye, Matt."

I hung up the phone, feeling for the first time that there may be some hope for getting Logan out of this mess. But I had to find Sam Cox, and figure out what he had been doing on Longboat Key the night Connie was killed.

The first thing was to find out something about Rundel Enterprises in the public records. You would be surprised at what a paper trail we leave with the bureaucracies as we go about our daily lives.

Chapter 15

If Rundel Enterprises was incorporated, it would have had to file all sorts of documents with the Secretary of State of the state in which it was incorporated. If it had been incorporated in some other state, but was doing business in Florida, it should have filed something in Tallahassee. If not, I would have to check all fifty secretaries of state if necessary, and see what I could get.

I fired up my computer and brought up the web site of the corporations division of the Florida Secretary of State's office. I got lucky. Rundel Enterprises, Incorporated, was indeed a Florida corporation. It had been incorporated about two years before, but had been involuntarily dissolved at the end of the last month for failure to pay its annual corporation fees to the state. It has been my experience that a corporation can get away with a lot of things, but withholding the annual state fees is not one of them. I wondered if Murder, Incorporated could have withstood the kind of scrutiny the bureaucrats in Tallahassee give.

The documents listed Hale Rundel as president, Samuel Cox as Vice-president, and Maria Cox as corporate secretary and treasurer. One thousand shares of common stock had been issued, at a par value of one dollar per share. There was no information of how the stock was distributed. Donald Jones was listed as resident agent for service of process. The corporate charter stated that Rundel Enterprises was in the business of leasing, buying and selling airplanes.

Rundel's home address was listed on Gulf of Mexico Drive in Longboat Key, Florida. Both Coxes were shown as living at the same address in Miami, and Jones' address was in Sarasota, obviously an office address, since a suite number was included.

I assumed Jones probably was the lawyer who drew up the corporation papers. It is not unusual that the lawyer who does the paper work is listed as resident agent. It makes it easier for the sheriff to serve process on somebody if the corporation is sued. Time to call Mr. Jones.

Jones' receptionist passed my call to his secretary who wanted to know what I was calling about. I know secretaries do this because their bosses tell them to, but it always gets under my skin. If the guy thinks he is too important to talk to anyone who takes time to call him, I wouldn't want him as my lawyer. My experience has been that the better the lawyer, the less rigamarole one has to go through to talk to him. I was about to make a sharp comment when it occurred to me that I needed this guy, and it made no sense to make him mad to begin with. I told her I was a lawyer and was calling in reference to Rundel Enterprises.

"I've heard a lot about you, Mr. Royal," Jones oozed. "What can I do for you?"

"I appreciate your taking your time to talk to me, Mr. Jones," I said. "I've got a client who is interested in buying an airplane that he heard Rundel Enterprises has for sale. We've tried to get in touch with someone from the company, but the phone has been disconnected and the letter I sent was returned. I checked with the Secretary of State and found that you were the resident agent, so I thought you might be able to tell me how to get in touch with them."

"I wish to hell I knew. They owe me a couple of grand, and the whole company seems to have disappeared."

Rundel had made a big mistake. Never stiff a lawyer on a fee. It makes the lawyer angry as a swarm of horny bees, and he will tell you anything you want to know about his client. It's a breach of professional ethics, of course, but the lawyer feels the biggest breach of all is when a client doesn't pay his bill. "What can you tell me about the outfit?" I asked.

"Not a whole lot. Guy name of Rundel had me incorporate the business and do a few other small items for him. Nothing big, but then if it had been big, I guess he would have gone to one of the larger firms here. I have a one man general practice, is all. I'm sure not in your league, Mr. Royal."

I'd been a pretty good lawyer, and pretty well known in the Orlando area, but I certainly didn't have a statewide reputation, and I couldn't figure out where this guy was coming from with all the compliments. However, I seemed to have some clout with Jones, and I wasn't about to blow it by asking him how he knew about me. I may have met him somewhere and didn't remember it. "What about the president, Rundel?" I asked.

"That's kind of funny, you know. He seemed to be a real money man. Drove a big Mercedes, and he lived in one of those high priced condos on the Gulf out on Longboat. But one day he came into the office with another guy, who didn't look like he had money for bus fare, and said this other guy was putting up money to buy the first plane for Rundel. They wanted me to hold the money in my trust account until they told me the name of the seller. I was then supposed to send a trust account check to whoever it was."

"What happened?"

"The guy gave me a cashier's check for one million dollars, made out to my trust account, and about two weeks later he sent me a certified letter telling me where to send the check. My first thought was that it may have been a drug money laundering deal, but you don't get a cashier's check when that is going on. Do you?"

"It doesn't sound like the usual way. Can you tell me who the check was made out to?"

"This was over a year ago, but my trust account records would show that. You know how the Bar is about keeping accurate records of trust accounts. They're probably in storage, but I can find them and call you back."

" Why don't I just call you back this afternoon. You wouldn't remember the name of the man who gave you the check, would you?"

"Sure do. It was John James. Don't know why that name has stuck with me. It was the only time I ever saw him. Lived in Gulfview, up in Ware County, in the big bend country."

I thanked him again for his time and cooperation, and told him I would call back later that afternoon. It had apparently not occurred to him to wonder why I needed the name of the payee on the check, if all I wanted was to buy an airplane.

The address given by the Secretary of State's office for Rundel was on the south end of the Key, an imposing ten stories of concrete, blocking the view of the Gulf. I entered a driveway off Gulf of Mexico Drive at a sign announcing that I had arrived at Gulf Breakers, Exclusive Condominium Living at its Best. About a hundred yard down the driveway I came to a gate, with a guard dressed in a khaki uniform. I told him I was going to see the manager, and he raised the gate, giving me a sloppy salute. The rest of the driveway was another hundred yards or so of brick pavers, lined with coconut palms. The grand entrance at the end of the driveway was fit for one of the finer hotels. I drove underneath a frescoed overhang and was met by a doorman wearing the same uniform as the gate guard. He was expecting me, apparently called by his buddy on the gate, and directed me to the manager's office on the first floor, next to the elevators.

A woman of about fifty, dressed as if she were twenty, invited me into her private office. She had blond hair, which had the dried out look of too many bleachings, done in waves falling almost to her shoulders. She wore a tight blouse of pale yellow, unbuttoned enough to show an ample cleavage. Her dark blue shorts were about three sizes too small and hugged a butt of a size and shape that cried out for a loosely draped skirt. Her feet were encased in plastic mules with six inch heels. She was the typical New Yorker, moved to Florida, with her youth recaptured.

"We have two nice units for sale, Mr. Royal," she said, "and right now the mortgage rates are about as good as we'll see."

I said, "Actually, I'm looking for an old friend, Hale Rundel. His brother gave me this address, and I thought that while I'm in the area I'd buy him a drink."

"Oh, goodness. You're not interested in buying a unit?"

"Sorry. Just looking for a friend."

"Well, you won't find him here." Her breezy mood disappeared as the thought of a nice sales commission danced out of the office. "He moved out three months ago in the middle of the night owing a months rent."

"He wasn't an owner?" I asked.

"No. He rented Penthouse A during the off season while the owner was living in North Carolina. I can tell you the owner was mad, getting stiffed on a months rent. He wants me to give him back the entire commission I made on the deal. Says if I'd been doing my job I'd have made sure the rent was collected in advance."

"How long did Hale live here?" I asked.

"About two months this time. But he rented the place two years in a row, for six months each year. He was supposed to stay six months this year. How was I to know he'd skip? He'd always paid the rent before."

"What did he do for a living?"

"Hey, I thought you were his friend."

"I was. I haven't seen him in several years, though. When I knew him, he was a pilot."

"Well, he wasn't flying airplanes while he was here. I don't know what he did. I always thought he was retired. He seemed to have plenty of money, and he threw a lot of parties. We got a few complaints about the noise from some of our residents, but if you called him about it, he was always polite and would quiet everything down real quick like."

"You haven't heard anything from him since he left, I take it."

"No. And I don't want to hear anything either. Unless he's calling to say he's sending me the rent. You sure you don't want to take a look at one of those units we got for sale?"

"Some other time, maybe."

"Sure."

I thanked her for her time and left.

I stopped by O'Sullivan's. It was still early, but the girls were always there.

Molly came over as I walked in. "Want something to drink, Matt?"

"No, thanks. I wanted to bring you up to date on your tip this morning. The man you saw is named Sam Cox, and he works for a guy named Hale Rundel who used to live on the Key. Do you know either one of those names?

"Sure, I know Hale. About fifty years old, getting fat and likes to wear those muscle shirts the kids wear. Looks pretty funny in them too. He's like a lot of the people that come down here, wearing clothes they shouldn't, and trying to stay young."

"What do you know about him?"

"It's funny, you know. He was a quiet type. He'd come in regularly for drinks at happy hour, and occasionally he'd have dinner. Always by himself. He'd sit at the bar, but didn't usually talk to anyone, and I don't think I ever saw him have dinner with anyone. He got to know one of our waitresses and invited her to a party at his condo one night. She later said she'd never go back there. Seems he had some pretty weird friends."

"What did she mean?" I asked.

"I don't know. She didn't say anything more about it, and I didn't feel it was my place to ask."

"Does she still work here?" I asked

"No. She left when the season was over and moved back north someplace."

"When did you last see Rundel?"

"I haven't seen him in several months. He just stopped coming in. I figured he might be embarrassed to see that waitress again, or figured she told us something about that party that made him not want to face us. I did see him a couple of times with Dick Bellinger at the bar at Pirates' Cove. He might know something."

"I need to stop and see Dick anyway. I'll check it out."

"Look Matt, I've got to get back to the drudgery. It was good to see you again. I hope this leads you somewhere good for Logan"

I called Don Jones from my cell phone as I drove north toward Pirate's Cove Inn and Marina. He told me that the one million dollar check he wrote on his trust account was made payable to Hawker Industries, an aircraft manufacturer.

On the bay side of Longboat Key, down a short road and across a narrow creek, sits a small island, perhaps five acres in size. It is protected from the open bay by a hook of the main island that comes out to the east and around to the south. The water between the hook and the little island forms a natural harbor called Pirate's Cove. The only establishment on the little island is the Pirate's Cove Inn and Marina. The Inn consists of a grand old restaurant and bar decorated as a Pirate's den dreamed up by Walt Disney. The marina has about fifty boat slips arranged in a semi-circle around the little island's protected shore. It was to here that I ran away from the world when Laura left. And it was here that Jason Clark rescued me.

A marina is always in a state of change, metamorphosing like a giant amoeba on a weekly basis. The liveaboards suddenly move ashore. The permanents, those who keep their boats in the marina, but don't live aboard, decide that the next marina down the line is a better deal. The regular transients sell their boats and don't come around anymore. The winter liveaboard decides to try the other coast this year. There's always somebody new at the bar. In the years since I'd sold my liveaboard boat and moved into the condo, there had been a complete turnover, except for me and the dockmaster, Dick Bellinger.

Dick had been a good friend during my down times after Laura left. He lived in the marina on a production boat that looked like a working tug boat, but was in fact a pleasure yacht of about thirty-six feet. He was my age, and the spitting image of a television series star, one of those balding guys with a gray beard who always looked distinguished. If a female tourist on the island happened to mistake Dick for the T.V. star, he was not one to disappoint her. I suspect that a lot of small town school teachers in Ohio still go to sleep nights, reflecting on their good fortune in having had an affair, although brief, with a television personality.

Dick had been a Navy fighter pilot in his youth, and then spent many years as an airline pilot. He woke up one morning and simply decided that he was finished with flying. He called his supervisor at the airline and quit. That day he loosed the lines from the mooring where he kept the sailboat on which he lived, and headed south. He spent a year traveling the Carribean, and then washed ashore at Pirate's Cove. When he heard the management was looking for a dockmaster, he took the job. Somewhere along the line he got rid of the sailboat and bought the tug. I was worried that Dick seemed to be slipping deeper into a bottle of vodka, but he had shrugged off my concern the one time I had voiced it.

Dick's small office looked out over the pool to the marina. This time of the week one could always find a number of the local women taking the sun by the pool. Dick was usually behind his darkened windows enjoying the fleshy view. At five he would move his portable radio to the bar for a few drinks of straight vodka with the regulars who always frequent any bar in any town.

The air conditioning in the tiny office puffed cold air, providing a respite from the June heat. Dick was on the phone taking a reservation from a boater who wanted to spend Independence day in the marina. He had his ever present filtered low tar cigarette burning in the ashtray. He looked up at me, grinned, and waived me to the only visitor's chair in the room. I remained standing and coughed a couple of times for emphasis. I had been telling him for years that his bad habits were going to kill him some day.

He hung up the phone. "Silly bastard. Thinks he can make a reservation this late for July 4th. I gotta get out of this business." Dick always groused, but he loved the Key and enjoyed his job. I had used Dick during my case with Jason to do some basic research on medical products, and to take telephone statements from some of the witnesses. He got himself qualified by the Circuit Court to serve subpoenas, and he took care of that for me when we needed depositions in Southwest Florida.

"I need some help, Dick. I'm looking into a guy named Hale Rundel. Molly O'Sullivan told me you might know him."

"Oh, I know him, but not well. A buddy of his brought a boat in here for a month winter before last, and Rundel spent a lot of time here in the marina. That was during the time you were so caught up in the doc's case that you didn't get over here for a time. I had a few drinks with him, and he invited me over to his condo for a party. Great party, but Rundel's a big sack of shit."

"What do you mean?"

"Well, Matt, you know I like to party. And I do love the girls. Rundel had these parties every now and then and would invite a very select crowd. Mostly folks from the mainland who had lots of money. The one I went to had a lot of drugs around. There was actually a dish of white powder on the coffee table, and people were sucking it up their noses with straws. If it wasn't cocaine there were sure a lot of people acting very satisfied with whatever it was. There were other kinds of pills and stuff to smoke and plenty of booze. Booze was being served by waitresses, who were all nude."

"Naked?" I asked rather stupidly.

"Buck-ass naked," said Dick. "Rundel told me that when he invited me. I figured I could get drunk and get laid without too much trouble. But the drugs scared me. You know how I feel about that, Matt." Dick's younger sister died from an overdose after she had put the family through years of hell. "I don't mess with them, and I won't stay around where they're used. I had one drink and left."

"Is Rundel in the drug business?"

"I don't think so, but who knows. He had a lot of money, and he didn't seem hesitant to spend it. I saw him after the party and told him I had left because I was not comfortable with the drugs. He told me he didn't do any drugs himself, but had to have them available for his business associates. He said he brokered airplanes, and that he suspected that many of his buyers were drug runners. He apparently hired a few of the girls from that topless place over in Sarasota to come over and walk around nude to kind of get things moving. He said that when everybody is standing around sucking coke and looking at nude chicks, there ain't no pretension and he can do business better. We got pretty drunk over at the bar the last time I saw him, and he was telling me that he had cameras hidden around the apartment. He said that it was amazing how cooperative some of his disgruntled customers would become once he showed them pictures of them and their wives or girlfriends standing around in a crowd of nudes snorting coke. Like I said, a sack of shit."

"Do you know why he left?" I asked.

"No. I didn't see him that regularly, and I guess he had been gone for some time before I heard about it. I ran into Sally, the manager down at Gulf Breakers, over at the Holiday Inn one night and she was bitching about him stiffing her on the rent. I figured maybe somebody caught up with him and he either ran, or somebody dumped him out in the Gulf one dark night."

"Did he ever say anything about where he came from or what he did before he landed on the island?" I asked.

"Nah. Like I said, I didn't know him well, and I really didn't care to. Sorry."

We chatted for a few more minutes about mutual friends, and I took my leave and headed home.

Chapter 16

Gulfview is a typical old Florida town, sitting on a part of the Gulf coast that has not yet been discovered by the developers and despoilers. It is home to a paper mill, which employs most of the men of the area. Inland, there is a little farming, and a few people still make their living fishing for mullet or taking oysters from the shallow bay. It is the county seat of Ware county. With a population of under twenty thousand, it is the smallest county in Florida. It is the kind of place that the northerners never see in the brochures put out by the tourist industry. It is also the kind of place where the sheriff knows everybody and everything that is going on.

I drove up from Longboat Key through St. Petersburg and Clearwater, and on up Highway 27. I had decided to see what I could find out about John James. If he were in fact involved in shady or illegal dealings, it was likely that a number of his fellow citizens would be aware of it. These people are very protective of their own.

As in many southern towns the courthouse sat on a square, with most of the stores and shops on the streets surrounding it. On the front lawn there was the usual statute of a Confederate soldier, facing his enemy to the north.

I parked on the street in front of the courthouse and went into the sheriff's office. I identified myself to the deputy at the desk, gave him my business card, and asked to speak to the sheriff. He was out but was expected back any moment, and I was welcome to wait. I had barely sat down on the hard bench when a small man in a suit walked in.

"Sheriff," said the deputy, "Mr. Royal here is a lawyer from Longboat Key. Wants to see you." He handed the sheriff my card.

"I'm Dave Tuten," said the sheriff, sticking out his hand. "I'll be right with you." He disappeared into his office shutting the door. A few minutes later the door opened and he invited me in.

Sheriff Tuten was not at all what I had expected. He was about five foot seven, one hundred forty pounds, with dark hair graying at the temples. He was dressed in a navy blue suit, white shirt, burgundy tie, and had a Phi Beta Kappa key pinned in his lapel. He was in his mid-forties.

"I appreciate your taking some time for me, Sheriff." I said. "I'm looking for a man named John James. He's not listed in the phone book, and the operator says his number is unlisted. I was hoping you might be able to help us."

"Why are you looking for James?"

"He was involved in a business deal that went sour, and I'm hoping he can give me some information I need about the company."

"I know who you are Mr. Royal, and that's the only reason I don't run you out of this office. I called Bill Lester, and he vouched for you. This county is clean. There was a time when it wasn't. You must have been surprised that the sheriff was not some good ole boy about seven feet tall with a pot belly and a six shooter. I grew up here." He went on to explain that his dad had been a shrimper. Tuten had played football at the high school and had made all-state his senior year. He was what they called a scatback in those days. He had been too small for college ball, but he had gotten an academic scholarship to Florida State. He earned a degree in Criminology and a commission in the Army Military Police. After the Army, he joined the Jacksonville police department and eventually became chief of detectives. He told me that his county had always been corrupt in small ways, but about five years before, some of the locals had gotten into the import business. They had been bringing in bales of marijuana in their fishing boats. The previous sheriff had been getting a nice percentage of the gross to look the other way. The governor sent in a special prosecutor who convicted the sheriff and about half a dozen others on drug charges.

Tuten came home and ran for sheriff. He always thought James was deeply involved in the local importing operation, but the only thing anybody had ever gotten on him was a vote buying charge. He had been giving five dollars and a fifth of liquor to anybody who would agree to vote for the old sheriff in the last election before the whole thing fell apart. It was a misdemeanor, and James pled guilty. The judge gave him ninety days probation. He was still in Ware County, running his motel.

"Now if I didn't know who you were I would think you were here to start up the import business again. Are you?"

"No, Sheriff," I said. "To be perfectly honest with you, I'm not sure exactly why I'm here. I just want to talk to James and see if he can help me find a man named Hale Rundel."

I told him everything I knew so far about the Rundel Enterprises deal and James' part in it. When I finished the sheriff shook his head and said, "There's no way in this world John James could get hold of a million dollars legally. Let's go talk to him."

We drove out of town on the main highway, which meandered southeast until it ran into U.S. 19. We turned into the dirt driveway of something called the James Motel. There were four separate tin roofed concrete block buildings, each of which held two rooms. The paint was peeling from the red doors of each room. A fifth building, with a sign in front announcing it to be the office, appeared to be the living quarters of whomever ran the operation. A rural mail box and a round newspaper box with a faded *Tallahassee Democrat* painted on its sides were attached to posts in front of the office. .

The sheriff said, "James' mother owns this dump. She used to make a small living out of it, but I doubt she's had an overnight guest in years. She had a stroke about five years ago, and John pretty much takes care of her and the place. He lives out back in a trailer. Once in a while, some politician from Tallahassee will drive down with his secretary and rent a room for a couple of hours. That's about all."

"How does he make a living?" I asked.

"He worked at the local Ford dealer's body shop until it went out of business. Now he teaches body work in the shop at the high school and runs the motel."

Behind the main building was an extra long mobile home set up on stacked concrete blocks. It was painted in alternating horizontal stripes of orange, white and brown. Each stripe was about two feet wide. There was a set of handmade wooden steps leading to the front door. There were gracious old oak trees surrounding the place, but grass only sparsely covered the ground.

We parked in the yard and got out of the car. The door to the trailer home opened to reveal a man wearing a sleeveless undershirt, khaki trousers and a pair of white socks without shoes. He had a beer belly, sparse brown hair going to gray, and a face that had lost its teenage bout with acne.

"Hello, John," said the sheriff. "We need to talk to you about an airplane."

"Hidy, Sheriff," said James. "Don't know much 'bout planes. I ain't never had to fix one."

"We want to talk about the one you bought, John," said the sheriff.

"You got to be kiddin', Sheriff. I hardly got the money to pay the light bill this month. Florida Power's already threatened to shut it off. 'Sides, what would I do with an airplane anyway?"

"John, this is Mr. Royal. He's a lawyer from Longboat Key. We have good evidence that you put up a million dollars for Rundel Enterprises to buy an airplane. You can tell us what you know about this, or I can get an affidavit from a lawyer in Sarasota named Jones and come back and arrest you. I don't think you really want to screw around with me."

"Now Sheriff, you know damn well I ain't never had a million dollars, or anything close to it. But y'all come on in and sit, and I'll tell you all I know."

The trailer looked, as my mother used to say, as if a cyclone had struck it. The sink was overflowing with dirty dishes, glasses, pots and pans. Several days worth of old newspapers had been discarded at random in the living room. There was a sour smell pervading the place, and I began to wonder if he had hidden the legendary Big Foot in a closet. There was an overstuffed sofa and two chairs in the room, each covered with a cloth cover that can be bought at Sears. Even the covers were old and worn. James sat in one chair, the sheriff in the other, and I took the sofa.

"Tell me about Rundel," I said.

"Look," he said, "All I did was to do a favor for a friend. He gave me the money, and I wrote a check for the whole thing. He gave me five hundred dollars for my trouble. If there was anything illegal going on, I didn't know about it, Sheriff. I don't want no trouble."

"Tell Mr. Royal about Rundel," said Sheriff Tuten. "If you didn't do anything wrong, and it checks out, you've got nothing to worry about from me."

James was obviously nervous. It was a testament to the power the sheriff held in this county. That is not always a good thing, but I thought this sheriff would use the power wisely.

"I don't really know this Rundel," James said. "I only saw him a couple of times. He had me open an account over in Palatka and he gave me a check for a million dollars to put into it. He had me set it up so that the only way I could get any money out was to have another friend of his sign on the check too. About two weeks after I opened the account, Rundel and this guy named Cox showed up, and we drove over to Palatka. Cox was the other guy on the checks. We wrote a check to the bank and they gave us a cashier's check. I didn't see how it was made out. Rundel handled all the paperwork, and Cox and I signed everything and showed the bank folks our driver's licenses. We drove on down to Sarasota and met with this lawyer Jones. Rundel told him I was an investor in something or other, but I didn't pay much attention to what they were talking about. We gave him the check and left. Rundel had me sign my name to some sort of letter and we drove back to Gulfplace. He gave me five one hundred dollar bills, and I ain't seen hide nor hair of him since. That's all there is to it, Sheriff. I swear."

"What did the letter say?" I asked.

"I don't know. I didn't read it."

"That was probably the letter of instruction to Jones," I said to the Sheriff. "None of this makes a whole lot of sense, unless they were just moving money around in an attempt to launder it or confuse the paper trail. Where did you meet Rundel, Mr. James?"

"My stepson introduced me to him up in Tallahassee. That's when he asked me to help him out with this little money problem he had. Said something about trying to keep it out of the hands of his ex-wife. I got a couple of those, and I know how it is."

"Who is your stepson?" Sheriff Tuten asked.

"John Noblin."

The name meant nothing to me or the sheriff. "He owns an insurance agency up in Tallahassee," said James. I filed it away for future reference.

We were back at the sheriff's office. It was spartan. There were no pictures of the sheriff with various dignitaries, such as you usually see in a politician's office. The desk was basic green metal government issue. There were two straight chairs facing the desk, and a vinyl covered swivel chair for the sheriff.

Tuten had loosened his tie and unbuttoned the top button of his shirt. His shoulder holster, with the nine millimeter semi-automatic pistol, was hung over the hat tree. He was sitting behind his desk with his feet propped up. I was in one of the chairs facing the desk.

"James is probably telling the truth," said the sheriff. "I think he's scared enough of me at this point that he couldn't pull off that big a lie.

Besides, if he had a million dollars of his own, I don't think he'd be hanging around here."

"I think you're right," I said. "But I don't understand why the money was being moved around like James says it was. If they were trying to launder it, they sure weren't doing a very professional job. I would think the bank might get suspicious about a guy like James coming in with a million dollars and then taking it out two weeks later."

"Probably," said the sheriff. "But there was nothing illegal in what the bank did, and the float, the interest the bank earned while the money was in a checking account, makes for a pretty good chunk of change. The bank officers wouldn't take any suspicions they had to the law, because they wouldn't want to disrupt what could become a fairly lucrative pattern.

"There is something that may be of interest to you, Matt," the Sheriff said. "About 6 months ago, a man named Bud Dubose and his wife died in his place out near the beach. The place burned to the ground after an explosion. I think it was caused by a gas leak they didn't know they had. But, I got a call from a lawyer down in Lauderdale a couple of months ago, who said she was Bud's sister, and felt that the deaths were murder. She said that a man named Rundel was responsible. I don't think there's anything to it, but it is interesting that the Rundel name comes up twice in two months. It's not a common name."

"No, it's not," I said. "Do you remember the lawyer's name?"

He pulled what appeared to be a call log from one of his desk drawers, and flipped through several pages. "Her name is Anne Dubose." He gave me her phone number.

I thanked the sheriff for all his trouble and headed back to Longboat. I ate a frozen microwave dinner, and collapsed into bed for a good night's sleep. I noticed that the message light on my phone was blinking, but I ignored it. I was too tired to deal with whoever or whatever the phone call was about.

The next morning was like most mornings in Southwest Florida - beautiful. I did my jog on the beach early, before it got too hot to even think about running in the sun. After my shower and first cup of coffee, I felt good enough to check my phone messages. There were two from people trying to sell me stuff, and one from Elizabeth Ferguson. I checked the time; 7:30. She'd probably be in the office by now. I called.

"Matt, I appreciate your getting back to me. I have a proposition for you."

I was about to make a smart retort, but decided this prosecutor would not appreciate it. She was all business. "I'm all ears," I said.

"My boss said we would take your offer of producing Logan, but we go to trial a week from Monday. I'll deliver the discovery material today."

"Good Lord, Elizabeth," I said, a sense of foreboding flooding my nervous system. "I can't possibly be ready to go to trial next Monday. It's Friday already."

"You can bring him in, move for a speedy trial and get yourself ninety days to prepare," she said.

"Will you agree to bail for Logan?"

"You know that's not going to happen, Matt. My boss is up for re-election next year. I'm supposed to tell you that if you don't produce Mr. Hamilton at the county jail by a week from Sunday, the deal is off."

I thought about it for a moment. If I didn't buy the deal, Logan would have to come in and sit in jail for months before trial, or spend the rest of his life as a hunted man. "Elizabeth, I have to run this by my client. Can I get back to you?"

"Gotta be quick, Matt. I can't hold this together very long."

"I'll give you a decision by noon," I said, without much conviction.

This was probably the best deal Logan was going to get, but I couldn't make the decision. It was his trial, his life, and therefore his decision. If he didn't call this morning, I'd have to make that decision myself. I might be putting his life in graver danger by agreeing to go to trial on such short notice, but the alternative was for him to remain a fugitive. I didn't think Logan was going to come in voluntarily, unless the trial started immediately. No wonder trial lawyers learn to live with ulcers.

My cell phone rang. It was eight o'clock, Logan calling. I would not have to make the decision. We discussed the pros and cons of the deal, and I urged him to turn himself in and go to trial in ninety days. That would give me plenty of time to get ready for trial.

Most people don't have any idea of the process that lawyers call "getting ready for trial." Lawyer dramas on TV give the impression that the lawyer walks into the courtroom cold, and by dent of his superior intelligence and lucky witnesses, wins the case. That is not even close to the truth.

A good trial lawyer has to know the law as it applies to his case, and be ready to instruct the judge. The law, though, is often painted in shades of gray, and the other lawyer will argue her case, trying to talk the judge into applying her view of the law to the facts. Witnesses are notoriously unreliable. Too often, a witness will make a statement from the witness stand that is directly in conflict with what he told investigators. The trial lawyer has to spend time with the witnesses in the days leading up to trial, making sure that memories don't change, and the carefully laid plan of attack is sunk by a misstatement from the witness stand. Even then, it is a crap shoot.

In this case, I did not even know who to blame, other than Logan, and truth be told, I wasn't sure Logan didn't do the deed. He was playing things awfully close to the vest, parceling facts out to me like a miser forced to spend a few pennies. Logan had something to hide, and he was hiding it from me.

I explained all this to my client, lobbying hard for the ninety days I needed. Logan was adamant. He wanted to go to trial. He would be at the sheriff's office to turn himself in on Sunday evening by six o'clock. We would start the trial at nine o'clock on Monday morning. I had nine days to get ready for trial.

I called Elizabeth, and left word with Mavis, her secretary, that we would take the deal. Mavis assured me the discovery material would be at my condo by noon. A messenger proved Mavis' word to be good.

I spent the rest of the day pouring over the contents of the file sent by Elizabeth Ferguson. There were really no surprises in the material. I spent the weekend talking by phone to the witnesses listed in the prosecution's witness list. I couldn't see where any of them had much to add to the case.

Chapter 17

MONDAY

Monday morning, the third Monday in June. A week until the trial starts. I awake with the feeling in my gut that every trial lawyer knows all too well. A feeling of not knowing enough, not being prepared, wishing he were anywhere but getting ready for a trial. Time always runs out. There is never enough time to prepare as much as you would like. Most trial lawyers, the good ones anyway, are paranoid and a little obsessive compulsive. We worry too much. We want to know all the facts, but we never do. I hoped that Anne Dubose could help in that department.

I called the number the Sheriff gave me. The receptionist answered by reciting the first two names of the firm, a relatively modern means of shortening the names of firms that hadgrown too long with the addition of all the egos who are the major rainmakers. I knew the firm, and was impressed that Anne was working there.

When she came on the phone, I identified myself and told her I was a lawyer in Longboat Key, working on a murder case, and I thought she might be of some help to me.

"What kind of help, Mr. Royal?"

"The name Hale Rundale has come up in my investigation. Sheriff Tuten in Ware County tells me that you think Mr. Rundel may have been involved in your brother's and sister-in-law's deaths."

"Are you with a firm over there, Mr. Royal?"

"No. Actually, I'm retired, but I'm trying to help a friend."

"Do you think Rundel had something to do with the murder you're investigating?"

"I don't know," I said. "But it's the only lead I've got right now."

"I can tell you a great deal about Mr. Rundel. Can we meet somewhere?"

"I can come to Lauderdale today, if that's okay. My trial starts a week from Monday."

"That'll work. Where will you be staying?"

"I like the Marriott Marina Hotel."

"Why don't I meet you in the bar at about 5:00 this evening?"

I threw my overnight bag into the Explorer and drove off the Key, through Sarasota and out to I-75. I headed south, and then west across the Everglades on Alligator Alley, now part of the Interstate system. I got off in Broward County on U. S. 1, and drove north to Seventeenth street, turning right toward the intracoastal waterway and the ocean. Just before reaching the draw bridge over the waterway, I turned left into the Marriott Marina Hotel.

I checked in, found my room overlooking the intracoastal, hung up my spare suit, and jumped into a cold shower. I dressed casually in a pair of tan slacks, a white polo shirt and blue blazer. Brown socks and cordovan loafers with tassels completed my wardrobe. Good enough, I thought, for South Florida.

I arrived at the ground floor restaurant overlooking the waterway right at five o'clock and took a seat at the bar. There were several tired looking men in suits sitting at a nearby table, drinking dark whiskey and discussing their business day. Three more men sat at the bar, quietly nursing mixed drinks, musing to themselves I guess. They were not talking to each other, and only glanced at me when I came in. The bartender was about thirty, with a bored look about him. He politely took my order, calling me sir. The Miller Lite was much needed.

About ten minutes after I arrived, a woman in her late twenties came in, looked quickly at me, and took a seat at the other end of the bar. She was dressed in a dark green skirt, a pastel blouse, and high heel shoes. Her black hair was cut short. Her face was pretty, her eyes dark and intelligent. She was tanned, with an athlete's body. One of the new breed of traveling businesswomen, I thought. She seemed so sure of herself in a place where only a few years ago a woman would never have ventured alone, unless she was what was known euphemistically as a working lady, a woman of easy virtue or a lady of the night. There are so many ways to describe a whore. This lady was certainly not one of those.

The men in the bar all looked quickly at her, each gaze lingering longer than it did on me. Then they went back to their drinks and their conversations. They appreciated a lovely woman, but they would not do anything more about it.

There was a time when I would have tried to strike up a conversation with any woman alone in a bar. My motives were certainly not pure, but then I could be reasonably certain that a woman alone in a bar was not exactly pure herself. No more. You see the businesswomen where ever you see businessmen. Including bars. And they are there for the same reason as the businessmen. To relax after a hard day. Nothing more. She'll have one or two drinks, dinner in the hotel restaurant, and up to her room to prepare for the customer she'll call on the next day. Typical business trip.

I had about decided that the lady lawyer Dubose had decided not to come, and was signaling for a check when one of south Florida's Latin cowboys sauntered in. He was about five ten, two hundred pounds, with biceps that attested to the number of hours he spent every day pumping iron. He wore black skin tight pants, black silk socks, black shoes with pointed toes, and a white silk shirt opened to his navel. He had masses of black hair on his chest into which snuggled four heavy gold chains. His hair was black, longish, and combed straight back. His head looked like it needed a lube job.

The great Latin lover surveyed the bar, spotted the businesswoman, and headed for her like a tiger after a staked goat. "Hi there, baby," he said.

"Buzz off," she said.

"Ah come on baby, you look like you need somebody to show you the town."

"No thank you. I've seen the town."

"Well, maybe you'd like to see what else I've got for you," he said, playing to the bar now, trying to salvage something out of an embarrassing situation.

She turned on her bar stool to face him squarely, one leg crossed over the other, swinging her foot slightly. She looked straight into his eyes, smiled, and said sweetly, "I told you I'm not interested. If you don't leave now, you're going to be singing tenor."

I think he got the message. He looked around and saw the bartender and me grinning, and the other patrons looking at him as if he had committed some terrible faux pas at an afternoon garden party. He gathered all the dignity he could find, muttered "bitch" and left. I didn't suppose he'd be down on Calle Oche later that evening, bragging about this encounter.

"Sorry," she said. "I don't usually talk like that. Bartender, have you had any messages from a lawyer named Royal? I was supposed to meet him here."

"Excuse me," I said. "I'm Matt Royal."

"You're Matt Royal? I was looking for an older gentleman."

"I'm feeling pretty old about now."

"But you said your were retired. People don't retire until they're actually old."

"I did. Look, lets get a table. I think we've got a lot to talk about."

Chapter 18

She was twenty-nine years old and a real estate lawyer in the Ft. Lauderdale office of one of Miami's big factory style law firms. She had graduated from the University of Miami Law School four years before, at the top of her class. While women lawyers were no longer a rarity, students ranked first in their class were rare enough that the big boys lost plenty of sleep trying to figure out how to lure them into their firms.

Anne Dubose had been offered $75,000 per year to start and promised that she would be considered for a partnership in eight years. At the end of five years she would become a senior associate, and in addition to a six figure salary, she would be provided with an automobile and a membership in any club she chose. They didn't tell her that she would spend all her time on the same minute point of law; doing it over and over again, while other young lawyers handled the other minute points of the same deal.

Anne was a child who had arrived unexpectedly during her parents' middle years. Her only sibling, her brother Bud, was eighteen years her senior and, her parents thought, an only child. Anne was welcomed into that family of middle class south Floridians as only a long despaired of dream can be. When she was two, her parents were killed by a drunk driver on the Palmetto Expressway. Bud dropped out of college to raise Anne. Three years later he married a young woman with the courage to take on the rearing of a five year old child. Bud and Marge had children of their own, and Anne was always treated as one of them. Bud had sacrificed his education to keep Anne out of foster homes, and he ended up as a construction worker. He insisted that Anne get an education, and he worked overtime to pay for her to attend Florida International University in Miami. She did well enough to earn a scholarship to law school at the University of Miami. Not surprisingly, she worshiped her brother.

Shortly after Bud and Marge married, they bought ten acres of land west of Miami, hard against the Everglades, and built a modest house. A year ago the city's growth reached their acreage, and the Duboses sold to a developer for one million dollars. Bud retired, and seeking a quieter lifestyle than could be found in Miami, moved north and rented a house near the beach in Ware County.

Somewhere along the line, he had met Rundel, who convinced him to invest in an airplane. Probably because the million dollars was the only asset Bud had, he was told by Rundel that if he put up the million dollars to make a down payment on the airplane, Rendel would lease it out to an air carrier, and Bud would get a twelve percent return on his money, plus a number of business tax deductions. This was substantially better than the banks were paying on certificates of deposit, and banks do not provide tax shelters on the interest they pay. He would be given a security interest in the airplane, so that if the deal ever went sour, he could simply repossess the plane and sell it for more money than he had in it. Bud did not tell Anne about this great deal, because he wanted to suprise her with what an astute businessman he was.

"So," I said, "Bud got one interest payment and nothing more. Neither Rundel nor the plane are anywhere to be found."

"Right," she said. "How did you know?"

"It's a variation on an old scam worked on trusting people." I explained the entire case concerning Logan, and told her what we knew so far about Rundel and James. "What makes you think your brother's death wasn't an accident?"

"After Rundel wouldn't answer his phone calls, Bud went to Longboat Key, and confronted Rundel. Bud told him that if he didn't get his money back, he was going to the police. Rundel told him that might end up being a very bad move, and that it could put his life in danger. He then told him that the plane had been stolen, and that there was an insurance policy that should pay off if the plane could not be found.

"My brother told him to go to hell, and left. He called me on his way home and told me about the conversation. The next day the house he was renting blew up."

"Did you ever hear anything about the insurance?"

"Oh, yeah. It turned out that the plane was on list of stolen aircraft kept by the Drug Enforcement Agency. They gave me the name of the insurance company." She had called the company and identified herself as a lawyer for her brother's estate. The claims people had been cooperative and sent her the documents showing that the company had paid the one million dollar loss benefit to Rundel, who was listed as the owner of the plane. She got the name of the agent who wrote the policy and called him. The agent had all the documents showing Rundel as the owner. There was no mention of Bud Dubose anywhere in the paperwork.

"What was the agent's name?" I asked.

"Noblin. He has an agency in Tallahassee."

The fog was lifting a little now, and I could begin to see the players a little more clearly. Obviously, Noblin was in on the plot to separate Bud from his money. It was a neat scam. They got the money from Bud, laundered it to some extent through the lawyer Jones, bought the plane, insured it, and then probably sold the plane to a drug dealer and claimed it stolen for the insurance money. We would never prove who bought the plane, and it would probably never be seen again. But Rundel made money twice, once on the sale of the plane, and then on the insurance payout. I told Anne my suspicions.

"Did you ever hear the names Sam or Maria Cox?" I asked.

"No. Who are they?"

"They're both affiliated with Rundel in some manner, and Sam Cox was the guy asking about Logan just before Connie was killed. I was heading for Miami to see what I could find out about the Coxes."

"How do you plan to do that?" she asked.

"I got their address from the documents in the Secretary of State's office. I thought I'd start there."

"You're just going to walk up and tell them you're looking for Rundel?"

"No. I think I've done about as much as I can without a little subterfuge. I have to come up with some sort of scam to get close to them. I have to know more about the operation before I can move at all."

"How do we start?"

"We? I think I'd better do this alone. It might get dangerous."

"I want a part of this. I know South Florida better than you do, and I've got some contacts around that you won't have. I've lived here all my life, you know. Besides, sometimes a couple is less menacing than a man alone."

"Let's have dinner and talk about it."

She drove us to an Italian seafood place overlooking the beach.

I was aware that Anne Dubose was beautiful the moment I saw her walk into the bar at the Marriott. Her law school academic record proved that she was very smart. Her sense of humor came bubbling out over dinner as she regaled me with tales of office politics in her law firm.

"Your stories make me glad I'm out of it," I told her over a dessert of canoli. "I'd forgotten how silly and petty a bunch of grown up lawyers can be."

"How are you able to get out of it? Did you hit the magic case and get lots of big bucks?"

"Something like that."

"You don't want to tell me. Listen, I don't care how you got the money as long as it was legal. If it wasn't legal, I could be opening myself up to a bad time with what we're about to get into. I've lived in South Florida long enough to know that everyone around can be at risk in drug deals."

"No, nothing like that." I really didn't have to explain, but I wanted this woman to like me. "I represented a guy on a big case and made a large fee. I was tired of the rat race and decided it could move on without me I'm dropping out, as the kids say."

"Then why are you helping Mr. Hamilton? You've dropped out."

"Because he's my friend."

"That's it?" she asked, a tone of incredulity slipping into her voice. "Because he's your friend?"

"Yes."

"Would he do the same for you?"

"I think so," I said. "I once told him that he was one of the few friends I had who would come get me if I ran out of gas in Hahira, Georgia. He said, 'Yeah, well, I'd probably send a limousine.'"

She laughed. "At least he'd take some action."

"Yep. That's Logan."

"Look," she said, "I really want to work with you on this deal. I want to find Rundel and ruin him. My brother worked hard all his life and got lucky once. When he sold his land. To think that some greedy con man can just take it away from him infuriates me. I really want to be there when Rundel gets his."

"It's late Anne. Why don't we think about this overnight and meet for lunch tommorow. We need a plan."

She dropped me at the Marriott and headed home. I stopped in the bar for a nightcap of good ole Miller Lite, and a meeting with an old friend. Jimmy Greene was at the bar. I had called him on my way to Ft. Lauderdale, and asked him to meet me late for a drink.

I had met James B. Greene, Jr. on my very first day at the University of Florida while standing in the registration line. "Hi," he had said. "I'm Jimmy Greene, and I've only got one leg. What you see hanging below my right knee is the world's best prosthesis. We don't call them wooden legs anymore, and its not considered polite to call me a cripple. I'm from New Smyrna."

Jimmy and I pledged the same fraternity and became good friends and occasional drinking buddies. He majored in building construction and went to work for a large firm of home builders while I went on to law school. I had not seen him in several years, but we kept up with each other through mutual friends. He was sitting alone at the end of the bar nursing a tall glass of something amber. He had put on a few pounds, but he certainly wasn't fat. His hair was still blond and still covered most of his head.

"Excuse me," I said, as I climbed onto the stool next to him, "but I assume this to be the handicapped section, since it seems to be filled with cripples."

He turned slowly toward me with a look of resignation on his face. "Fucking lawyers," he grumbled. "I got to start hanging out at a better class place. How the hell are you, Matt?" We shook hands and hugged. It was very good to see an old friend.

"Couldn't be better. How about you? I heard you had made it real big in the home building business."

"Can't complain buddy. Can't complain."

As a matter of fact Jimmy Greene had made it very big in the construction business. He was president and only stockholder of Greene Constructors, one of the largest companies of its kind in the southeast. He had divisions that built houses, office buildings and roads. He had built his business on the basis that his customers got exactly what they contracted for, on time and within budget. He was an honest and competent builder.

"It's been too long, Jimmy."

"It has. It's a terrible thing to get so busy that you never see those who meant the most to you in times past. I've kept up with you though. Hot shot lawyer. I'm proud of you. What brings you to Lauderdale?"

"Trying to help an old buddy who's in a lot of trouble."

I told him that I was looking for Rundel, and also told him about Bud Dubose and the scam he was caught up in. "I don't guess you ever heard of Hale Rundel, did you?" I asked.

"No, can't say that I have. But if he's really been in the airplane business anywhere in South Florida, I'd bet Paul Jensen would know."

Jimmy explained that his business had grown to the extent that he had to have a small fleet of airplanes to ferry him and his executives around the country. Jensen was his chief pilot and had been flying in and around South Florida for forty years.

"Why don't we meet for breakfast in the morning, and I'll take you out to the Executive airport to meet him. It can't hurt to ask."

We agreed to meet in the hotel coffee shop at eight the next morning. We spent the next hour reminiscing about college friends and laughing at the memories.

Chapter 19

TUESDAY

Jensen was one of those beefy guys in his early sixties who had always had to fight to keep his weight down. He was losing the battle now, but hadn't completely gone to fat. There was a lot of muscle still there, but it was inexorably being replaced by lard. He was sweating in the hot hangar and wiping grease off his hands as he came toward us. His right arm had the scars of a long ago burn running from the elbow up into the sleeve of his yellow golf shirt. He was wearing dirty jeans held up by a wide leather belt with a large metal buckle onto which had been etched the outlines of a P 38 fighter plane in flight. Wispy gray hair tried without much success to cover his scalp.

"Hello, Mr. G. Flying today?" he asked Jimmy.

"Afraid not, Paul. I want you to meet an old friend of mine, Matt Royal. Matt, Paul Jensen, our chief pilot. Matt would like to ask you some flying questions."

His handshake was strong. "Nice to meet you, Mr. Royal." His voice was deep, and an accent of the deep South rumbled my way. "Come on into the office. Don't let the title fool you. I don't do a lot of flying anymore. I'm sort of a jack of all trades these days."

Jimmy had told me that Jensen had failed his flight physical two years before, and he couldn't fly passengers anymore. It had something to do with his heart. Greene kept him on to oversee the other pilots and mechanics, and to take care of scheduling the aircraft.

There were several planes in various stages of repair, scattered like toys over the hangar floor. The office sat to one side, with the only door opening into the hangar. There was a window to the outside taken up almost

123

entirely by a groaning air conditioner pushing a swath of cold air into the tiny room. A rusty metal desk sat in the corner completely covered with parts manuals and old aviation magazines. A metal swivel chair covered in cracked green vinyl was in front of the desk and an old wooden straight chair that had probably once graced someone's dining room was placed to the side. The current Sports Illustrated swimsuit calendar was tacked to the wall. Miss June was climbing out of a swimming pool showing tits and teeth. "Have a seat, gentleman," said Jensen.

Jimmy took the swivel chair, and I took the other. Jensen hoisted himself onto a two drawer metal filing cabinet in the corner. "What can I do for you, Mr. Royal?" he asked.

"Have you ever heard of a man named Hale Rundel or of Rundel Enterprises?" I asked.

"Nope. Can't say I have. Is he supposed to be based in this area?"

"I'm not sure. I assumed that he might be flying out of one of the airports in Dade or Broward, but I don't know that for sure."

"I think I'd know of him if he had been around here for any length of time. You get to know most of the airplane people sooner or later. What kind of outfit is Rundel Enterprises?"

"A charter outfit. Leases jets out to corporations."

"Never heard of it. You never know though. These little fly by night outfits are always changing their names. Lots of them are into shady deals running drugs."

"What about Sam or Maria Cox?" I asked.

"Sure, I know Sam. Used to hang out down at the Opa Locka airport. He was mostly a mech, but he had a license and did some flying. He worked out a deal with one of the marine supply stores in Miami, where he would fly boat parts and groceries to the islands to deliver to boaters who couldn't get what they needed down there. I think he made a pretty good little living out of it. I haven't seen him in five or six years though."

"Is Maria his wife or sister?" I asked.

"I don't know. I never heard of him with any woman named Maria."

"Do you have any idea what he's doing now?"

"No, but I could call around and maybe find out."

"Don't tell anyone why you're looking for him. If we find him, I'd like to surprise him a little bit. How long will it take you?"

"I'm not sure, but I'll get right on it and call you as soon as I know anything. Where can I reach you?"

I gave him my cell phone number. Jimmy dropped me back at the Marriott and said he'd get in touch later in the day to see about dinner.

A small tingle of anticipation had been rooting around in the back of my mind all morning at the thought of seeing Anne again. I arrived back at the hotel shortly before noon to find her sitting in the lobby. She stood as I approached and stuck out her hand.

She was wearing a beige linen dress, beige pumps and a small diamond pendant hanging from a gold chain around her neck. "Hello, Matt," she said as we shook hands. "I called your room and didn't get an answer. I was about to think I had been stood up."

"Not a chance," I said. "I've been doing a little legwork this morning. I'll tell you about it over lunch."

The restaurant at the hotel was not a simple coffee shop, but it did not quite make it to the level of a top eatery either. The view, however, was hard to beat. We had a table next to the high windows that overlooked the intracoastal waterway. We could watch boats of just about every description ply their way north and south. It was early yet for the annual southerly migration of yachts from the north, but Ft. Lauderdale boasts a wealth of boats at any time of the year.

We ordered iced tea from the cocktail waitress and perused the menus. I ordered a hamburger and Anne asked for the chef's salad. While we waited for our food I told her about my morning and Paul Jensen's offer to help.

"You've been busy. What's your plan if Mr. Jensen can find Cox?" she asked.

"I don't know yet. I'll come up with something."

"We'll come up with something. You're not going to leave me out of this. I told my boss this morning that I was going to take the next few days off. I don't think it'll cause any problems with the firm, but I really don't care if it does. I want a piece of Rundel."

I guess I had already made up my mind on some unconscious level to work with Anne, but it seemed at the time to be a split second decision. "Okay. But you work with me. Don't go off on any tangents of your own. I need to know everything that's going on, so I don't shoot myself in the foot. It's like a trial. One guy has to be in charge, and everybody else reports to him. Deal?"

"Deal," she said. "But you keep me informed, too. Deal?"

"Deal."

As we were leaving the restaurant, my cell phone rang. It was Jensen.

"Sam Cox is still living in Miami. Old buddy of mine at Opa Locka says he hit it rich and is living in one of those expensive condos on Brickell Avenue. Sam says he inherited some money, but everybody else thinks he's in the drug business. He doesn't work out of Opa Locka anymore."

"I appreciate your help, Paul. You didn't alert anybody down there that we're looking for him, did you?"

"Nope. I called this buddy of mine who runs a flying school at the airport and just chewed the fat. Told him I had been thinking about some of the old crowd and wondered what happened to them. I asked him about several people, including Sam Cox."

"Good thinking, Paul. I appreciate it."

"Oh, by the way, Maria is Sam's wife. Got married about a year ago, just before he struck it rich. Cuban girl."

"Thanks Paul. I hope I can return the favor."

I called the Miami information operator and was told that she had a listing for a Samuel H. Cox at a Brickell Avenue address. I jotted down the number.

"Well?" asked Anne.

I related Jensen's end of the conversation. "I think we ought to go on down to Miami and see what we can come up with. I think the Coxes will be our key to Rundel. We just need to come up with an approach."

Anne went to her apartment to get some clothes, and I went back to my room and called Jimmy Greene. I told him that Paul Jensen had come through and that Anne and I were heading for Miami. He said to call him if we needed anything.

I drove over to Anne's apartment complex to pick her up. I thought it better to be driving the Explorer than her little Nissan with the sun roof. She had given me directions and was waiting in front when I arrived. I put her one bag in the back seat, and we swung out toward I-95 South.

Chapter 20

If they ever give I-95 through Broward and Dade counties a name, it should be called Avenue of the Idiots. Otherwise sane Americans seem to go over the edge when they get behind the wheel of an automobile. My favorite moron is the slot jumper. He is the one who weaves in and out of traffic, going from lane to lane trying to get into any open slot he sees. It's as if he thinks that the act of putting on his turn signal gives him the absolute right to move into the adjoining lane. The slot jumper always uses his turn signal, and always seems to be driving one of those little square foreign jobs that looks as if it were made of tin.

The road south had plenty of slot jumpers and other assorted maniacs. I put the Explorer in the right lane and drove a steady sixty miles per hour. It was another scorcher of a day, but dark clouds were moving in from the east. With any luck we'd get some rain to cool down the afternoon. The SUV's air conditioner was going full blast, and I wondered briefly how we had survived Florida in the days before everything had become air cooled. I remembered a lot of sweaty nights and car trips with the windows all down trying to catch the air.

"Have you got a preference for a hotel in Miami?" I asked.

"I've got a key to my friend Mandy's apartment. She's in Europe for the Summer. I thought if you didn't mind we could stay there."

"I don't mind if Mandy doesn't."

"She won't. She asked me to stay there when I'm in town. Gives the place a lived in look."

"You won't feel compromised?"

"There are two bedrooms, thank you. Have you decided how we approach the Coxes?" she asked.

"It has to be natural," I said. "We can't just go up to him and ask if he knows where Rundel is."

"And how do we do that?"

"I don't know yet. Let's stop by that Brickell Avenue address and see what it looks like. If we can find out more about what Cox is doing these days, maybe we can come up with something."

The apartment building was one of those glass towers designed by an architect with no imagination and a small budget. It was twenty stories tall, and it was apparent that the top floors commanded an expansive and expensive view of upper Biscayne Bay. I found a parking space on a cross street about three blocks from Cox's place, and Anne and I strolled up the street gawking as if we were tourists. There was a revolving door at the front of the building opening into a large lobby that was two stories high. It contained several large Oriental rugs of varied hues situated tastefully on a marble floor. Large indoor plants were placed around the area, growing out of ornate containers. There were four sofas and half a dozen wingback chairs arranged in seating groups that encouraged conversation. In front of the elevator bank sat a security guard at a desk that contained television monitors and other electronic gadgetry that apparently controlled the elevators. He wore the uniform of a local security firm that closely resembled that worn by Miami cops. I guessed that was a conscious decision of the part of someone. He was about forty years old, and he wore captain's bars on his collar points. He was not a big man, but he had long arms and large hands that I thought would give him an advantage in a fight that would surprise most who took him on. He had dark hair with specks of gray, and when he opened his mouth I knew he had spent his formative years in Brooklyn.

"Can I help you?" he asked.

"I hope so Captain," I said. "You're the fourth building along here we've stopped in. We're looking for an old friend named Jonathan Cox who is supposed to live in one of these big buildings in this area. I had the address, but I forgot to bring it down with me." An old Florida accent, the kind spoken by those of us who grew up in the state before the Northerners took it over, is essentially Southern. I learned a long time ago that most New Yorkers, even those from Brooklyn, think all Southerners are a little slow, and are therefore often willing to tell us things they wouldn't normally tell a stranger.

"I'm afraid not, sir."

"Are you sure? The is the last building it could possibly be. Would you mind checking the directory just to be certain? I promised his sister we'd look him up while we're in town."

"I know everybody in the building, sir. There ain't no Jonathan Cox lives here."

"Well, I swear. The security officer next door said he thought surely there was a Mr. Cox in this building. Guess he was wrong."

"Oh, he's thinking about Mr. Samuel Cox who lives here. But I never heard of a Jonathan Cox."

"Does he live in 16-B? That's Jonathan's apartment number. I remember that."

"No, sir. Our Mr. Cox lives in the penthouse."

"Well, sorry to bother you. I really appreciate your help, Captain."

"No problem," he said.

We walked back into the afternoon heat and headed for the car. "We didn't accomplish much there, did we?" Anne asked.

"Sure we did," I said. "We've established that Cox lives there and that he's done well enough to have acquired the penthouse. Even if he's only renting, it costs a bundle. A lot more that he ever made ferrying groceries to boaters in the islands."

"What now, Sherlock?" she grinned.

"We have to get close enough to him to give him an opportunity to try to sell us an airplane. If he thinks we have a lot of money, not too much sense, and a little larceny in our hearts he may try to scam us. Where ever Rundel is, you can bet Cox can get hold of him. And I don't think they would've stopped running a lucrative scam after just one score. There are probably other people out there that have been taken, and I imagine Rundel and Cox are always looking for more suckers. Let's move into Mandy's apartment and find a good restaurant. We can talk about it over dinner."

Joachin Jiminez, known as J.J., had come to Miami with his mother and father in 1959, in the first exodus from Cuba. He had been the pampered sixteen year old son of a prosperous lawyer who was on Castro's earliest hit list. Because Oscar Jimenez was not licensed to practice law in the United States, he had gone into the restaurant business. As was the custom of those early Cuban refugees, the entire family worked at the restaurant, which was housed in a store front on Miami's Eighth Avenue. Oscar's passion however, was not food, but freedom for Cuba. He became an active member of the anti-Castro exile community, and when he heard that the

American Central Intelligence Agency was recruiting an invasion force, he signed on. His son J.J., then eighteen, joined as well. After training in the jungles of Nicaragua, father and son landed with Brigade 2506 on Playa Giron in Cuba, known to Americans as the Bay of Pigs. The force ran into heavy resistance from Cuban troops, and was abandoned by President Kennedy and the Americans. Oscar was among the twenty percent of the Brigade who were killed. J.J. saw his father fall during the retreat to the beach. With most of the remaining men, J.J. disappeared into the swamps. He was caught by Cuban soldiers three days later, and spent the better part of two years in prison. He was among those survivors ransomed by the American government for fifty-three million dollars in 1963.

J.J.'s mother, Carmen, had kept the restaurant open during his imprisonment. When he came back to Miami, J.J. took over, and he built it into one of the finest Cuban restaurants in the city. In the late 1960's he bought an old house near the University of Miami campus in Coral Gables and moved the restaurant there. Over the years J.J. and his food became legends. His mother, now in her eighties, still presided over the dining room, and J.J.'s wife and teenage son helped out.

J.J. never lost his contempt for the Kennedys, and he loathed the Democratic Party. He became a tireless worker for the Republican Party. I had gotten to know him well in my days in politics, and I ate at his restaurant every chance I got. Anne had enjoyed the place while a law student at the University, and she was quick to accept my suggestion that we eat there.

Carmen Jimenez greeted us at the door with a whoop and a big hug for me. "Matthew Royal, where have you been? And who is this beautiful young lady? And why didn't you call me if you wanted to get married?" she gushed in her slightly accented way.

"Carmen Jimenez," I said, "Meet Anne Dubose, a colleague, not a date."

"Why, you're just too pretty to be a lawyer, and probably too nice to be with this guy anyway."

"Why, thank you Mrs. Jimenez. He was the best I could do on short notice. I'm surprised that a lady of such obvious refinement as yourself even admits to knowing this scoundrel," Anne said.

"I think we're going to be friends," laughed Carmen. "Come on. Let me get you two seated and tell J.J. you're here. He was talking about you just the other day."

The restaurant is spread out among several rooms of the old house and some additions that had been added over the years. Carmen led us to a table isolated from the room by several tall plants. She left menus and told us she would send J.J. right over.

In moments, a waiter approached our table. He was a young man with a shock of black hair and a noticeable Spanish accent. I knew that J.J. always hired recent refugees from Cuba, trying to give them a good start in their new country. He took our drink orders and departed. By the time he returned with a Miller Lite for me and a glass of Chablis for Anne, I saw J.J. working his way across the room, stopping to talk briefly to each guest. He hadn't changed much in the five years since I had seen him. He was maybe a little heavier, and perhaps a little grayer, but he still carried himself like a soldier and grinned like the happy man he usually was.

"Good Lord," he said, as he grabbed me in a bear hug. "How long has it been, old friend? Five years? I knew you had dropped out of politics, but I had begun to think you had dropped off the world as well. Introduce me to your friend." His words fell from his mouth slightly askew, sibilant with the vestigious memory of his mother tongue.

"Anne Dubose, this is J.J. Jimenez, the legend."

"It's nice to finally meet you, J.J. I used to eat here occasionally when I was a student."

"Glad to have you with us, and very nice to meet you."

"Pull up a chair, J.J., and let me buy you a drink," I said.

J.J. sat. "I hear about you now and then from some of the people from the old days. They tell me you're doing great."

"I'm sure they also told you about the bad times. I seemed to have survived them. Anne knows about my sordid past."

"I'm glad to hear you're alright. We miss you at the political meetings. What brings you to Miami?"

I gave him the shortened version of our stories, but left nothing of substance out. I told him we were trying to get a line on Hale Rundel and that Cox seemed to be our best bet.

"I know them both. Cox married Maria Domingo. He father Jorge was part of the Brigade. After we were released from prison he started a business mowing lawns." Jorge was part of the Cuban renaissance of Miami. He had owned one old pick-up truck and a Snapping Turtle mower, and had two teenage sons who worked their butts off. He built his business into the largest landscaping business in Dade County. He had one daughter, and she seemed to go out of her way to cause him anguish. When she was seventeen, she dropped out of school and married a young man who was working for a company that supplied a pilot and plane for the daily traffic watch on one of the local radio stations. He was the pilot. One day he left Opa Locka in a Piper heading for the Bahamas and was never heard from again. There were a lot of rumors flying around about him being in some kind of a drug deal that went wrong.

"I guess no one will ever know whether he was murdered or just crashed at sea. At any rate Maria got a job as a secretary at one of those flying services out at the Opa Locka airport and moved in with one of the mechanics. She refused to try to patch things up with her father, and the family kind of wrote her off. Jorge died about two years ago of a heart attack. He completely cut her out of the will. About a year ago she came in here with her new husband, Sam Cox. She's about twenty-five now, and absolutely beautiful. Cox is old enough to be her father, but they seem happy enough. We see them about once a week. They come in, have dinner and a drink or two, chat a little with Mother or me, and leave. He drives a Mercedes, one of the big ones, and based on the tips he leaves, he either has a lot of money or wants to give the impression that he has. He has never indicated what he does for a living, but I've heard rumors that he supplies muscle for some bad people."

"It is truly a small world, sometimes," said Anne.

"Not really," said J.J. "The first wave of Cubans who came after Castro make up a relatively small community here, and the Brigade survivors are a very small group. Anyone related to either group usually makes his way into this restaurant. Even though Maria was cut off from her family, she is still part of a small group of Cubans."

"What do you know about his business?" I asked.

"Nothing really. Only what I heard. He works for this guy Rundel, who is on the fringe of Republican politics down here. Nobody likes him much, but he seems to have a lot of money, and that buys him entree to most of the events," J.J. said. "I think he's also using Maria to help him get close to the Cuban community. There're a lot of Republicans there, and they always vote."

"Why would that be important to an Anglo like Rundel?" Anne asked

"We have the Presidential primaries coming up in March of next year," J.J. said. "The Cuban vote can swing a close race, and Florida is one of the most important primary states."

"Does Rundel have a candidate?" I asked.

"I haven't heard anything about that," J.J. said. "But he's kind of a sleaze ball, and I can't imagine any serious candidate getting to close to him."

"Can you think of any way to set us up with Cox that wouldn't seem suspicious?" I asked.

"He and Maria are regulars on Wednesday night for our seafood special. If they hold true to form, I expect they'll here tomorrow evening. They always make a reservation. I could let you know when it is and seat you and Anne at a table next to them. That would give me a good excuse to introduce you. You would have to take it from there."

"That's the best offer I've had so far. Why don't we try it," I said.

We talked a little bit about old times and old faces and friends, and then J.J. had to get back to work. I gave him my cell phone number and told him to leave a voice mail if he couldn't get an answer.

We had a delicious chicken dish whose name I could not pronounce, and would not have known what it was except for the English translation on the menu. The waiter refused us a check, declaring that Senor Jiminez had insisted that we were his guests, and that it had been his honor to serve any friend of a hero such as Senor Jiminez, and that he would not even consider accepting a tip. J.J. was a hero, but he was also one hell of a nice guy.

"We got lucky," said Anne as we drove back to Mandy's apartment.

"Yeah," I said, "and I think we're going to have to have a lot more luck to pull this off. I'd like to find out more about Rundel, and I'd sure like to know why Cox was looking for Logan on Longboat Key."

We stopped at a Publix supermarket on the way to Mandy's and bought coffee and pastries for breakfast. The apartment was in one of those upscale garden complexes that had a large pool next to a room that was used for meetings and parties. Most of the tenants were young couples who drove BMW's and went to the currently in South Beach clubs for their entertainment. They spent the weekends around the pool, soaking up the sun and ensuring that their skin would be as dry and wrinkled as an alligator by the time they were forty. An unlucky few of them would develop melanoma and not live to see their fortieth birthdays. But what the hell, they were in Florida and living for the moment. Every Northerner knows that a deep tan is the trademark of those of them who escaped the frigid winters of their birthplaces. They need to show them off when they go home for

Christmas. The natives knew that summer in Florida was no time to be spending their days off in the sun.

Mandy was single and lived in the complex when she was in Miami. She apparently was an heiress of some sort and was not required to hold a regular job. Consequently, she traveled a great deal. The apartment was just a place to stay when she was in Miami. It was a sterile sort of place, devoid of personality. There were no pictures of loved ones, no books or even magazines; none of the things you normally find in someone's home. This was not a home. It was a place for a transient to occasionally park herself.

There were two bedrooms, one with a bath. Anne had put her things in this one when we had stopped by earlier that day. I took the smaller bedroom, with a bath in the hall next to it. There was a kitchen stocked with utensils, but no food.

"I'm really tired, Matt. Would you think me terribly rude if I went on to bed?" Anne asked, as we entered the apartment.

"Not at all," I said. "I wouldn't mind a little time to read." I was reading Randy Wayne White's latest novel and wishing I were more like Doc Ford.

"Well, goodnight then," she said, and disappeared into her room. Moments later I heard the shower running, and wished briefly that I was in it with her. I told myself that she was my partner in a gamey enterprise, and that I really did not want to gum up the works by getting involved with her. Yeah, right.

I read for an hour and drifted off to sleep. I had a disturbing dream, but could not remember it the next morning. I woke up vaguely troubled, but could not bring the dream out of the murky depths of my mind.

Chapter 21

WEDNESDAY

Thirty minutes later, I was showered and shaved and followed the smell of coffee into the kitchen. Anne was sitting at the table, reading the morning paper and having a breakfast of pastries. "Good morning, sleeping beauty," she said with a smile. "I've already run three miles and picked up the paper."

"Well, I'm older," I said. "Anything new in the paper today?"

"Same old stuff," she said. "The police busted a ring of prostitutes who were slipping mickeys to their johns and stealing their gold Rolex watches. They would only go to their pads with guys wearing Rolexes. The cops got them before they could hock the watches. They had ten, but eight were fakes, worth about ten bucks a piece."

"See, crime doesn't pay."

"Yeah, and a girl's got to be real careful who she goes out with. Fake watches. What's next?"

My cell phone rang. It was J.J.

"Hey Matt," he said. "I got a call last night from Sam Cox, making a reservation for 7:00 this evening. I've arranged for you to sit next to him and Maria."

"I've been thinking about this, J.J. I'm afraid if you introduce us, he may make the connection between me and Longboat or between Anne and her brother. Have you got a digital camera?"

"Sure."

"Why don't you take a picture of Anne and me at the table, but angle the camera so that you get both Sam and Maria in the picture."

"No sweat, Matt. See you at seven."

I hung up and related the conversation to Anne. "I'd like to take a picture of Sam back to Longboat and see if anybody recognizes him."

"Do you think he's the killer?" she asked.

"Not if he was the one with Logan at the time Connie was killed. But he would sure as hell be part of it."

"I can't see any connection to Connie in any of this. It was obviously not just a random murder."

"You're right, but there must be some connection we're not seeing. I don't think Logan was the target, or they'd have just killed him. Logan was purposefully set up, but I suspect it was because he was available. Serendipity. But someone had watched Connie long enough to know that she and Logan were tight. But, why?"

"The answer to that will tell us who the murderer is," she said.

Anne headed for the bedroom and a shower just as my cell phone rang again.

"Mr. Royal, this is Will Ledbetter, the probation officer in Chicago."

"Yes, Mr. Ledbetter. How are you?"

"Fine, thanks. I figured I owed you a favor, so I thought I'd pass along some information I just got."

"I appreciate that, but I can't imagine what sort of favor I did for you."

"Since you were in the office that day, Carol has been a vision of cooperation. I sort of forgot to tell her you weren't a real senator."

"Ah, yes," I laughed. "I'm glad that did you some good. What's your news?"

"I found out what happened to that pimp, Golden Joe, and thought you'd like to know. He was found dead back in April down in Miami. Nobody got real excited about finding out who he was, but they did take fingerprints. The system finally worked the information through to this office. The body was one Joseph Dean Johnson, aka Golden Joe."

"Thanks Will. I appreciate the call. I'll see what I can find out in Miami."

Anne came out of the bedroom wearing peach colored capri pants, a sleeveless blouse and matching sandals. My professional detachment was taking a beating. I related my conversation with Will. "Do you know anybody on the Miami Police force that might be able to help us get some information real quick? I hate to call in another favor from the Longboat chief."

"Carl Merritt is a detective for Miami-Dade. I dated him some in high school. He'd probably help us if he thought it might be connected to my brother's death."

The Miami-Dade police department is located in a new headquarters building several blocks west of Miami International Airport. Carl had agreed to meet us and bring the file with him. He was also going to see if he could find the detective who worked the case, and bring him along.

Carl met us in the lobby and passed us through security. We took the elevator to the homicide division. Carl was a large man who had been a pretty good linebacker in high school, but not quite good enough for college. He had earned a degree in criminal justice from Florida International University and settled into a career with the county police department. He had risen to homicide detective in a relatively short period of time. He was glad to see Anne, but she had mentioned that they had maintained their friendship over the years, and she saw him and his wife every month or so.

Carl introduced us to Ryan Mallard, the detective who had worked the homicide. I told them both about my involvement in the case and the connection to Anne's brother's death. Mallard was a little embarrassed that his investigation was so skimpy, but he told us that the body had been found in a drainage ditch on the edge of the Everglades, with one of its legs missing. There were no personal effects or identification on the body. The victim had been shot in the back of the head, execution style. Mallard had run the fingerprints and found that the victim had been released from an Illinois prison a couple of weeks before his death.

The trail, and the investigation, ended there. There was no evidence to pursue. Golden Joe had been dead only a day or so, but a heavy south Florida thunderstorm had passed over the area during the evening hours, and any tire tracks or other evidence on the ground had been washed away. Mallard sent his paperwork through channels, trusting that the proper people in Illinois would be notified in due time. He put the file in open cases, and moved on to other investigations.

"Did you do any ballistic testing on the bullet that killed him?" I asked.

"Sure. If we ever find the gun, we could match it up," Mallard said, "but that's like finding a needle in a haystack. And this county is a mighty big haystack."

"Do you know what kind of gun was used?"

"Nine millimeter is about all I can tell you."

"Any idea how Joe got from Illinois to Miami?" I asked.

"No. I did check the airlines, but there was no record of him flying in. But he could have come by bus or train, or hitchhiked and we'd never know. The airlines are the only ones that require some ID to board."

"And you haven't heard anything from any snitches?"

"No. My guess is that he was killed as soon as he arrived in Miami. Lots of people float through here like ghosts, leaving no trail at all," Mallard said. "We figured he probably had run afoul of somebody in prison, and it was payback time."

"But, then, why not kill him in Illinois? Why follow him all the way to Florida? I wonder if someone might have lured him here somehow just so they could kill him."

"Could be. We'll never know unless we get lucky on another bust somewhere, and somebody has some information about this one. We end up with lots of unsolved murders of transients in this county."

"Wouldn't it have made sense to drop the body somewhere in the 'glades where it likely wouldn't be found?" I asked.

"We think that was the plan. That ditch usually has a lot of gators in it, but for some reason, they didn't take the whole body. My guess is that a gator chewed off his leg, and left him on the bank for a snack later, but a fisherman came by and saw the body and called us."

We thanked the detectives for their courtesy and took our leave.

"I don't understand any of this," Anne said as we drove out of the police parking lot. "What connection is there among the three murders?"

I had thought about this same thing since hearing about Joe's murder in Miami. If Rundel and Cox were involved in Bud's and Connie's murders, that might be the only connection. Connie and Bud had not known each other as far as either Anne or I knew, and neither Logan nor Connie would have had any reason to do business with Rundel. They might have met during Rundel's stay on Longboat, but I could come up with no reason for Rundel to murder Connie.

On the other hand, Connie/Vivian was connected to Golden Joe. Maybe these two murders were connected, and Bud's death was either an accident, as the sheriff thought, or he was murdered just to keep him quiet about Rundel's shady business dealings. The questions then were, who would want Connie and Joe dead, and why. They had not seen each other in years, and while Joe might have reason to kill Connie/Vivian out of revenge, who would kill him, and why. And why in Miami. Any why would Rundel and Cox be interested in Connie and Joe. It was all circular, and I was getting nowhere.

I explained my thinking to Anne. She said, "Forget the part about Bud's death being an accident. He knew too much about living in isolated places to not check on his propane tank regularly. Plus, he had an alarm that would have sounded at the first sign of a propane leak. Rundel killed him, or had it done."

"Okay," I said. "I'm just thinking out loud. Do you remember J.J. saying that he heard that Cox was hired out as muscle? Maybe he's graduated to contract killings. Maybe Rundel set things up and uses Cox to do the dirty work."

"Yes, but Cox didn't kill Connie if he was with Logan at the time of her death."

"True, but he was involved. Maybe Cox is the set up man, and he has someone else actually do the killing."

"But why would he be interested in killing Connie and Joe?" she asked.

"The answer to that question might get Logan acquitted."

We arrived at the restaurant right on time, and after a hug from Carmen, we were escorted to our table. There was an older man and a young Cuban woman at the next table; the Coxes, I presumed. We were situated so that I was sitting back to back with the woman, with the man sitting across from the woman and Anne sitting across from me. A waiter stopped by to get our drink orders, and in a few minutes J.J. came to our table.

"Matt," he said. "Good to see you. I meant to ask you last night if you remembered John Allred up in Orlando."

"Sure," I said. "I haven't seen him in a long time. What do you hear from him?"

"He's doing well. I talked to him today and told him I had seen you. He asked that I send him a picture of you the next time you came in. Do you mind?" He brandished a small digital camera.

"Go ahead," I said, laughing. "God knows why John wants a picture of me."

J.J. put the camera to his eye, said, "smile," and snapped off two quick shots. My guess was that he had gotten a pretty good shot over my shoulder of Sam Cox. And of course, John Allred had never asked for my picture.

We enjoyed our meal, and left before the Coxes had finished their after dinner drinks. We had already cleaned up at Mandy's and had our gear in the Explorer, so we headed for I-95 and Ft. Lauderdale. There was nothing else to be accomplished in South Florida, and I had a trial looming in Bradenton. We had decided over dinner that I would let Anne know if I came up with anything in Longboat, but otherwise, I would be getting ready for trial.

I dropped Anne at her place and checked into a hotel near the airport. I wanted to get an early start on the three hour drive to Longboat. I left a wake up call for five a.m., and fell into a deep and dreamless sleep.

Chapter 22

THURSDAY

I was on the road, the Explorer pointed due west on Alligator Alley, as the dawn seeped into the black world of the nighttime Everglades. Within minutes, the sun rose over my shoulder, bathing the River of Grass in gold and burnt orange. Off to my right, four vultures rode the air currents, circling low, no doubt eyeing the remains of some animal who had met its demise during the night. The early sunlight danced on the water, glittering like so many small diamonds among the sawgrass blades.

I had not heard from Logan in several days. I was hoping he would keep his promise, and turn himself in to the Manatee Sheriff on Sunday. If he didn't, I would look a little foolish; but worse, the State Attorney would look foolish too. And he was a politician, and politicians do not like to look foolish. He would chase Logan with the resolve of a wounded elephant charging its tormentor, and he would stay on him until, finally, some day, Logan would be brought down. There would be no mercy, in either the hunt or the aftermath. And Logan would not have me as his lawyer, because I would not be suckered twice.

Near Naples, I-75 turns north, to run parallel to the Gulf coast and the old federal highway known as the Tamiami Trail. Traffic was light, and by eight o'clock I was crossing the wide Caloosahatchee River just east of Ft. Myers. By nine, I was taking the off ramp at Fruitville Road, driving west into Sarasota. As I neared downtown, I opened my sunroof and put the windows down in the Explorer. The morning air was spiced with the scent of the Gulf. I crossed the Ringling Causeway and bridge to St. Armands Circle, glancing briefly at the shops, not yet open. I headed north across the New Pass Bridge and onto Longboat Key. I stopped at Publix for a bag of donuts and headed on up the island to my condo. I brewed a pot of coffee and sat on my balcony munching donuts and sipping coffee. A nutritious breakfast it was not.

When I finished eating, I booted up my computer and checked my email. There were several spams offering me an opportunity to increase the size of certain body parts and a note from J.J. with attachments. Sure enough, the attachments were both pictures of Sam Cox. One caught him full face, and the other about quarter face, as he turned to talk to Maria. J.J. had cropped the pictures, so only Sam was visible. I printed up several of each.

I called Molly and asked if it would be convenient for me to stop by her home. She lived in snug little house on a canal near the south end of the key. Coffee was brewing as I entered the front door. She poured us cups, and we sat at a table on the porch overlooking the canal. I showed her the pictures of Sam Cox.

"That's the guy I saw at the Town Hall the other day. I'm almost positive he's the same guy who was looking for Logan."

"Are you certain enough to testify in court if necessary?" I asked.

"Yeah. I'm certain, Matt. Who is he?"

"I'd rather not tell you just yet, in case the police start asking you questions. I want to play some of my cards close to my vest. I'd appreciate it if you wouldn't mention the pictures to anyone else."

"I understand, Matt. I know Logan didn't do this."

I finished my coffee and left, heading to mid key and the police station. Iva was at her desk and greeted me with a smile. "Good morning, Matt. I heard you'd been off the Key for a while." There are no secrets on a small island.

"Morning, Iva. Just got back. Is the chief in? I just need a couple of minutes."

"He's in, Matt, but he's up to his fanny in paperwork. Let me see if he can see you." She picked up the phone and told the person on the other end that I would like a couple of minutes of the chief's time. She hung up, and said, "Go on back, Matt."

Bill Lester was at his desk, tie askew, a cup of coffee in his hand. "Counselor, you're getting to be a pain in the ass." He was grinning.

"Guess so, Bill," I said. "As soon as we get through with this mess, we need to go fishing."

"You can say that again. What can I do for you this morning?"

"I don't want to presume on an old friendship, but I'm trying to get a line on a guy named Sam Cox. I understand he came to visit you. I wonder if you can tell me what he was doing here."

"I guess you haven't seen yesterday's *Observer*." The *Longboat Observer* is our weekly newspaper. It keeps the island politicians in the sunshine and dutifully reports most of the gossip on the Key. "We've got Governor Wentworth coming to visit. He's going to be at the Colony for a few days this weekend. Cox's company is providing security. He stopped by to give me a heads up about the visit and to coordinate the security." The island was a favorite spot for politicians, and their visits always stretched the police budget. The chief was not happy. "More overtime for the cops and more paperwork for the chief. Why do you ask, Matt?"

"He's a friend of a friend, and I was just wondering if he was in some kind of trouble."

"Trolling for business, Matt?"

"Nah. Just curious," I said, heading for the door. "Thanks Bill. See you soon."

"Take it easy, old buddy."

I picked up a copy of the *Observer* from the free box outside the Town Hall and sat in the Explorer reading the front page story of the governor's visit. There wasn't much to it. The governor had been campaigning hard and was taking a mini vacation with his wife and two children at the Colony. He would be here for three days, starting Friday. The Longboat Key police department was handling security.

More pieces of the puzzle fell into place. Rundel was a political type, Wentworth was a politician, Cox worked for Rundel, Rundel provided security for Wentworth. But why had Cox been looking for Logan in early April? I really needed to talk to Logan, and he had not called in several days. I was beginning to worry about him.

It was almost lunchtime, so I headed for Bradenton Beach and Dewey's. I could count on a pretty good Philly cheese steak sandwich, a couple of laughs with Dewey, and perhaps another identification of Sam Cox.

Dewey was at her usual place behind the bar. "Hey Matt, I was asking K-dawg about you just last night. Said you were off island for a few days."

"Just got back. How're you doing?"

"Without," she cackled. She was always complaining about how lousy her sex life was. I guess if I live to be eighty-five, I might figure out whether she was just kidding around, or dead serious.

"How about one of those famous steak sandwiches and a diet coke?" I asked.

"Coming up. She called to the kitchen, placing the order and set my drink on the bar.

"I want to show you a picture and see if you know this man," I said, laying the two pictures of Sam Cox on the bar.

"That's Logan's Army buddy," she said without hesitation.

"You sure, Dewey?"

"Absolutely. I might be old, but my eyesight is twenty-twenty."

"Would you testify to that in court if it became necessary?"

"To help Logan? You know damn well I would. How's he doing?"

"As well as can be expected. I think he's anxious to finally get his trial started."

"You going to get him acquitted?"

"I certainly hope so, Dewey," I said.

My sandwich came and we chatted as I ate. I told Dewey I'd let her know about the trial, and left to see Slim Jim at Frisco's with the picture of Sam Cox. He was certain that Sam was the guy with Logan on the night of Vivian's death. He also agreed to testify if I needed him. This would cut my window in which Logan was without an alibi to less than an hour between the time Logan left Frisco's and the latest time Vivian could have been killed. I was making a little progress, but that hour could put Logan in the death chamber.

I headed back to Longboat to email Anne with what I'd found out. As I was pulling into the drive leading to my condo, my cell phone rang. It was Logan.

"Where the hell are you?" I asked, my anger boiling up. He had left me hanging on a thin limb, and I wasn't happy about it.

"Whoa," he said. "I'm still in New England, but I'm planning to be in Florida by Sunday. I'll give you my ETA as soon as I know it. What kinda bug you got up your ass?"

"Goddammit, Logan," I exploded, "You haven't called me in a week, and I can't get in touch with you. What the hell kind of deal is that?"

"I've been busy, Matt."

"Busy? Busy? Are you out of your mind? It's your life on the line here, not mine. I don't want another day to go by without hearing from you. Understood? Or so help me, I'll withdraw from this case so fast you'll be wondering if I was just a figment of your imagination."

"Okay, Matt. Sorry. I'll call you every day. What's so important?"

My anger was fading. "I've found your Army buddy. Ever hear of a guy named Sam Cox?"

"Never. I sure as hell wasn't in the Army with anybody by that name."

"How about Hale Rundel?"

"I know that name. He used to hang out at O'Sullivan's some. I had a few drinks with him once or twice, but that's all."

"Would you have talked about your Army experiences with him?"

"Probably. He was a pilot himself. Fixed wing guy, I think. He was interested in how I got into choppers and what kind of training I had. What's he got to do with this?"

"Did he know about you and Connie?"

"He knew we were friends, I guess. She was at the bar at O'Sullivans with me one night when Rundel was there. What's going on?"

"Cox works for Rundel down in Miami. They are both tied into the Wentworth campaign somehow. I don't know what it all means, but it's too much of a coincidence not to be looked into. Can you think of any connection?"

"Nothing. None of it makes sense to me."

"I'll stay on this. Call me tomorrow."

An idea had been buzzing around in my head since I left Miami. I decided to call Will Ledbetter and see if he had any thoughts. I identified myself as Senator Royal, and was put right through to him. I just couldn't help myself. Will answered, laughing, "Senator, you are sure shaking up my office staff."

"Glad I can help. Will, I've been trying to make some connection between the deaths of Vivian and Golden Joe. You told me Joe was not happy with Vivian, because she testified against him. Could he have reached out to her from prison?"

"I doubt it. He was a real loser; no friends and no money to pay anybody. He might have gone looking for her when he got out, though."

"No, the time frame isn't right. Somebody was after Vivian months before Joe got out of prison. They probably found her through Vivian's dad. I was just thinking that maybe Joe set it up."

"I don't see how, Matt. Could there be a connection between the john who messed Vivian up and her killer?"

"I've wondered about that too, but I don't have any way of checking that out, since we don't know who the john was."

"Let me do some checking. I've been here a long time, and I can call in some favors. Maybe there're some rumors out there that'll help. I'll let you know. When does your trial start?"

"Monday morning, Will. I'm on a short string here."

"Gotcha. I'll get back to you soon."

As I was putting the phone back in my pocket, it rang again. Anne Dubose showed up on caller ID. "Hey, Matt. How's it going?"

"Nothing new. How're you doing?"

"A little depressed, I think. I thought we were onto something, and I could help put those bastards away. I guess I'm just disappointed. I was thinking about driving over to Longboat. Maybe I can help with your trial."

My heart did a little jig. It was happy to think about seeing Anne again. "I'd love to have you. I've got a guest bedroom and bath in my condo that you're welcome to use."

"What'll the neighbors think?"

"If they think I'm sleeping with you, I'm not going to deny it. Wouldn't want to hurt my reputation, you know."

She laughed that delightful trill that made me want to see her. "I'll be there this evening," she said.

Anne arrived in the late afternoon. We went to the Hilton for drinks with my friends who always gathered there on Thursday evenings. Dallas was there, being the absolute gentleman, but grinning wickedly at Anne. He told her stories about Logan, and some about me, and they got along famously. I thought the stories about Logan would humanize him some to Anne. To her, Logan was really just an accused felon, his story written in the dry legalese of the indictment. We lingered longer than we should have, and went to Moore's for a late dinner.

Dottie Johansen was at the bar, and she took to Anne immediately. She announced that it was about time I brought a lady around, and that while Anne could probably do better, I might be worthy of spending some time with. After dinner, we drove to the far end of the key to the Colony Beach, where we sipped our after diner drinks and listened to the smooth voice of Debbie Keaton, singing jazz and oldies.

"You've got a lot of friends here," Anne said, looking over her Kahlua and Cream.

"Yeah. The locals are really a good bunch. Every one takes care of every one else.

"They all seem to think a lot of you."

"That's a very mutual feeling. I think they were a little surprised to see me with a beautiful lady. I didn't have the heart to tell them we're just professional colleagues." I laughed.

"What's so funny?"

"I think the average person thinks of a lawyer as a rich man in an expensive suit. They haven't gotten used to the new order - good looking women kicking ass in a court room."

"I think the feminist idea is that a woman can do anything a man can."

"Yes, and I agree with that, mostly. I think what they missed is that there is always a sexual tension between a man and a woman."

"Always?" She chuckled. "And I thought you were tense about the trial."

"Well, that, too." I had made a fool out of myself, and I didn't even have booze to blame it on. I was ridiculously sober. Not only was she a colleague in a dicey situation, I was years older than she.

"Would you be less tense if I went back to Lauderdale?"

"I'm sorry. I guess that did sound like a proposition, and I didn't mean it that way. You're a very attractive lady, but you don't have to worry about me. I'll respect the boundaries."

"I wasn't worried," she said, smiling.

We drove back north toward my condo. The key was quiet, with only an occasional car headed in the other direction. The lights were on at the 7-Eleven store, the only all night establishment on the island. Two Longboat Key cop cars were parked in the lot. Dinner time for the night shift, I figured. I had the sun roof open and the windows down. The sweet air off the Gulf saturated our space. Soft classical music played on the radio. We didn't talk; just enjoyed a fine evening as it wound down toward bedtime.

As we entered my condo, I told her I'd see her in the morning, and headed for my room. "Matt," she said, "about that sexual tension. I felt it too."

"Thanks, Anne. I'm sorry I made a fool out of myself. Just chalk it up to bar talk."

"Matt? Do I have to sleep in the guest room tonight?"

My heart did that little jig again, and old Mr. Lucky started stirring. "Um, what did you have in mind?" I asked, not daring to assume the answer.

"Can I sleep with you tonight? No boundaries."

Chapter 23

FRIDAY

Will called on Friday morning, waking me from a sound sleep. He told me that he had talked to the police lieutenant who had overseen the investigation into the beating of Vivian and the murder of the other prostitute. The lieutenant had moved on to the intelligence division of the Chicago Police Department.

"They play things real close to the vest over there," Will said, "but he and I were classmates at the police academy."

"I didn't know you were a cop," I said.

"Only for a couple of years, and I moved to Probation and Parole. The lieutenant told me some interesting rumors picked up by the intelligence people. It seems that when Golden Joe was released from the pokey, he went right back to his old ways. He began to deal in drugs, but then suddenly disappeared within a few days of his release."

"Do the cops have any idea what happened to him?"

"Well, that's the funny thing. Joe was bragging that he had made a connection with a big time drug importer in Miami, and he was headed down there to put together a deal that would make him rich."

"And he ended up dead."

"Yes, but the Intel Division didn't know that. The word hadn't gotten through channels to them."

"Did they have any idea who Joe was dealing with in Miami?" I asked.

"No, but he did say they were a bunch of white guys. I thought most of the drug importers in Miami were Hispanic."

"I thought so, too. Thanks Will. If you hear anything else, let me know."

"There was one other thing, Matt. I don't know if its important."

"Shoot."

"The lieutenant told me that there had been some pretty heavy pressure coming down on him to close the case. He wanted to find the john, but some people in high places were pulling a lot of weight to get him to back off. It didn't sit well with him, but he had a career, and he didn't want to piss off the bosses. He's always thought the john was somebody high up in the police department."

"Okay, thanks, Will. See you later."

I put in a call to Carl Merritt, Anne's detective friend in Miami. "Good morning, Counselor," he said, picking up the phone. "How're things on the west coast?"

"Puzzling Carl, very puzzling. I have it in my mind that the big drug importers in Miami-Dade are all Hispanic. Am I wrong?"

"You're right. There are probably some small time scumbags in the business who aren't Hispanic, but they don't last long. The competition is tough, and most of the new guys end up dead."

"Do you know anything about some white guys getting into it in a big way?"

"No," he answered. "Some try it now and then, but we usually find their bodies pretty quickly."

"Have you ever heard the names Hale Rundel or Sam Cox mentioned in the drug context?"

"Hang on," he said, and put me on hold. He was gone for several minutes, while I listened to a jazz station piped into their phone system. Suddenly he was back. "Sorry that took so long. I checked with our drug enforcement division. They don't know anything about Rundel, but Sam Cox showed up on their radar a couple of years ago. They thought he might be flying drugs into the country from the Bahamas, but they could never nail him. Even if he was, it was probably such a small operation that it never got the interest of the Hispanics."

"Thanks, Carl. I appreciate the effort."

"No problem, Matt. Tell Anne I said hello."

"Carl said to tell you hello," I said to Anne, who was sitting up in bed beside me.

"How did he know I was here?" she asked.

"Video phone, maybe," I said.

She blushed, and pulled the sheet up over her naked breasts.

I laughed.

"I did tell his wife I was sweet on you. Maybe he just assumed," she said.

"Sweet? That's a little old fashioned, isn't it? Hot would be more au courant."

"Yeah, but I didn't want to tell her I had the hots for an elderly gentleman," she giggled.

"I'll show you elderly," I said, as I reached for her.

After I proved, apparently to Anne's satisfaction, that I wasn't that old, we dressed and headed for breakfast at the Blue Dolphin. Over pancakes and sausages, I told her my thinking. There had to be some connection between Vivian's and Golden Joe's deaths. The link might very well be Cox and Rundel, but the only connection I could make was that Joe died in Miami, and Cox and Rundel lived there. I suspected that Joe had been lured to Miami with the hope of striking it rich in the drug trade, but was really being brought there to die. But, if somebody wanted to kill Joe, why do it in Miami? Why go to all that trouble when they could have wacked him in Chicago? Unless, the idea was to get Joe a long way from his home turf, so that his murder would seem random. The only reason that made any sense was that the killers were trying to erase any connection between the murder of the prostitute in Chicago, and the murder of her pimp in Miami. Besides, if the gators had done a better job, nobody would ever have found Joe's body. That still left the question of why Rundel or Cox would be interested in a Chicago pimp.

Anne didn't say much during my soliloquy, letting me ramble in a stream of consciousness discourse that left a lot of loose ends. As we were leaving the restaurant, my cell phone rang. It was Logan, checking in. The conversation was short, since I had nothing to report. He told me he was on his way south, and would call on Saturday to arrange to meet me.

After breakfast, we boarded my boat. I wasn't going to accomplish anything in Logan's defense that day, so I was taking the opportunity to show Anne Sarasota Bay. Over the years, I have driven and boated to every nook and cranny in the state of Florida. Nothing compares with the Sarasota Bay area.

We spent the day sunning, while floating alone in the bay. Anne wore a striking red bikini that made me feel younger every minute. When I mentioned this, she laughed and flashed her boobs at me. Except for the nagging feeling in the back of my mind that time was slipping by, and I still didn't have a good defense plan for Logan, it was a day that you put away in the memory banks. I knew I would roll out that memory for the rest of my life, and it would put me back into a glorious day on the water with a woman who was better than I deserved.

At mid-afternoon we called it quits and headed for home. As you travel north, the channel meanders through the shoals, and narrows as it runs across the bay and into the constricted channel between the Sister Keys and Longboat. As I made the wide right turn that would take me into the narrow channel, I noticed an Anhinga cutting across the flats toward me. He came up on my beam and raced my boat along the waterway at 30 miles per hour. He was working mightily, his wings flapping rhythmically, his left eye fixed on me, daring me to go faster. I had the feeling he would strain his heart to a stop if I kept pushing. I slowed for a larger boat coming my way, its wake frothing a wave dangerous to my small boat. The Anhinga seemed to sigh with relief, and grin at his victory, as he settled, like a small plane, flaps down, on a waiting channel marker. Anne was delighted.

"You remind me of that bird," she said.

"Oh, thanks a lot."

"No, I mean your tenacity. That bird was out to beat you, and he would have killed himself if you hadn't slowed down. That's the way you are about this case. Have you always been so intense?"

"Pretty much. I think that's why I burned out early. I want to win, and I want to do justice. Sometimes they're not the same, and that adds to the tension. With Logan, I just can't think about my friend going to prison for life, or worse."

"I've got an idea that I don't want to talk about yet. I need to go to Miami in the morning. Will you trust me on this?"

"Of course, I'll trust you. But don't you think you ought to let me in on the big idea?"

"It might not work, Matt. I'll know tomorrow."

We had an early dinner at the Hayloft, listened to the sweet jazz piano of Skip Cook for a while, and headed home to bed, where I did my best to demonstrate my youthfulness. I think she appreciated the effort.

Chapter 24

SATURDAY

Anne left after breakfast, headed for Miami. I spent the morning with my files, thinking hard about the confluence of events that put Logan on trial for his life, and me with my hands around his neck. Could Logan really be the guilty party here? Was I grasping at straws, seeing connections where there were none?

Logan had been very vague with me during this whole ordeal. I couldn't figure that out. There was no reason for him not to tell me everything, to hold back nothing. But he had been evasive, and maddening. Was he playing me for a sucker? Did he have a reason to kill Vivian? Was their relationship more complicated that he had led me to believe? Had he found out about her past and snapped?

I wasn't getting any answers sitting there, but a vague plan was taking shape. Logan had to present himself to the Sheriff's office by six the next evening. I was expecting a call from him to give me his time of arrival. I wanted to meet him at the jail and get him situated. I called Dick Bellinger and ran the plan by him.

At mid-afternoon, Logan called. "I'm getting off the interstate and headed for Longboat," he said. "My brother Fred is with me. I'll be at your place in thirty minutes. We need to talk before I head for the hoosegow."

And talk he did. We spent the rest of the afternoon with him telling me about where he had been for the past month, and me telling him my plan of attack for the trial. We were both surprised with what the other had to say, but everything seemed to be falling into place. I knew better. The trial lawyer part of my brain was braying tocsins, screaming at me about having missed something. Elizabeth was going to lay a big surprise on me, and I wouldn't be ready for it. I was going to get Logan convicted. Trial lawyers suffer from chronic heartburn.

Fred took a flight back to Boston late that afternoon. Logan and I spent the evening on my balcony talking. On Sunday, we simply relaxed. The plan was in progress, and there was nothing left to do. I knew the following week would be rough, and I needed the rest.

Chapter 25

MONDAY

The Manatee County courthouse sits on its square in downtown Bradenton. It is a stylish old pile of yellow bricks with white trim that had been built more than seventy years ago. It has large white columns at the four entrances on each side of the building. A Confederate soldier stands watch on his pedestal, facing north, an engraving telling us that he is enshrined in the hearts of his grateful countrymen. I throw him a mental salute as I walk by, trial bag in hand, thinking briefly of my forebears who wore the gray.

The courthouse had recently been remodeled, and while everything had been upgraded, the essential beauty of the old place was intact. There was a security station at the entrance, and a metal detector that scanned my bag. The security guard was a minimum wage rent-a-cop, and probably would not know a bomb if he saw one. It was a measure of how much stock the Manatee County high sheriff put in the security of judges, that he refused to waste valuable deputy time on guard duty. Instead, the county hired a private security company and let them worry about it.

I suspected that the judges found little solace in this. As a practical matter, if I wanted to take out a judge, I'd simply wait until he headed for the golf course and blow him away in the parking lot. That thought had sustained me on many a sleepless night.

I took the elevator to the third floor and pushed open the double doors guarding the place where Logan's life would be on trial. The court room had a high ceiling, from which dangled fans that were once used to stir the fetid air, made rank by fear and anger. Old polished wood adorned the walls, and there was a balcony, that at one time had been reserved for black folks.

I was early, and the room was quiet. I always get to court early. I like to sit alone in the courtroom, soaking up the atmosphere, communing with the ghosts of lost causes that had played out here for so many years. There is a somberness to old court rooms; a sense of history permeates them. I wondered how many men had gone from here to the gallows that had once stood in the square, or later to old Sparky up in Raiford. I hoped Logan wouldn't be making that trip.

In Florida there is no requirement that counsel sit at a given table. The first ones there get the pick. I had never much cared at which table I sat, but since I was first today, I took the one farthest from the jury box. It was a great slab of polished walnut, surrounded by cane back chairs with green cushions and casters. The chairs were rockers as well, and thus made one as comfortable as one could be in a pit that was about to explode with the drama of a man on trial for his life.

Judge T. Johnson O'Reilly was to preside over the trial. I'd heard of him over the years, and since learning that he would be our judge, I had talked to lawyers who regularly practiced in the Twelfth Circuit. Every judge has a history, and those lawyers who knew him as an attorney or appeared before him as a judge, whispered to each other the secrets they learned. You could always get a pretty good idea of who and what a judge was by simply asking the local trial lawyers.

Judge O'Reilly was tired, a lawyer with too many battles behind him. He wore his cynicism like some ancient amulet designed to ward off any errant appeal to the notion of justice that resides in the soul of those who love the law. He had battled mightily and often, sometimes even finding himself fighting for principles in which he believed. Too often, however, he was the one who perverted justice at the whim of his client. He consoled himself with the money he made, and with the belief that he had never committed an unethical act.

But he knew in his gut that he misused his powerful intellect and his courtroom presence to prevail over lesser lawyers with better causes. It ate at him until he became rich, and then he quit the law. Still, he loved the law, which was in truth his only mistress; a mistress who demanded devotion; who could not be controlled and who was always ready to embrace inferior rivals.

So he came back to the law. He took the bench, and saw a prostitution of the law that surprised and overwhelmed even him. A large number of the lawyers appearing in his court were shameless charlatans, and he treated them with towering contempt. He got to the point that he was so disenchanted with the poor lawyers that he could not distinguish between them and the good lawyers who found their way into his courtroom. With this, he became a tyrant, and an object of derision among the members of the bar.

I was not too concerned by this thumbnail sketch of a tired and obstreperous judge. I was sure that I could appeal to that small kernel of justice that was surely buried deep in his heart. Do your job, I thought. Know your facts and know your law and the judge will embrace you for the lawyer you are. Boy, was I wrong.

After a while the door near the judge's bench opened, and a lady with an armful of files came in and took the seat next to the bench reserved for the clerk. During the trial she would be the custodian of all the evidence submitted to the court.

"Good morning," she said. "I'm Bonnie Moore."

"Good morning. I'm Matt Royal, defense counsel."

"Nice to meet you Mr. Royal. As soon as everybody gets here, we'll bring in the venire. Judge O'Reilly likes to start on time."

Elizabeth Ferguson came through the double doors, followed by a young assistant carrying their trial bags. She came over and I stood to shake hands. She introduced me to her assistant, Richard Wightman, a singularly unprepossessing young man whose handshake was like that of a sick fish. I didn't think he'd be handling much of the trial.

"I can still do a deal on a plea," Elizabeth said.

"No can do, Elizabeth. Logan is innocent."

"We'll see," she said, going to the other counsel table to instruct young Richard on how to get the files out of the bags.

The door opened again, and in came two deputy sheriffs, with a handcuffed Logan between them. He was wearing one of the suits we had brought from his condo. He looked wan and humorless. A night in the county jail does that to a man. As they entered the rail, Logan smiled faintly, and said, "Good morning, Matt."

"Morning Logan," I said. One of the deputies uncuffed Logan, gave him a hard stare, and took his seat at the desk reserved for the court deputy who used to be called the bailiff. Another deputy entered from the door beside the bench, looked around, and asked, "Are we ready for the judge?" Elizabeth and I both nodded assent, and the deputy disappeared.

At exactly nine o'clock, there was a knock on the back door, a signal that the judge was about to enter. The door opened and the deputy stepped out, with the judge right behind him. We all jumped to our feet. The deputy intoned the formal greeting that always sends chills up my spine. "All rise. The Circuit Court of the Twelfth Judicial Circuit of Florida, in and for Manatee County, is now in session, the Honorable T. Johnson O'Reilly presiding." The battle was about to be joined.

The judge climbed the three steps to the bench, his black robe floating behind him like a priest's cassock. He was a big man, probably six feet two, and two hundred pounds with a head full of snow white hair. He sat in his chair, high above the trial pit, as seemingly befitted the man who would preside over the life and death struggle that would play out here over the next few days. He looked out at the courtroom, and in a deep voice said, "You may be seated."

"Good morning, Ms. Ferguson," the judge said. Then looking at our table, "And you must be Mr. Royal."

"Yes, I am, your Honor. Good morning."

"Good morning. Now before I bring in the venire, I want to lay some ground rules. You will not take more than thirty minutes a side on your voir dire, and then we will take fourteen jurors, including two alternates. Do I make myself clear?"

Uh-oh. This was not starting out too good. I stood, "With all due respect your Honor, I believe that restriction will constitute absolute reversible error. The State vs. Morgan case clearly gives the defendant an unlimited time for voir dire."

"You're wrong, Counselor. That case stands for the proposition that you are entitled to a reasonable time on voir dire, and I think thirty minutes is reasonable."

"Your Honor, I have a copy of that case with me if you'd like to see it. It clearly says that even a three hour time limit is unreasonable, and the concurring opinion says that the defendant is entitled to unlimited time." I handed him and Elizabeth copies of the case, and returned to my table. I knew I was playing with fire by challenging the judge this early in the trial, but on the other hand, I had to establish that I was not one of those marginal lawyers that didn't mind getting pushed around by judges.

After scanning the case, the judge scowled down at me, and said, "I'm not sure I entirely agree with your reading of the case, Counselor, but I'll give you all the time you need to pick this jury. But be aware that I like to move trials along. Bring in the venire."

They trooped through the double doors, all sixty of them, and took seats in the pews that made up the court room gallery. Most of them were not happy to be here, but all had come in response to the notice sent by the Clerk of Courts notifying them that they would be held in contempt of court and jailed if they did not come at the appointed time. A few years before Florida had gone to a system of selecting potential jurors from the driver's license rolls instead of the voter's rolls. It made for a decidedly less intelligent jury pool, but lawyers were learning to live with it.

Voir dire, the act of picking a jury to try any case, much less a capital felony, is a laborious task. Since Logan was on trial for his life, the state and the defense were entitled to ten peremptory challenges each. That meant that I could get rid of ten prospective jurors for any reason, and I didn't have to state the reason.

We settled in to trying to determine which of the twelve people in the gallery would be able to fairly try the case. Neither Elizabeth nor I were concerned about fairness. We wanted those people most likely to find in our favor. I was still concerned about agreeing to Logan's demand that we not try to change the venue because of all the pre-trial publicity. The trick was to find fourteen people, including the alternates, who had not read or heard enough about the case to form an opinion as to Logan's guilt. Looking at the panel we had to work with, I was convinced that I could pick fourteen people who did not know they were in Manatee County. I wasn't sure whether that was good or bad for our side.

By the end of the day, I had exercised six peremptory challenges and Elizabeth four. One of my biggest fears was that the jury would think that Longboat Key was peopled only by the rich, and would not be sympathetic to Logan. I was trying to find jurors with some assets. The only way I could do that was by matching them to addresses in the more affluent areas of the county. I didn't know if Elizabeth had figured this out, but she had stricken two of the people who lived in upscale neighborhoods along the Manatee River.

At five o'clock on the nose, Judge O'Reilly dismissed the venire with a warning not to talk among themselves or read or watch any accounts of the trial in the press. I knew in my bones that every one of them rushed home to catch the six o'clock news to see if somehow the cameras had picked up his or her image. Who knew how this would affect them.

"Counsel," the judge intoned after the court room was cleared, "I don't want to be here all week picking this jury. We need to move it along. Do you think we can finish voir dire tomorrow?"

Elizabeth conferred briefly with her protege, then stood and said, "Maybe, your Honor." Well, I like certainty in a lawyer.

The judge looked at me. I stood and said, "Maybe."

"Well, let's move it along. We'll be in recess until nine tomorrow." He rose and left the court room.

Chapter 26

TUESDAY

The next day was no different. It dawned hot and humid. As I drove from the Key across the Cortez Bridge, headed for downtown and the courthouse, there was not a ripple on the bay. The sun was already high at 7:30, and I had the Explorer's a/c blasting. I was tired, and I was only starting the second day of a long trial. I had not slept well, my mind refusing to stop churning Logan's case.

Elizabeth and I plodded along for most of the day, and by late afternoon, after exhausting all my peremptory challenges, we had a jury of twelve, and two alternates seated. They did not look all that promising to me, but it was the best I was going to get out of that pool.

The judge seemed relieved that we were through, but he couldn't leave the bench without chastising the lawyers. He warned the jurors about reading or listening to or watching any news about the trial and dismissed them until 9:30 the next morning. Then he turned to the lawyers. "Counsel," he rumbled, "You've taken way too much time to pick this jury. I expect you to move this case along a lot faster from now on. Do you understand me?"

Elizabeth and I both murmured a "Yes, your Honor," and he left the bench. I was standing there wondering how the hell he thought he could hurry up a first degree murder trial without committing reversible error, when I sensed Elizabeth standing next to me. "Still don't want to plead?" she asked.

"Not a chance, Counselor," I said.

"I don't know, Matt. That looks like a hanging jury to me."

She was right, and all I could say was, "We'll see."

160

Chapter 27

WEDNESDAY

Wednesday morning. Fatigue was etching my mind with a blunt stylus. I had to get a better grip on myself. This was the first day of testimony, and I had already begun to think about some way out of this trial. There wasn't any, of course, but the trial lawyer's mind always seeks solace in the knowledge that a settlement or plea is possible, and the trial would end immediately Not in this case. I was here for the long run, however long that took. And Logan had put himself in my hands, simply because he was broke. Ah, well, I thought, maybe some part of him actually thinks I can do this.

All the players were on the stage; the jury in its box, the judge on the bench, the lawyers ready for action. Opening statement. This is not supposed to be argument, but lawyers have a way of weaving some of their closing argument into what is supposed to be simply an outline of the proof they plan to present during the trial. Elizabeth was a past master at this, and I let her run. She smiled when appropriate, and would occasionally glance sternly at Logan and me, as if signaling to the jury that she could not understand murder nor those who represented murderers. She made some statements that I thought would be hard for her to prove, but that would work to my advantage. She spoke for thirty minutes and told a tale of murder and circumstances that gave the jury a framework upon which to hang Logan.

I rose, shuffled some papers on my table, looked at the jury, looked at Logan, cleared my throat. "Ladies and Gentlemen," I said, "Logan Hamilton did not commit this terrible crime, and the state cannot prove he did. Keep in mind that Ms. Ferguson must prove beyond and to the exclusion of any reasonable doubt that Logan killed his friend. She cannot do that. Hold her to the proof she just told you about. Make her show you why all the evidence she presents points only to Logan, and not to some one else.

"The constitution of the United States says that Logan does not have to testify in his own defense. If he were to take that witness stand, Ms. Ferguson could open up his life like a can of peas. No secret would be safe. Fine. Bring it on. Logan will testify. Thank you."

I kept it very short, not wanting to tip my hand to the jury. I did not want the members thinking about what I was going to prove while listening to the prosecution's case. In a courtroom where formalities are important, I wanted to make Logan human. Calling him by his first name was part of that process. I also intended to show the jury that Logan not only had no reason to kill Vivian, but that she was his friend; our friend, part of an island community that took care of each other.

The first witness was Dave Beemer, the Longboat Key cop who had taken the call from Logan. He testified to that fact, to his arrival at Logan's condo, and to his call to Chief Lester. Short and sweet.

On cross, I asked, "Am I correct in understanding that Logan is the one who called the police that morning?"

"Yes, sir. He called the 911 dispatcher."

"What was Logan's demeanor when you arrived?"

"Confused."

"What do you mean?"

"He couldn't understand how the victim got onto his balcony."

"The victim being his friend Vivian?" I asked, sincerity pouring out of my mouth.

"Yes."

"Did he say anything to you that led you to believe he killed Vivian?"

"No. Just the opposite. He was crying. He was obviously very broken up."

"No further questions," I said, sitting down.

Elizabeth got to her feet. "Could the reason he was crying be that he was remorseful that he had killed this lady?"

Now, that was an objectionable question. It called for a conclusion among other things, but I had talked to Dave Beemer, and I knew his feelings about the charges against Logan. I kept my seat.

"No ma'am," he said. "Logan had lost a friend, and it liked to have killed him."

Score one for the home team, I thought. We won the first round. Lots more to come, though, and I didn't expect all of them to go as smoothly.

Bill Lester came to the stand. He was dressed formally for the occasion, in a blue uniform. Two stars garnished each collar point. Elizabeth established who he was, what his job was, and how he came to be notified of the death of Vivian Pickens.

"Did you know the victim?" Elizabeth asked.

"Yes."

"What was her name?"

"I thought it was Connie Sanborne."

"It wasn't?"

"No, I later ran the fingerprints, and found out she was Vivian Pickens."

"Did you make the call to Manatee County on the morning of the murder?"

"Yes."

"Did the county send someone out?"

"Yes. Detective Michael Banion got to the scene within a few minutes of my call."

"The scene being the defendant's Condo?"

"Yes."

"Did anyone else show up?"

"Yes. Matt Royal."

"The same Matt Royal sitting there beside Mr. Hamilton?"

"Yes."

"Do you know how he came to be there?"

"I suggested to Mr. Hamilton that he might want to call a lawyer."

"And he called Mr. Royal?"

"Yes."

"Nothing further, your honor," Elizabeth said, and returned to her table.

"No questions," I said, standing. I could see no benefit in having the chief testify that I was the one who put him onto the right name of the murdered lady, or to have him admit to being a friend of both mine and Logan's.

Then, as if changing my mind, "Well, excuse me your honor. I think I might have a question of two for the chief after all. May I proceed?" When the prosecutor is focused on her facts, and quite succinctly laying out her case, totally in control, it never hurts for the defense lawyer to bumble a bit. He hopes that it makes him look human. I don't know about that, but a little bumble never hurt anything.

"Chief," I said, "When you found out that Connie Sanborne was in reality Vivian Pickens, did you find out anything else about her?"

"Objection, your honor. Relevance. Hearsay." Elizabeth was on her feet. I knew she would not like the jury to hear about Vivian's record.

"If I might lay a predicate, your honor," I said.

"Go ahead, Mr. Royal, but be careful. I haven't ruled on the objection yet."

"Yessir. Chief, did you learn certain information about Ms. Pickens?"

"Yes."

"Was this the kind of information that you as a police officer rely on daily in pursuing your profession?"

"Yes."

"Did you get the information from another police agency?"

"Yes."

"Was it information that the other agency compiled in the pursuit of its professional obligations?"

"Yes."

"Is this information that is routinely shared among law enforcement agencies?"

"Yes."

"Your honor," I said, "I think this clearly falls into the business records exception to the hearsay rule."

"I agree," said the judge. "Now, I want to hear the relevance of this testimony. Deputy, please take the jury out."

After the jury left, I turned to the bench. "Your honor, the whole thrust of the prosecution's case is that a very nice lady was killed on Longboat Key by her lover, my client. I knew the lady, and I will attest to the fact that she was very nice, but, your honor, she had some large skeletons in her closet that included jail time, prostitution, drug abuse, and an outstanding warrant for her arrest. I think the jury needs to hear this, not to stain the memory of a decent woman, but to understand that my client is not the only one who had the means, opportunity, and most of all, the motive to murder her."

"What say you, Ms. Ferguson?" asked the judge, turning to Elizabeth.

"Your honor, we're not here to try the reputation of the victim. It wouldn't matter if she was a prostitute or a drug dealer, or whatever Mr. Royal wants to make her out to be. She was a human being, and she was murdered."

The judge pondered this for a moment, and said, "I agree with you Ms. Ferguson that the victims reputation has no bearing on her death, but it may have a bearing on why she was murdered, and who did it. Overruled. Bring the jury back."

Big win. I was chipping away little by little from the foundation of facts Elizabeth was building. "What did you find out, Chief?"

"Vivian Pickens had a warrant out for her arrest. Should I go on and explain why?"

"Proceed," said the judge.

Bill then told the story of her past, including the crimes, arrests, convictions and disappearance.

"Thank you, Chief. I have no further questions," I announced.

"Nothing further," said Elizabeth.

"The witness is excused," said the judge.

The next witness up was Banion. He had dressed for his starring role in a tan polyester suit, white shirt with a red stripe, and a red white and blue striped tie. He looked a little like a barber pole. He strode through the gate into the pit, confident, arrogant and mean. His face was as red as usual, and he gave Logan a look of contempt as he walked by on his way to the witness stand.

After he was sworn, Elizabeth said, "State your name please."

"Michael Banion."

"By whom are you employed?"

"The Manatee County Sheriff's Office."

"In what capacity?"

"Homicide detective."

"How long have you been in law enforcement?"

"Thirty years."

"How many murders have you investigated in that time?"

Uh, oh. I came to my feet. "Objection, your Honor. Assuming facts not in evidence." I didn't want the jury getting used to the M word.

"What facts, Mr. Royal," the judge asked.

"Your Honor, we don't know if Mr. Banion has been investigating suicides, accidental deaths or what. Ms. Ferguson just assumed they're all murders."

"Overruled."

I sat down. That's about all you can do in that situation.

Elizabeth continued, "Before we were interrupted, I was asking you how many deaths, if you will, you have investigated in your career."

"Three hundred or so."

"Did you investigate the death of Vivian Pickens?"

"Yes."

"How did that come about?"

"The Manatee Sheriff's office always investigates homicides that occur on the Manatee end of Longboat Key. We do this in cooperation with the Longboat Police."

"How were you notified of the death of Ms. Pickens?"

"I live in West Manatee, and I was about to leave for work when dispatch called and told me there was a homicide on Longboat Key. I went right to the scene."

"What time did you arrive?"

"May I look at my investigative notes?"

"Of course," said Elizabeth. I didn't object. I had already seen the notes in the discovery material the state had provided me.

"I arrived at the scene at 6:55 A.M.," Banion said.

"What day was this?"

"April 16, of this year."

"You mentioned the scene. Where was that exactly?"

"9640 Gulf of Mexico Drive, Apt. 401, Longboat Key, Florida."

"Was anyone else there when you arrived?"

"Yes. The Longboat Key Chief of Police Bill Lester, Police Lt. Dave Beemer, and the defendant Logan Hamilton."

"Did you find a body on the premises?"

That was a leading question, but one thing trial lawyers learn is that you don't object to every objectionable question. If the answer is one that the prosecutor can get by asking the question a different way, why object. It pisses off the jury, and you gain nothing. I kept my seat.

"Yes, the body of a female was on the balcony overlooking the Gulf," said Banion. I guessed that that answer was rehearsed. They wanted the jury to know that Logan lived on Gulf front property, which was some of the most expensive real estate in Florida.

"What was the cause of death?"

"Objection, Your Honor. This gentleman has not been qualified as an expert to give an opinion on cause of death, and I doubt that Ms. Ferguson can qualify him as such." I was standing, trying to look outraged for the jury.

"Withdraw the question," said Elizabeth. "We'll wait for the medical examiner to testify." She was good. I couldn't let Banion testify as to cause of death, but the prosecutor had set me up so that now the jury was anticipating the M.E.'s testimony. The jury was probably figuring that an experienced cop would know a thing or two about cause of death, and that I was trying to hide something for them.

Elizabeth said to Banion, "I think you're qualified to say whether she was dead or not. Was she?" Some of the jurors chuckled.

"She was dead," said Banion, with a smile.

"Did you collect evidence at the scene?"

"The crime scene technicians did, under my supervision."

"What did you find?"

"The only thing of significance was some hair from Mr. Hamilton's comb."

"Why was the hair important?"

I was on my feet again. "Objection. The witness is not qualified to testify to that."

"Well," said the judge, "We don't know why he thinks it's important, do we?"

"May we approach, Your Honor?" I asked.

"Come on," the judge said, motioning us forward.

Elizabeth and I huddled at the judge's bench, while the court reporter got her machine so that she could hear our whispered conversations and get it all on the record. "Judge," I said, "The witness is going to testify about DNA, and Lord knows what else. He isn't qualified to do that, and we need to wait until someone who is can take the stand."

"I wasn't going to ask him about the results of testing, Judge," said Elizabeth.

"Where are you going with this Ms. Ferguson?" he asked.

"Chain of custody, Your Honor," she replied. "I'm simply asking the witness to tell me what he did with the hair sample."

"She asked him about the importance of the hair sample, not what he did with it," I said.

"Okay," said the judge, "Don't ask him about the importance of the hair. Establish your chain of custody, and let's get this show on the road."

I went back to my chair, and Elizabeth turned to the witness, who had heard the entire conversation at the bench. "What did you do with the hair, Detective Banion?"

"I took it to the Florida Department of Law Enforcement Crime Lab in Tampa for DNA testing." He planted the DNA question in the minds of the jury. Now they would be primed to hear the rest of this, because everybody knew DNA was solid evidence. I thought Elizabeth was pulling a fast one on me and the Judge, but it wouldn't do me a lot of good to object now. It's impossible to put that cat back in the bag. But Elizabeth surprised me again.

"Detective Banion," she said, her voice cold, the words flung like cubes of ice into the face of the witness, "I didn't ask you why you took the sample to Tampa. I asked you what you did with it. Please answer my questions, and do not elaborate."

"Sorry Counselor," Banion said.

"To your knowledge did the lab conduct DNA testing?"

"Yes."

"I have no further questions of Detective Banion," said Elizabeth.

"The judge turned to the jury. "Ladies and Gentlemen, we'll take our lunch break now. We'll reconvene at 1:30."

Banion was back on the stand, swelled with his own importance, glowing in his flashy haberdashery. I stood quietly for a moment, giving him time to wonder at my first question.

"Were you still drunk when you arrived at the crime scene?" I asked.

"Objection, your Honor." Elizabeth was on her feet, eyes flashing. I had struck a nerve.

"What are your grounds, Counselor?" asked the judge.

"This is absurd. Detective Banion is a respected law enforcement officer," said Judy, glowering at me.

"Those are not legal grounds. Objection overruled."

I looked at Banion, waiting. "Absolutely not," he said. His face was red with anger, the little capillaries of the drunk standing out like major thoroughfares on a road map.

"But you were hungover," I said.

"Your Honor," said Elizabeth, coming to her feet.

"Let him answer the question," the judge said.

"No, sir," said Banion.

"Where were you on the evening of April 15, the night before you arrived at the crime scene?" I asked.

"Your Honor, may we approach?" asked Elizabeth.

The judge waived us forward. The court reporter moved in close for the whispered conference with the judge.

"I hate to keep objecting, but this all seems completely irrelevant to me," whispered Elizabeth.

"I agree, Mr. Royal," said the judge. "Where are you going with this?"

"I intend to show that Detective Banion was so hungover the morning of April 16, that he could not have overseen a murder investigation."

"Do you have evidence to back this up?" asked the judge.

"Yes, sir," I said.

"Proceed then, but don't overstep Mr. Royal."

We returned to our places. "Where were you on the evening of April 15?" I asked Banion.

"I don't remember," he responded.

And with that answer, he sprung the trap.

"Detective, are you familiar with Gary's Sports Bar on Cortez Road?"

"Yes."

"As a matter of fact, you spend a lot of time in that bar, don't you?"

"I go there occasionally."

"If some people testify that you were at Gary's on the night of April 15, would you dispute it?"

"No. I don't remember being there that evening, but I might have been."

"And if the same people testify that you did not leave the bar until after closing at 2:00 A.M., would you dispute that?"

"I don't remember." He was losing some of his bluster.

"But would you dispute that testimony?"

"I'd have to hear it, first." I had him now. The jury could see that he was waffling in his testimony, and that is usually devastating. If a witness will lie about one thing, he will lie about others. A lie, or a convenient loss of memory, always undermines testimony that the witness is so sure of.

"And if people testify that you were drunk when you left the bar would you dispute that?"

"I would." Drunks never admit they were ever drunk.

"Tell us about the fight you got into that night."

"What fight?"

"The fight where you punched a tourist from Indiana."

"I don't remember that." He was talking low now, his confidence eroded.

"You don't remember it because you were drunk?"

"Maybe."

"Do you remember the owner of Gary's driving you to your home at 3:00 A.M.?"

"If you say so." He was totally cowed now.

"And you arrived at the scene of the crime less than 4 hours later."

"Yes, sir."

"No more questions, your Honor."

Banion left the stand with a lot less confidence than when he took it. Elizabeth ignored him as he walked from the courtroom.

"Call your next witness," said the judge.

Elizabeth called the director of the Florida Department of Law Enforcement's crime lab in Tampa. She asked him about his qualifications, his academic background, and offered him to the court as an expert on DNA. She established that the lab had taken custody of a sample of sperm taken from Vivian's vagina and a few hairs from Logan's comb. The DNA matched. The hair and the sperm came from the same man.

There were some holes in the testimony, since the comb had not been directly connected to Logan. I could have made a case that the hair in the comb was from a visitor to Logan's condo, but I had agreed with Elizabeth not to do that. In fact, I had stipulated that the hair was Logan's, and she reported that to the jury after the director finished testifying. If I had not agreed, Elizabeth could have forced a DNA sample from Logan, and put the trial off until the lab work was done. This could have taken weeks, as she mentioned to me, given the back log in the lab, and Logan would have enjoyed the hospitality of the county jailer during that time. Since I was not going to argue that Logan had not had sex with Vivian on the evening of her death, I could see no harm in moving things along.

Elizabeth called a couple more unimportant witnesses dealing with the DNA and then we broke for the day.

I had ordered a dinner of subs and diet cokes from the deli across the street from the courthouse. Logan and I ate an early supper in a witness room, with an armed guard outside the only door. They would go directly from here to the jail for the evening. I thought Logan would like the sub better than the crap served by the county to its inmates.

"You're knocking them out of the park," Logan said, speaking around a large bite of cheese steak with all the fixings.

"No, we're not," I said. "We're just playing defense. Elizabeth is building her case, and I'm just trying to punch small holes in it."

It was true. A case is built a small brick of evidence at a time. Elizabeth was getting in everything she needed to make the prima facie case for murder. I had, to continue Logan's metaphor, only hit a couple of ground balls, and nobody was on base. Elizabeth had spent her time establishing that there had been a dead body in Logan's condo, and that the DNA proved that Logan had had sex with Vivian shortly before her death. She would continue with the technical details for the rest of the day and probably the next. She still hadn't established motive, and that was going to be harder to do. On the other hand, she did not really have to establish a reason for the murder, only that a murder occurred and that Logan probably did it.

"Don't put too much into what is going on in the early part of the trial," I said. "Elizabeth has a way to go to prove her case, and then we get our turn at bat." I hate to waste a good baseball metaphor. "We're still in the first inning."

"We're going to win, right?"

"Logan, that is the sixty-four dollar question."

We finished our dinner in silence.

Day three was over. I had scored a few points, but I still had an uphill battle. I headed for Longboat, looking forward to a beer, a late dinner, and a good night's sleep. I knew I could count on the first two, but would probably sleep fitfully, if at all. Trial lawyers are prone to nightmares.

Anne was at my condo when I arrived. I had told her where I hid the extra key, and she had let herself in. Grocery bags were strewn across the counter top. She was barefoot, wearing shorts and a halter top. She looked delicious. "Hey Counselor," she said softly, as she folded herself into my arms. "You look beat."

"I am. I'm getting too old for this crap." That's the lament of every trial lawyer over thirty, but I think we all feel it during a trial.

"Sit down and take off your shoes and tie. I'm going to make dinner tonight."

I went to the living room and did as told. She was right behind me with a cold beer. "When you finish that, go get a hot shower. It'll make you feel better, and dinner will be almost ready." I didn't tell her about the sub with Logan.

Anne had called on Sunday evening to fill me in on her Miami trip. She needed a couple of days to get everything set, and she would be back in Longboat on Wednesday evening. I was glad to see her.

Over dinner I filled her in on the day's events, and told her I was still worried about what Elizabeth had that I didn't know about. "I always think there is something the other side knows that I don't. Usually they don't have anything, but I stay awake nights thinking about it. I just can't figure out why Elizabeth went into this with what seems to me to be a thin circumstantial case."

"Well," said Anne, "they did find Vivian's body on Logan's balcony. How did she get there? And why? Then you have a State Attorney running for reelection next year, and you probably have the makings of a case."

"You're pretty cynical for a real estate lawyer."

She laughed. "I think the cynicism starts in law school."

"Is that what made you decide to go into real estate law?"

"Not really. The firm made me a great offer, and I had a lot of educational debt to pay off. I just took the job without thinking too much about it."

"What do you think now?"

"I think the loans are almost paid off, and I'm ready to start representing real people for a change. Do you know how boring it is to do the same thing over and over again for the same big company, and still have them question your bill every month? I spend as much time explaining my bill to the company bean counters as I do practicing law."

"What are you going to do?"

"I don't know, Matt. I don't have any anchors. My brother was the only family I had, and he's gone. I've got my nieces and nephews, who are more like siblings to me, but they're spread all over the country now, with lives of their own. I'll wake up some morning and know that that is the day for me to make a decision, and I will. We'll see."

We made small talk for awhile, and then headed for the bedroom. I could get used to this. Anne was a good cook, and sex before bedtime always makes the trial lawyer sleep better.

Chapter 28

THURSDAY

Thursday. Day four. I was in the courtroom early, reviewing statements from the trove of documents Elizabeth had given me. The court deputy came in and said that Logan wanted to talk to me before court began. I met him in the witness room.

He was looking more and more haggard. He was handcuffed, a rule I had already been told could have no exceptions. He would only be let out of the cuffs when he was in sight of the jury. "How's it going, old buddy?" I asked.

"I'll survive, Matt, but not for long if I'm locked up."

"Try to be patient. We'll be through by the end of this week."

"I know. And you're doing a good job. I just wanted you to know that I'm glad you're my lawyer."

"Thanks, Logan. You ready for court?"

We walked into the courtroom to start the next segment of this fight for life or death.

Elizabeth called Dr. Bert Hawkins as the first witness. After qualifying him as an expert in forensic pathology she began the examination.

"Doctor Hawkins, do you hold an official position with the government?"

"Yes. I am the Chief Medical Examiner for the Twelfth Judicial Circuit, which is made up of Sarasota, Manatee and Desoto counties.

"Doctor, did you have occasion in your official capacity to perform an autopsy on a body identified as that of Vivian Perkins?"

"Yes."

"Did you reach a conclusion as to the cause of her death?"

173

"Yes."

"What was that conclusion, Doctor?"

"She died from manual strangulation"

"You mean somebody choked her to death?"

"Yes."

"How did you determine that Doctor?"

"The small U shaped bone in her neck called the hyoid bone was fractured, and she had bruising around the neck that was consistent with someone's hands exerting a great deal of pressure on her throat. Also, petechiae were present in the conjunctivae."

"What are petechiae and what are their significance, Doctor?"

"Petechiae are pinpoint-sized hemorrhages of small capillaries, in this case in the conjunctivae, which are the thin, transparent tissues that cover the outer surface of the eyes."

"Were you able to determine a time of death?"

"Within reasonable probability, the time of death was between 11 P.M. on April 15, and 3:00 A.M. on April 16."

"You mentioned the bruising on the victim's neck. Was there any other bruising on the body?"

"Yes. The area around the vaginal opening was bruised."

"Did this lead you to believe she had been raped?"

"No."

"No?" Elizabeth seemed surprised. Had she missed something? Was this her Achilles heel? "Doctor, doesn't that kind of bruising usually result from rape?"

"Not always."

"Doctor, I'm a little confused here. If a rape didn't cause the bruising, what did?"

"It could have been any number of things. She could have engaged in rough sex; she could have fallen on something, straddling it and getting the bruises."

"Nothing further," said Elizabeth, obviously in a snit.

She had just made what could be a fatal error. She had violated the first rule that every trial lawyer learns. Never ask a witness a question to which you do not know the answer. Even seasoned trail lawyers make this mistake sometimes. It is usually because the lawyer assumed she knew the answer, when in reality she had not fully prepped the witness. I could see how that happened here. Elizabeth and the Medical Examiner had tried a lot of cases together. They knew each other well. Elizabeth had read his report, and gone along with the conventional thinking, that bruising around the vagina meant rape.

I was going to have to begin to get into the personal lives of Vivian and Logan. I rose, walked to the podium and said, "Good morning, Doctor."

"Good morning, Counselor."

"You don't think Vivian was raped, do you?"

"I don't have an opinion either way."

"Would it be fair to say that if a rape had occurred you would have expected to find tearing of the vaginal tissue?"

"That would be fair."

"You didn't find that in this case, did you?"

"No, but that is not always dispositive."

"What do you mean by that?"

"I have seen rape victims that didn't have the vaginal tearing."

"But those were always live victims who told you they had been raped, right?"

"Yes, that's right."

"Tell the jury why vaginal tearing is of some importance in the diagnosis of rape?"

He turned in his seat to face the jury. "When a woman is ready for sex, she secretes a lubricant into the vaginal tract. When there is no lubricant, the forceful penetration of the vagina causes tearing of the delicate tissues."

"You said that rough sex could cause the bruising you found?"

"Yes," said the M.E.

"If there is testimony in this case that Vivian and my client Logan had engaged in rough sex shortly before her death, would you agree that given everything you know about this case and about Vivian, you would have to form an opinion that rape did not occur?"

"Objection!" Elizabeth was on her feet, fuming. "That is assuming facts not in evidence."

"Your Honor," I said, "I will tie this up in my case."

"Overruled," said the judge.

I turned back to the witness stand. "You may answer, Doctor."

"Correct."

"In other words, with that evidence you would be of the opinion that Vivian was not raped."

"That is correct."

Big time win on this one. I thought I may have just shot down Elizabeth's motive. I still figured she had something else. She was too good a prosecutor not to have a fall back position on something as important as motive. Still, even experienced lawyers make mistakes.

"I'd like to move on to another issue, Doctor," I said. "You told Ms. Ferguson that in your opinion the time of death was between 11:00 P.M. on Thursday night, and 3:00 A.M. on Friday morning. Can you be more exact than that?"

"No, sir."

"Would you agree with me that you cannot fix the exact time of death?"

"Yes."

"So the best you can do is approximate."

"That's correct," said the doctor, "but it is a scientific estimate as opposed to a guess."

"I understand that, but wouldn't the chances of pinpointing the exact time of death diminish as you moved toward the outer edges of the estimate? For example, wouldn't there be a greater possibility of the death occurring between midnight and 2:00 A.M.?"

"Yes."

"So, an estimate of time of death as between midnight and 2:00 A.M. would be a better scientific estimate than the four hours between 11:00 P.M. and 3:00 A.M."

"I would agree with that." said the witness.

"Can you narrow that time span any more?"

"No, not with any kind of scientific reliability."

"Thank you, Doctor. That's all I have." I returned to my seat as Elizabeth was rising.

"Doctor," Elizabeth said, "based on the evidence you've seen, you can't say whether the victim was raped, can you?"

"Based on the evidence I've seen, and what Mr. Royal suggested the evidence will be, it would be my opinion that she was not raped."

He was good. He really didn't like lawyer word games, and he was showing it. Elizabeth had tried to set him up to testify as she wanted, and he had slid right by her. I guessed there would be hell to pay when the trial was over. Prosecutors don't like their witnesses to testify truthfully, if the truth hurts their cases.

Elizabeth had had enough of the Medical Examiner. She sat down and the witness was excused by the judge. We broke for lunch, and Elizabeth stormed out of the courtroom without a word, her assistant trailing behind.

Anne had been in the courtroom all morning, and she and I joined Logan in the witness room for another lunch of sandwiches. I introduced them, and explained to Logan Anne's involvement, including her brother's death. "And," I said, "she's sweet on me."

"Geez," said Logan, grinning, "I'm on trial for my life, and you bring a date."

That was the first flash of humor I'd seen from Logan since the indictment, and I thought it was a good sign. "You seem a little more chipper today," I said.

"That was a great cross examination of the M.E.," said Logan. "I'm beginning to think we can win this thing."

"We made some good points," I said, "but we still have a way to go."

Anne asked, "Do you have enough for a directed verdict of acquittal?"

"I don't think so," I said, "but I'll make the motion anyway. You never know, and it will be a ground for appeal if we lose."

"We're not going to lose," said Logan. "I feel it."

"I think the prosecution is winding down," I said. "I don't know what else Elizabeth can put on. We have a decision to make, Logan, and it's your call."

I explained to him my plan for the defense, and the fact that I thought this might be the only way to open the way for a prosecution of the real killers. I told him that I thought with the thin case Elizabeth had put on, we could remain moot, not put on any evidence, and argue to the jury that the state had not proved its case and that they had to acquit. I could excuse Logan's not testifying as I had promised, by the fact that there was no need for him to do so, since there was no case to begin with. I told him that there is always the chance that a plan will go off the rails; that a witness might testify differently than expected; that the prosecution might bring out something in cross examination that we did not know about. There was also the chance that the jury would not buy my argument that the state had not proved its case and convict if we didn't put on any evidence.

"If we quit now, what happens to the killers?" Logan asked.

"In all probability, they'll walk," I said.

"And you think the same people who killed Vivian killed Anne's brother?"

"You can bet on it," Anne said.

"Then we need to go ahead with the evidence," he said. "I want the bastards who killed Vivian, and I know Anne wants to see them hang."

"You sure?" asked Anne.

"I'm sure," said Logan. "Go for it, Matt."

Elizabeth rested her case when we came back from lunch. I made a motion for directed verdict of acquittal, which was promptly denied. The judge asked me if I was ready to proceed with my case. When I responded that I was, Elizabeth rose to object.

"Your Honor," she said, "Mr. Royal provided me with a witness list on Monday morning. I've had investigators interviewing these witnesses since, and most of them wouldn't talk to us. I object to the late notice of witnesses and ask the court to disallow their testimony."

"Denied," said the judge.

"But your Honor, how am I supposed to prepare my case if I don't have access to the witnesses?"

"Your Honor," I said, rising to my feet, "Ms. Ferguson gave me nine days lead time to get ready for trial. I asked her for ninety days. She said no. If we had had that time, she could have deposed the witnesses. I think she has hoisted herself on her own petard."

"Mr. Royal is the one who wanted the quick trial," Elizabeth said.

"Children, children," said the judge, "I've ruled. The motion is denied. Sit down. Deputy, bring in the jury."

Things were not going well for Elizabeth, but I knew this trial had a long way to go. She was an able prosecutor, and I was still worried that she had held something back, and would spring it on me at the worst time.

I called Will Ledbedder. Will had flown in the night before from Chicago, taking vacation time to help me out. I had him state his name, occupation and place of residence. He told the jury about Vivian's background, her conviction, her incarceration and her rehabilitation. He also told them that she had disappeared from Chicago and that at the time of her death there had been a warrant out for her arrest.

"Who is Joseph Dean Johnson?" I asked.

"He was Ms. Pickens' pimp, known as Golden Joe."

"Where is Golden Joe now?"

"Dead," said Will.

"What do you know about his death?"

"Shortly after he got out of prison, he disappeared. A few days later his body was found in Miami, shot through the head."

"What was he in prison for?"

"Objection," said Elizabeth. "What possible relevance could this have to the case we're trying?"

"I was wondering that myself, Mr. Royal," said the judge.

"May we approach the bench?" I asked.

He waved us forward. Leaning in, whispering, I said, "Judge, I can tie this all up with the next few witnesses. I'm going to show the jury that someone else killed Vivian."

"Okay, Mr. Royal, but tread lightly. If you don't tie this up, you're going to have to send for a toothbrush, because I will jail you for contempt of court."

"But..." said Elizabeth.

"No buts, Ms. Ferguson. I've ruled. Proceed, Mr. Royal."

I returned to the podium. "Do your remember my last question?" I asked.

"Yes," said Will. He then told the jury the facts surrounding the death of Vivian's co-worker, Vivian's vicious beating, and Joe's sentence. He also told the jury that Vivian was the key witness against Joe.

"Who was the customer who killed Vivian's friend?" I asked.

"Nobody knows," said Will. "The investigation hit a dead end."

"Nothing further, your Honor."

Elizabeth rose and walked to the podium, reviewing her notes. "Mr. Ledbetter, are you here under subpoena?"

"No ma'am."

"You came down voluntarily from Chicago to help Mr. Hamilton?"

"No ma'am."

"Then how did you come to be here?"

"Oh, I came voluntarily, but I came to tell the truth, not help anybody."

This was not going well for Elizabeth, and she wisely sat down, announcing that she had no further questions.

Next up on the stand was Maria Cox. Anne had gone to Miami on Sunday, with the hope of getting Maria to open up about Cox. She had called J.J. Jimenez on her way to Miami, and met him at the restaurant. She asked him if he thought Maria Cox would be mixed up in murder plots. J.J. didn't think so. She had been raised right, as they said in the old South, and even kids who stray from their family's values are in some sense tethered to those ideals forever. J.J. also thought Maria had been beaten, and showed Anne the pictures he had taken of her and Cox when we had been in the restaurant. J.J.'s camera was high resolution, and he had used his computer to manipulate the pictures of Maria, so that Anne could see the bruising on her right cheek, beneath the makeup she had applied.

"Who would she go to for help?" asked Anne.

"I don't know. She cut herself off from her family, and there is some bad blood there, but she is still family, and her brothers would take her in," said J.J.

"Cox is in Longboat Key this weekend," Anne said. "Would you go with me to visit Maria?"

"If we can figure out where she lives."

"I know where," said Anne.

"Let me make a call," answered J.J.

Hernando Domingo, Maria's eldest brother, had been twelve when Maria was born. He had doted on his little sister, and was devastated by the way her life had turned out. He had taken over the family business after his father's death, and with the help of his younger brother, had overseen its continued growth.

He arrived at the restaurant thirty minutes later and hugged J.J., who introduced him to Anne. He was a large man, tall and muscular, the result of years of hard work. He had a head of dark hair, olive skin, black eyes and the facial features that advertised his Cuban heritage.

J.J. explained that Maria might be in trouble, and he thought it a good idea for the three of them to go see her. He told Hernando that Anne was a lawyer working on a case that would likely put Maria's husband in jail for years, and that he had reason to believe that Cox had beaten Maria.

That was all Hernando needed to hear. They took his vehicle, a big Chevrolet Tahoe that he used in his work, and headed for Brickell Ave. At the door, they told the same Brooklyn born security guard that J.J. Jimenez was there to see Maria Cox. And no, she wasn't expecting him. After phoning upstairs, the guard directed them to an elevator.

At the door to the penthouse, the only one opening off the elevator lobby, Hernando knocked on the door. Maria opened it, wearing a flowing caftan decorated with palm trees, and a Rolex watch. She was barefoot. She was expecting J.J., and here he was with a big Cuban she had not seen in years. It took her a moment of puzzlement, but then her face took on a look of shock, and perhaps wonder. Anne wasn't sure.

"Hernando?" Maria said in Spanish. "Oh my God! What's wrong?"

"Hello, little one," Hernando answered in English. "Everything is fine. May we come in?"

"Of course." She opened the door, and Hernando grabbed her in a bear hug. Letting her go, he introduced her to Anne.

The living room was enclosed on one side in glass walls, giving the visitor a view of lower Biscayne Bay that only the wealthy usually enjoyed. They sat in furniture upholstered in silk fabric that must have cost a fortune. J.J. looked at Maria, and said, "Who hurt you?"

"Nobody hurt me."

"Take the makeup off and we'll see bruises," said Hernando.

"Is this what this is about? Big brother come to the rescue?" Maria was loud.

"No, little one, it's more than that. We think you're in trouble, and I'm your family, and I'm here to help, and take you home if you want."

"Home?" Tears began to well in her eyes and run over, making little rivulets in her makeup.

"Yes, little one. Home. Do you want to tell us what is going on?"

"Oh Hernando, it's such a long story, and so bad. I don't know what to do."

"Maria," Hernando said, "Anne is a lawyer and is here to help you out of this mess. Will you talk to her?"

"Yes." said Maria, relief in her voice.

Anne explained to Maria her involvement in the matter; the fact of her brother's death, Vivian's and Joe's deaths and how Cox and Rundel appeared to be involved. "Does your husband have a gun?" Anne asked.

"Yes. A big one."

"May I see it?" asked Anne.

Maria left the room, and returned in a couple of minutes, carrying a nine millimeter semi automatic pistol wrapped in an oil cloth. "Sam keeps this in the safe in the bedroom." She handed it to Anne.

"May I keep this?" Anne asked.

"Yes, please. Get it out of the house. When Sam gets drunk, I'm always afraid he'll use it on me."

"He's been beating you, then," said Hernando.

"Yes, not often, but more, lately."

"Get packed," said Hernando. "We're going home."

Maria left the room, and Hernando asked Anne what she was going to do with the pistol. She said she was going to give it to a detective friend of hers for analysis. Hernando was worried about his sister's involvement, but Anne assured him that if this turned out to be the murder weapon, Maria would not have any involvement. In fact, since she was the one who turned it over to the police, Maria could count on the authorities to see her as another victim.

Anne went to see Carl Merritt, and told him she thought she might know where the murder weapon used on Golden Joe could be found She would only tell him if he agreed not to arrest the gun's owner until he could testify in court in Manatee County. After that, he could shoot the bastard, for all Anne cared.

Merritt agreed to the deal, got the gun, and his ballistics department matched it to the gun that had killed Golden Joe.

Maria's brother had taken her back into the family, and she had agreed to testify at this trial. She and Hernando had been sequestered alone in a witness room since lunch.

After getting her name and address, I asked, "Who is your husband?"

"Sam Cox."

"Does he own a gun?"

"Yes sir."

"Where is that gun now?"

"I gave it to Miami-Dade Detective Merritt."

"Thank you, Ms. Cox. I have nothing further."

Elizabeth had no questions, and I called Carl Merritt to the stand. He testified that he had had the gun tested by the ballistics lab, and was sure that it was the same gun used to kill Golden Joe. I had no further questions, and neither did Elizabeth. Carl was excused by the judge and sat down in the back of the courtroom.

My next witness was Sam Cox, who had spent the week in the Sarasota County jail. That had worked out better than I had anticipated.

On Sunday I had asked Dick Bellinger to serve some subpoenas for me. He had agreed, and gone to the Colony Beach to find his quarry. Cox was in the bar when Dick approached him with the subpoena, and told him that he had to appear in Manatee County Circuit Court the following week. Cox ripped up the subpoena without looking at it, and walked out of the bar.

Dick then called the Sarasota County Sheriff's department and explained that he was a licensed process server, told the dispatcher what had happened, and asked that a deputy be sent to the Colony. By the time the deputy arrived, Cox was by the pool drinking vodka. He had apparently been at it for most of the afternoon, and was drunk. The uniformed deputy explained that the subpoena had been served, and that he would be glad to give Cox another copy of it, but he had to agree to abide by it. Cox cold-cocked the deputy, knocking him into the pool. Dick grabbed Cox in a full nelson and held him, sputtering and cursing, until the deputy got out of the pool and handcuffed him. The deputy took Cox to jail while Dick raced for the airport.

In southwest Florida, it is considered bad form to attack uniformed deputy sheriffs, and Cox was thrown into jail. Somehow, his paperwork got lost by the jailers, and he was not brought before a judge as required by law. No matter how much Cox screamed about constitutional rights, he was kept in solitary confinement, with his meals brought to his cell. I thought the jailers would have a hard time explaining the lack of prompt first appearance to a judge, but since trial judges are elected in Florida, I thought it would not make much difference in whether he was charged with battery on a law enforcement officer.

I had discussed this with the chief jailer earlier in the week, and told him I would still need Cox to testify. The jailer agreed and arranged for Cox to make his first appearance before a Sarasota County judge that morning. Bail had been set, but again the paper work got rerouted in some manner, so that Cox was still in custody when he was brought to the Manatee County courthouse.

Cox was led into the courtroom by the court deputy. He looked a little hollow eyed, and a faint stubble covered his chin. He seemed docile enough, and I thought that sometimes a few days in jail can do a man some good.

"State your name and address, please," I said, after Cox took the stand.

"Samuel Cox, Brickell Avenue, Miami, Florida."

"Why did you kill Golden Joe Johnson?"

Elizabeth was on her feet. "Assuming facts not in evidence and irrelevant."

There was a slight buzz from the audience, mostly made up of local reporters. This trial was a pretty big deal for the sleepy town of Bradenton, so the local newspapers had reporters sitting through the proceedings. There was one reporter from the only T.V. station in the circuit, but the big boys in Tampa had not thought a local murder trial was worth their valuable time. Certainly not when there were gory traffic accidents to put on the six o'clock news.

"Overruled," said the judge, motioning Elizabeth to sit down.

Cox was sputtering. "What the hell do you mean?"

"Mr. Cox," said the judge, leaning over the bench to look directly at the witness, "There will be no profanity in this courtroom. Do I make myself clear?"

"Yes, sir. Sorry, Judge." Cox was calming a bit, his rage dissipating like mist in the sunshine. "I didn't kill anybody."

"But you know who Golden Joe Johnson is, or was, don't you?"

"Never heard of him."

"Then explain to the jury why a bullet from your pistol was found in his head?"

The anger flashed again. This was a guy with a short fuse, and I was setting it off with every other question.

"I don't have any idea," Cox said.

"If I told you that your wife had given the gun to the police, and that Detective Merritt of the Miami-Dade police department had testified here today that your gun was used in the murder of Joe Johnson, would you think them liars?"

That question was borderline objectionable, but Elizabeth did not rise. I think it was about this time that Elizabeth figured out where I was going with my case. Prosecutors are sworn to get to the truth, not just convict the accused. A few, the really good ones, take that oath seriously and will hesitate to keep out evidence that may prove the innocense of the accused. Besides, Elizabeth had been shot down so much that I didn't think she wanted to test the judge's patience any more.

Cox sat silent. "Did you not hear my question, Mr. Cox?"

"Please repeat it."

I repeated the question, and when I mentioned Merritt's name, I pointed to him in the back of the courtroom. I wanted Cox to know that the detective was there.

"I can't explain it," he said. Then he did exactly what I expected him to do, because he was a clever guy who had operated on the margins of the law for many years. He said, "I'm not going to answer any more questions. I'm invoking my Fifth amendment rights."

The Fifth Amendment to the Constitution of the United States provides that no one can be forced to testify to matters that might incriminate him in a violation of the law. It is the criminal's best friend, but it is part of a package of Amendments that limits the government's rights. I think they are some of the most important thoughts ever devised by man. And sometimes, the criminal mind, hiding behind a constitutional right, can be a force of good for the defense lawyer.

"Are you sure you want to do this, Mr. Cox?" asked the judge, leaning again over the bench and pinning Cox with those piercing blue eyes.

"Yes," said Cox.

"Okay," said the judge with a sigh. "I need to instruct the jury."

He then told the jury that everyone has the right not to incriminate themselves, and that the jury should not think Mr. Cox guilty of anything on account of him exercising a right given him by our constitution. Right, I thought. The jury knows to a man that Cox is guilty as hell, or he wouldn't have taken the Fifth. Just because Cox refused to answer did not mean I couldn't ask my questions, and that was a very big part of my game plan.

"Did you arrange for Golden Joe Johnson to come to Miami?" I asked.

"I stand on my Fifth amendment rights and refuse to answer the question."

"Did you meet him when he got to Miami?"

"I stand on my Fifth amendment rights and refuse to answer the question."

"Mr. Cox," I said, "I'm going to ask you a bunch of questions. If you are going to assert your Fifth Amendment rights after every one, why don't you just say 'Fifth Amendment' and save us all some time."

"Okay."

"Did you put your pistol to the back of Golden Joe's head and shoot him?"

"Fifth Amendment."

"Did you then dump his body into a canal in the Everglades?"

"Fifth Amendment."

"Did you plan for the alligators to eat the body?"

"Fifth Amendment."

"Were you in Longboat Key the night of April 15, of this year?"

"Fifth Amendment."

"Did you meet Logan Hamilton in Dewey's Five Points Bar and tell him that you were a member of his Army flight training class?"

"Fifth Amendment."

"Did you also go with Logan to Frisco's Bar on Bridge Street?"

"Fifth Amendment."

"Do you work for Hale Rundel or Rundel Enterprises?"

"Fifth Amendment."

"Think about that Mr. Cox. I can easily prove you were employed by Rundel, and I can think of no reason why that fact, in and of itself, would incriminate you."

"Fifth Amendment."

I surely wasn't going to get anything else out of Cox, and I thought I had made my point to the jury, that this was a bad guy. "No further questions," I said.

Elizabeth stood. "Under the circumstances, I have no questions."

The court deputy escorted Cox to the back of the room and had him sit next to Carl Merritt. The deputy stood at the back of the room, next to the door to the hall.

"I'll recall Chief Bill Lester, of the Longboat Key Police Department," I said.

I put a few questions to the chief, establishing that Cox had introduced himself to the Chief as head of security for Rundel Enterprises, and told him his company had been employed to provide security for the Governor Wentworth's visit to the key. On cross, Elizabeth made the point that in fact Cox had headed the private security detail for the governor's weekend getaway.

I then called Molly O'Sullivan who testified about the man who had come into her restaurant one night and asked about Logan, telling her he was his old Army buddy. "Do you see that man in the courtroom?" I asked.

"Yes, he's sitting in the back of the room," she said, pointing right at Cox.

I asked no further questions, and neither did Elizabeth.

I next called Dewey Clanton, who told the jury about the night that Vivian died, when Logan sat in her bar drinking until 11:00 o'clock, with a man who had identified himself to Dewey as an old Army buddy of Logan's. "Do you see this man in the courtroom, today?" I asked.

She pointed to Cox, saying, "That's him, right there."

Elizabeth passed on questions, and the next person up was Slim Jim Martin from Frisco's Bar on Bridge Street. He identified Cox as the man drinking with Logan until closing time on the evening Vivian was killed. I took him through how he knew the exact time Logan and Cox left, and put his bank receipt into evidence. Elizabeth had no questions.

I had timed things so that my last witness of the day would be Logan. I knew his story was compelling and exculpatory. I wanted to finish the day on a high note, and leave my last witness, a surprise blockbuster, for Friday morning.

I called Logan to the stand. He was dressed in a light gray suit, a blue button down oxford cloth shirt and dark blue silk tie. He looked like the executive he was. We had gone over his testimony the evening before in the jail's interview room. He was well aware of my approach, and knew that he was not to volunteer any information outside our script. I also made it very clear to Logan that he was to tell nothing but the truth. Otherwise, he would get tripped up on cross examination by a very experienced prosecutor.

"State your name," I said.

"Logan Hamilton."

The jury had perked up. This was some of the testimony they had been waiting for all week. They were trying to take the measure of Logan, and I knew that the next few minutes would very well determine my friend's fate.

"Did you kill Vivian Pickens?" I like to get right to the meat of the subject.

"Absolutely not," Logan said, looking right at the jury.

"Do you know how her body came to be in your condo?"

"No, sir."

"Tell me about your relationship with Vivian."

Logan gave us the whole thing. They were friends who would occasionally share a bed. Vivian, and a lot of people on the island had keys to Logan's condo, and besides, he seldom ever locked it when he was in town. He had no idea how Vivian's body ended up on his balcony. He had come in that night very late, at around 2:00 a.m. He was drunk and did not pay any attention to his balcony. He awoke as the sun was coming up and went to the kitchen for a drink of water. He looked out toward the Gulf and saw the body on the balcony. He thought Vivian was asleep and went to wake her. She was dead, and Logan called 911.

He told us about the sex on the boat the night of her death, and about getting drunk with a man who said he had been in flight school with him at Ft. Rucker.

"Did you remember him?" I asked.

"No, but there were a lot of guys going through flight school at that time, and I could have known him and not remembered him. I didn't want to look like a jerk to somebody who remembered me, so I didn't tell him I didn't remember him."

"What was his name?"

"He told me it was Bill Smith."

"Did you later try to find out about Bill Smith?"

"Yes, I called some of my old army buddies, and none of them remembered him."

"Have you seen this so called Army buddy since?"

"Yes. I saw him today in this courtroom. Sam Cox."

"Are you sure Sam Cox was the man pretending to be your Army buddy?"

"Positive."

"Nothing further, your Honor," I said, regaining my seat.

Elizabeth was obviously taken aback. She was expecting me to elicit a lot more testimony from Logan, and normally a defense lawyer would do that. I had set a little trap, and would wait to see if Elizabeth would step into it.

"If you didn't kill Vivian Pickens, why did you run and hide after you found out that the grand jury had indicted you for her murder?" the prosecutor asked, rising from her seat.

"I didn't," Logan said.

"You didn't?" Elizabeth was incredulous. "Am I right that you turned yourself in to the county sheriff just this past Sunday?"

"That's right."

"Okay, if you didn't flee the jurisdiction, where in the world have you been for the past six weeks?"

I could hear the jaws of the trap closing. It was sweet music.

"In the hospital in Boston, and then in a rehabilitation facility there."

"Hospital? For what?"

"I had a heart transplant."

"Heart transplant," Elizabeth sputtered. "Judge, can we be heard outside the presence of the jury?"

"Take the jury out," said Judge O'Reilly.

I could see the look of disappointment cross the faces of several of the jurors. This was just getting good, and like children, they were being sent to their room so the adults could talk.

"Judge," said Elizabeth, after the room was cleared of jurors, "This is a complete surprise. I would like to either continue this trial until I have had time to look into it, or to bar any further testimony about this alleged heart condition."

"Your Honor," I said, in all innocence, "She asked the question."

"That you did, Ms. Ferguson."

"He set me up, Judge," said Elizabeth, pointing at me.

"That he did," said the judge, "But you know the old saw about not asking a question to which you don't know the answer."

"I don't know why it is a surprise, Judge," I said. "I provided Ms. Ferguson with the entire medical records on Monday morning."

"There must be a thousand pages there, your Honor," said Elizabeth. "I got those just as I was leaving for the courthouse. The first few pages had to do with his childhood measles. Are you telling me that there is record of a heart transplant in there?" She was looking at me.

"Yes, its all there, and I was going to offer the entire record into evidence at the appropriate time."

"Unless Mr. Royal has a witness to authenticate the records, I will object," said Elizabeth.

It would be necessary for me to put a representative of the Boston hospital on the stand to testify that the records were in fact true and correct copies of the original hospital records. Since Logan had only given me the records and told me his story on Saturday evening, I could not get any one from the hospital to come and testify. I was winging it, but I had planned on not being able to get the records into evidence, so Logan's testimony was very important.

"Do you have a witness to authenticate the records, Mr. Royal?" asked the judge.

"No sir."

"I'm going to allow the testimony. Bring in the jury," said the judge.

The jury filed back in, wondering, I'm sure, what they had missed. Elizabeth took up where she left off. "Tell me about this heart transplant," she said.

"I have suffered from congestive heart failure for more than a year. I've been treated for it both here and in Boston. I was put on a transplant list some months ago in Boston, and Friday, the day I was indicted, I got a call to come to Boston. There was a man there who was clinically dead, and his family had agreed to allow the hospital to harvest his organs. There was a tissue match, and if I could get to Boston that day, they could do the transplant."

"So you went to Boston. Did you tell anybody here where you were going?"

"No. I had planned to call on Saturday when I was sure the surgery was going forward."

"When was the surgery performed?"

"Saturday morning ."

"So you were in the hospital when you found out about the indictment. Who told you about it?" asked Elizabeth.

"I honestly don't know. I was going to call Dallas Mahoney on Longboat to tell him about the surgery. I called to check my messages first."

"And there was a message about the indictment?"

"Yes, but I didn't recognize the voice of the person who left the message."

"What did you do then?"

"I called Mr. Royal and retained him to represent me."

"Did you tell him where you were?"

"No ma'am."

"Why not?"

"I was afraid he would be constrained by ethics to tell you or the police where I was, and I couldn't take the chance that I'd be arrested. There was a heart that would work for me, and they were going to take me to surgery in a matter of hours. I couldn't risk that being stopped."

"Did you ever tell Mr. Royal or anybody else where you were?"

"No. After I got out of the hospital, I was in a rehabilitation facility for several weeks. I didn't want to be taken out of there before the anti-rejection drugs had taken hold, and I knew that I was going to live."

Elizabeth sat down, her case blown wide open. The DNA had been explained, and Logan's absence was not a flight to avoid prosecution, but a legitimate and reasonable effort to save his own life. I could have probably rested right there, but trial lawyers are a nervous bunch. Sometimes we overdo the evidence, putting in everything we know, even when we don't need to. I felt that I still needed to give the jury a reason to point the finger of guilt in a direction other than toward Logan.

"Who will be your next witness, Mr. Royal?" the judge asked.

"I'll be calling Governor George Wentworth," I said. "We have him scheduled for first thing in the morning."

There was a murmur of surprise in the courtroom, but the judge took it in stride. On Sunday afternoon, Dick Bellinger had raced to the airport in time to get to the governor before he flew out in his campaign plane. Dick had shown one of the deputies on security duty the subpoena and was escorted to a room where the governor and his family were relaxing. He shook the governor's hand and handed him the subpoena.

"What's this all about?" the governor had asked.

"Don't really know, sir," Dick said, "But you've got to be in court next week in Manatee County."

"Where the hell is Manatee County?" asked the governor.

"You're standing in it," said Dick.

""I don't understand," said the governor.

"The airport is partly in both Sarasota and Manatee Counties..." Dick started to say.

"I don't give a shit about the geography of the airport. What I want to know is what this subpoena is about."

"I really couldn't say, sir. I'm just the process server," replied Dick.

"We'll see about this," said the governor. "No two bit judge in Mana what the fuck county is going to keep me here." He stormed off toward the plane.

Dick turned to the deputy, grinning. "Did you hear that?"

"I sure did," said the deputy.

"Do you want to know who the two bit judge is that's presiding at this trial?"

"Who?"

"T. Johnson O'Reilly," said Dick.

"Oh shit," the deputy said, laughing, "and that guy is a mere governor. Old T. Johnson is going to have his ass."

And sure enough, that is what happened. By the end of the first day of trial, a lawyer for Governor Wentworth had filed a motion to quash the subpoena. Judge O'Reilly had set a hearing for noon on Tuesday, and Elizabeth and I were in the judge's chambers, along with Dick Bellinger and a lawyer from one of Tampa's megafirms, representing the governor.

"What goes on in this hearing is going to be sealed," said the judge, "and I'm imposing a gag order on all of you. I don't want to embarrass the governor if this is some kind of publicity stunt on Mr. Royal's part."

"It is not, Judge," I said. "I have every reason to believe the governor can shed some light on my client's innocence, and I need him on the witness stand."

The judge turned to the governor's lawyer, and said, "What say you, Counselor?"

"The governor is a very busy man, and it would be an imposition to have him return to Florida for a trial about which he knows nothing.

Moreover, I don't believe he was properly served, and the subpoena is therefore no good."

"What about that, Mr. Royal?" asked the judge.

"Your Honor, I have the process server, Mr. Bellinger, here. He can testify as to what he did," I said.

Turning to Dick, the judge said, "Raise your right hand." Dick did, and was sworn in by the judge. "Tell me about the service of the subpoena," the judge said.

Dick took him through the process, testified that he was a duly licensed process server in the state of Florida, and that he had personally handed the subpoena to the Governor.

"What was the governor's response?" the judge asked.

Uh oh, I thought, here's where the subpoena gets upheld. "The governor said he was not going to let some two bit Florida judge keep him in this state," said Dick. "His words, not mine, your Honor."

Judge O'Reilly seemed unfazed by the comment. He turned to me, and said, "Mr. Royal, I swear by all that's holy, if this is some kind of stunt, if the governor really doesn't have anything to add to this trial, I will hold you in contempt and put your ass, strike that last word Madam Court Reporter, rear end in jail. Do I make myself clear?"

"Crystal clear, your honor." I said.

Turning to the governor's lawyer, the judge said, "Work out a time with Mr. Royal for your client to appear, Counselor. We'll take him out of order, if necessary. And don't forget the gag order."

We had chewed up the afternoon, and Judge O'Reilly recessed for the day. Elizabeth flounced out of the courtroom. She was seething. She had renewed her objection to each of my witnesses and the judge had overruled each one. I didn't know if she had completely figured out where I was going with my witnesses, but I doubted it, because I hadn't known until the weekend before.

After the jury and judge had left the courtroom, Carl Merritt formally arrested Cox and read him his rights. They would head back to Miami that evening, and Cox would be charged with the murder of Golden Joe Johnson. He wouldn't be making bail in Sarasota County.

As I left the courtroom, I was mobbed by the local press. They were all yelling at me, asking why I was calling the governor. I waved my hands in a downward motion, telling them to quiet down. "I can't answer your questions. Not now. Come to court tomorrow, and you'll find out. That's all I can say for now."

I walked off. They followed, like a pack of rabid dogs, yelling questions. I guess there hadn't been any decent car wrecks that day.

Chapter 29

FRIDAY

My body protested as I dragged it out of bed that morning. I was exhausted. The mental effort of a trial is so intense that the trial lawyer's mind tries to shut down, and knowing it can't, sends signals to the body to shut down instead. I have read that the second highest rate of suicides in the country is among trial lawyers. I can believe that, and the thought of suicide crossed my mind, briefly, as I rose to face another day in the pit.

Anne slept next to me, curled into a fetal ball, her dark hair mussed. Every few minutes, a delicate snore would slip from her. It was kind of cute, I thought, but if I told her about it she would be so embarrassed she might decide not to sleep with me any more. That did not seem like something I wanted to contemplate.

When I got out of the shower, she was awake, and padded naked to the bathroom. I felt a bit of stirring in places that didn't need to be awakened on the morning of the final day of a trial.

As we neared the courthouse I saw several large TV transmission vans, some bearing the logos of national networks. I wasn't surprised. Governor Wentworth had been in the news a lot lately, and the media would be excited, like a school of piranha, hoping to chew the flesh from his bones. The fact of his being a witness in a murder trial was just too juicy to pass up.

As Anne and I neared the courthouse steps, I was mobbed by the reporters, throwing stupid questions in my direction. I did not respond, walking quickly and quietly toward the security station at the entrance. The mob was left behind as I passed through security. Perhaps these rent a cops had some use after all.

The courtroom gallery was packed. Most of the observers had press passes hanging around their necks. There was a TV camera set up in one corner of the courtroom, aimed at the pit. Elizabeth and her assistant were at their table. Anne came inside the rail and sat in one of the chairs behind counsel table. As a member of the bar, she was allowed entrance to the pit, and I had already introduced her to Elizabeth and Judge O'Reilly.

The court was called to order, and the judge entered. Taking the bench, he told us to be seated, and said, "Ladies and Gentlemen, this is a most unusual event, to have this many members of the press in a Manatee County courtroom. I want to caution each of you that I will countenance no outburst, no talking and no running out of the courtroom during the testimony of Governor Wentworth. I have instructed the deputies to seal the courtroom. If you want to leave, do so now." No one stirred.

"There is a pool camera in the corner," the judge continued. "If counsel has any objection, I will hear it now." There was no objection. "Bring in the jury."

The jury entered, anticipation written across their faces. This was probably the most exciting event of their lives, and they would be telling their grandchildren about it. They took their seats, intent on the proceedings. The judge said, "Mr. Royal, call your witness." I did and the court deputy made a big deal out of walking to the door at the back of the courtroom,

"Governor George Wentworth," the deputy called, and then stood aside as the governor strode into the courtroom. He was wearing a navy blue suit, a bright white dress shirt, and a red silk tie. His hair had obviously been styled that morning, probably by his traveling hairdresser. He had that arrogant air about him that emanates from many politicians, especially when they are campaigning. It was clear that the governor saw his court appearance as just another campaign stop; one that he was determined to turn to his advantage. He took his seat on the witness stand, was sworn, and turned and smiled at the jury as he promised to tell the truth and nothing but.

State your name and occupation, please sir," I said.

"George Wentworth, Governor of Iowa and candidate for the Presidency of the United States." He smiled directly at the camera in the back corner of the courtroom. He was probably thinking about the six o'clock news. He seemed very sure of himself, the arrogance oozing from every pore. It was time to start chipping away at the stone exterior. I wanted to see him sweat a little. I had heard stories about the hair trigger temper he was careful not to show in public. Trial lawyers love explosive tempers in witnesses. If you can gently goad a witness into exploding on the stand, you have him in your arena. You're in charge, and the jury is forever after a little skeptical of his testimony.

"Where were you on October 6, twelve years ago?" I asked.

"I have no idea."

"If I told you you were at the Lakeview Hotel in Chicago on that evening would you disagree?"

"I have no idea, Counselor."

I walked to the witness stand and handed him a piece of paper. "Can you identify that document, Governor?"

"It appears to be a computer printout from the Lakeview Hotel for the evening October 6."

"Does it show the name of the person registered in suite 1101?"

"Yes."

"And what is the name?"

"It's my name, Counselor. So, I guess you proved your point." He was close to snarling.

"Do you remember that a prostitute was beaten to death in that hotel on the same night you stayed there?"

"What's your point, Sir?"

"Just asking, Governor. Do you remember that?"

"Vaguely, " he said.

"And do you remember Governor, that some john had two prostitutes in his room and they were all snorting cocaine?"

"What are you implying, Counselor?" The snarl was closer to the surface now.

"Nothing, Governor, just asking."

"Well, ask something else. I'm tired of this line of questions."

"Your Honor?" I said.

Judge O'Reilly leaned over his bench, his face grave. "Governor, you will answer the questions put to you unless I rule otherwise."

"Judge, these questions have no bearing on anything," said Wentworth.

"I'll make that decision, Governor," said the judge.

Turning to me the governor said, "Ask your next stupid question, Counselor."

"Governor," said the judge, "You will sit there and conduct yourself like a gentleman. You will answer the questions put to you, or so help me, I will hold you in contempt of this court."

I had turned and was walking back to counsel table. I saw one of the governor's handlers standing in the very back of the courtroom, making calming hand signals to the governor. The governor was trying to control himself, willing himself to calm down, to present himself as the strong leader with a steady demeanor.

"Where were you on the evening of May 5, 1979, Governor?" I asked.

"I have no idea."

"Where did you live at the time?"

"I was in college then."

"At Georgetown University in Washington D.C.?"

"That's right."

"Lived in a dorm on campus?"

"Yes."

"Then why were you checked into a sleazebag hotel on that night?"

"I'm not sure I was. I guess you have a registration card for that as well."

"I sure do, Governor." I handed him the registration card.

"Okay. That's my name. So what?"

"Are you aware that a prostitute was beaten to death in that hotel on the very night you were there?"

"This is getting tiresome, Counselor."

"Can you answer the question?" I asked.

"I don't have any memory of that."

"Were you aware that cocaine was found in both hotel rooms where the dead prostitutes were found?"

Judge O'Reilly was getting a little restless. "Do you have a point, Mr. Royal?"

"Yes, sir, your Honor," I said. "Just a few more questions."

"Governor, where were you on the evening of September 6, 1984?"

"I'm sure you're going to tell me."

"Does Moline, Illinois sound familiar?"

"Maybe. I've been to Moline a number of times. It's right across the river from Davenport, Iowa. I was working on my father's campaign for reelection to the United States Senate at the time. I was traveling the whole state of Iowa."

"Do you remember that a prostitute was beaten to death in the same hotel in which you stayed on the night you were there?"

"No. I'm not aware of that."

"There was cocaine residue found in the room. Does that ring any bells?"

"Just what are you getting at, Counselor?"

"Are you still using cocaine, Governor?" I asked.

That was it. He came out of his chair, screaming, "You two bit pissant. I'm the Governor of Iowa. Just who the hell do you think you are?" Spittle was flying out of his mouth, his eyes blazing. Out of the corner of my eye, I saw the court deputy move toward the witness stand. Two members of the jury flinched at the fury of the governor's response.

"Sit down, Governor!" said the judge.

"Don't you tell me what to do, you small time tyrant. I make and break judges like you every day." The governor had lost control. I could not have asked for a better display of a witness out of control.

"Not in this state, and not in this courtroom," said Judge O'Reilly. "Either you sit down or I'll have the deputy arrest you. Now, Governor. Right now!" The judge's voice was calm, but his words flowed out of his mouth like steel javelins.

Suddenly, the governor sat down. He had pulled himself back to reality by strength of will, but he must have known that he had done terrible damage to himself. His outburst would lead the national news shows that evening. "I apologize, your Honor," he said.

"Proceed, Mr. Royal," said the judge.

"Governor, are you aware of the progress made in DNA evidence during the last ten years?" I asked.

"Only in the vaguest sense."

"Did you know that the Chicago Police Department had recovered semen from the room in which one prostitute was beaten to death and Vivian Pickens was almost beaten to death?"

He didn't know that. His eyes reflected something that I had seen a long time ago in the eyes of a North Viet Namese regular soldier who was about to die. It was the acknowledgment that his life was over.

"No," he said quietly.

"Would you be willing to give a DNA sample to the Chicago detective that is here in the courtroom?"

"I think I'd better seek legal counsel, Mr. Royal," said the governor.

"Were you responsible for the death of Vivian Pickens and Golden Joe Johnson?"

"No."

"Governor, you sent your goons to Chicago to find Vivian four years ago, and when they did, she disappeared. Your people picked up her trail through her father down in Pahokee, and they found her on Longboat Key. You had her killed, because you were afraid she could identify you as her attacker and the murderer of her friend. You had Sam Cox waylay Logan on the night of Vivian's death, so someone could strangle her and leave her in Logan's condo. You wanted it to look like a lover's quarrel, so the police would look no further. Am I right, Governor?"

"I refuse to answer that without advice of counsel."

"I have nothing further, your Honor," I said.

"I have no questions, your Honor." said Elizabeth.

"You may be excused, Governor. Under the circumstances there will be no contempt citation. I imagine you'll be going to Chicago for awhile," said the judge.

"Your Honor," said Elizabeth, still on her feet, "The state dismisses all charges against the defendant Logan Hamilton."

"Case is dismissed," said the judge. "The defendant is forthwith released from custody. The jury is dismissed." He rose and left the bench.

Just like that, the trial was over. Since a jury had been empaneled before the dismissal, jeopardy had attached, and Logan was as free as if the jury had acquitted him. I breathed a large sigh of relief. Logan leaned over to me and said, "What just happened?"

"Case is over," I said. "You're a free man."

Pandemonium erupted in the courtroom as the judge left. Cell phones appeared, and reporters were calling in their stories. The pool camera was being broken down, the live feed having been sent all day to the trucks parked in front of the courthouse. Programming would be interrupted on all the network and cable channels, so that the feed of the governor imploding his campaign could be given to the American people without delay.

The court deputy walked over, smiling. "That was great, Mr. Royal," he said. "That SOB had it coming. I can't imagine him ending up as president."

"I don't think it'll happen now," said Anne.

I had turned to find Elizabeth, who was packing up, getting ready to leave. "That was a courageous thing you did," I said. "I wonder how your boss is going to take it."

"I don't really care, Matt," she said. "Maybe it's time I moved on."

"Don't do anything rash, Elizabeth. You're a hell of a prosecutor. The state needs you. Why don't we let the dust settle and have a drink. I'll call you the first of the week."

"I'd like that Matt. You're a hell of a lawyer, for a beach bum." She was smiling.

Logan, Anne and I walked out of the courthouse, reporters vying for our attention. We ignored them, and headed for Longboat Key. I was breathing easy for the first time since I had agreed to represent Logan. The trial was over, and my friend was free. Anne was the bonus I did not expect when the case started, and I thought I could get used to having her around. We'd have to explore that.

Chapter 30

As I expected, the national news on Friday evening was dominated by the turn of events for Wentworth. The governor was not available for comment, and the media was frantically trying to find him. I knew that he had been arrested by a Chicago Police lieutenant of detectives named Miles Leavitt, and that he would be transported to Chicago before the night was over.

The morning papers ran large headlines announcing that the governor had been arrested for murder and had withdrawn from the presidential race and resigned his governorship. Longboat Key was prominent among the stories, and I had my fifteen minutes of fame. It was a little unsettling, but so is life.

I called David Jarski on Saturday morning.

"I saw you on TV. I thought you were in the insurance business," he said.

"I'm sorry about that, Dr. Jarski. I was under the impression that you might have killed Vivian, who I then thought was your wife Connie."

"It's not a problem, Mr. Royal. I'm glad you found Vivian's murderer. And I appreciate your taking the time to call."

We chatted for awhile, and I asked him to give my regards to Mrs. Gibbs. He was not a man to hold a grudge, and he seemed genuinely pleased that Vivian's murder would not go unpunished.

Sam Cox was going to be charged with the murder of Golden Joe Johnson and with conspiracy to commit murder in the Vivian Pickens case. Nobody had figured out who actually killed Vivian. Cox had an ironclad alibi for most of the time in which the murder could have occurred, since he was with Logan. No one doubted though, that Cox had put it all together.

The key was quiet on Saturday. Dottie Johanson put together a party at one of the local gin mills to welcome Logan home. All the regulars were there, including some who had probably thought Logan guilty. It was a celebration, and the key breathed a collective sigh of relief over Logan's acquittal.

While we would never know exactly what was going on with Connie/Vivian during the last days of her life, Dallas probably came up with the best guess. "I think she must have realized that somebody was after her in Chicago, and when she found out about the real Connie's death, she decided that was her way out. She turned herself into Connie Sanborne and started a new life."

"But why was she so strange just before she died?" asked Dottie.

"I think Rundel's people found her through her father. All they had to do was wait until Vivian came to the post office to get her mail, and they could follow her home. It wouldn't take a whole lot of nosing around on this island to find out all they needed to know about Connie, or actually Vivian, and her new friends."

"Maybe she had given up," said Dottie. "Maybe she knew she had been found by whoever was looking for her, and was just tired of running. That last night at Moore's, she was so quiet, and then she went to listen to Pearl. Even Logan said all that crazy sex was a surprise. Maybe she was just saying good-bye."

I thought that was probably as close to the truth as we were likely to get.

Anne left for Miami on Sunday afternoon, and Logan, K dawg and I went fishing. It was an easy afternoon floating around Terra Ceia Bay, drinking beer, telling the same old stories, and catching a few fish. Logan told us more about his heart problems, and that he had not told anyone on the Key, because he wasn't sure he would get a new heart. He didn't want to be treated as if he were dying, so he kept it all to himself. During the year leading up to the transplant, a lot of the time when we all thought he was out of town on business, he was in Boston doing medical things. He thought the new heart would give him fifteen or twenty more years.

Logan left for somewhere on Monday morning, back to work. He said he had to make some money to pay his defense attorney. I told him that I didn't need the money, and that the pizza he gave me for a retainer was payment enough. I suspected I would never be able to buy another drink when he was in the bar. Logan was a good guy.

Elizabeth called me on Monday morning and asked if I could meet her at O'Sullivans for lunch. I accepted immediately. She had been an honorable and tough adversary, and I always respected that in a lawyer.

I was at the bar talking to Glenda when Elizabeth arrived. She was wearing shorts and a tank top, with her hair in a pony tail. I stood as she approached the bar, and she gave me a hug. "You're one hell of a lawyer, Matt Royal," she said.

"You too, counselor," I said.

"I'm glad it worked out for Logan, but how in the world did you get the evidence on the governor?"

We ordered lunch, and I told her the story. I had become friendly with Will Ledbetter, the probation officer, and his friend, Lieutenant Miles Leavitt, had overseen the investigation into Vivian's beating and the murder of her friend. Leavitt had moved on to the intelligence division of the Chicago Police Department, and when I told Will of my suspicions about all the ties from Cox and Rundel to Wentworth, he passed it on to Leavitt. The police had collected semen samples from the murder scene involving Vivian, but even with the advent of better science, they had nothing to compare it to.

Leavitt went into the computers and found the similar murders in Washington and Moline. When he compared the guest lists of the three hotels where the murders occurred, he found that Wentworth had been registered at all three on the night of the murders. It was just too much of a coincidence. We figured that the DNA from the crime scene would match Wentworth's, but there was no way we were going to get a sample from a sitting governor. That is why is was so important to put him on the stand, under oath. I was betting that at some point he would crack. I could publicly ask him for a DNA sample. No innocent man, especially one who wanted to be president, could refuse.

"That was a hell of a strategy," Elizabeth said.

"Yeah, but it could have all crumbled if you had objected to the questioning of the governor. I was betting you wouldn't."

"What made you think that?"

"You're an honorable person, Elizabeth. You want to put the bad guys away, but you care about the system. You don't want good guys going to jail, even if you can notch another win on your belt."

"Thanks, Matt. I'm quitting, though. I'm burned out."

"Take a vacation, Elizabeth. You're tired. We need good career prosecutors like you."

"Matt, I did some things in this case that I've never done before. I didn't review the medical records. I got caught out on a limb with the Medical Examiner. I just wasn't doing my job."

"I've been there, Elizabeth. Trial lawyers burn out. Usually, it just takes some time off to get your head back together. Think about it before you give up a career that makes a difference."

"I've been thinking about becoming a beach bum. It seems to work for you."

"Actually, I live on the bay."

"I hear you, Counselor, I hear you," she said. "Thanks for lunch. I'll let you know what I decide."

Summer moved on into the dog days of August. The key was hot, and the sea breezes did little to bring relief. We all looked forward to the afternoon thunderstorms, regular as sunrise, to give us relief from the heat that baked our island. Elizabeth Ferguson had taken a leave of absence from the State Attorney's office and gone to the north Georgia mountains to try her hand at writing a book on criminal law.

John Noblin had been arrested for fraud, and the insurance companies were planning to pay Anne the money that should have gone to her brother when his plane was stolen. Anne had rented Elizabeth's house and moved to Sarasota. She was working for a small law firm, making less money and enjoying it immensely. She was actually representing real people, handling their problems, and feeling like a real lawyer for the first time in her career. Our relationship was ongoing, but sporadic. The heat of the first days, stoked by the rigors of the trial, had cooled. We both knew that over time the physical side would play itself out, and we would end up friends.

Wentworth was going to be tried for murder in Chicago, and there were holds on him for D.C., Illinois and Florida. Cox was being prosecuted in Miami, with a trial set for the fall. Rundel had disappeared. Cox had told Miami-Dade Police that Rundel was the one who actually killed Vivian. He had followed her from Bradenton Beach marina to Anna Maria island. When she left Pearl's piano bar, Rundel had grabbed her in the parking lot, pulled her into his car and strangled her. He then took her to Logan's condo, while Cox and Logan drank on Bridge Street.

Afterwards, Cox had driven Vivian's car to her condo parking lot, parked it and left with Rundel.

Cox also told the police that Rundel had tampered with the propane line into Bud Dubose's house, and disabled the gas warning alarm. Rundel had killed Bud over the million dollar investment. He could not take the chance that Bud would go to the police.

There were bulletins out for Rundel all over the country. The cops figured it would be just a matter of time before they picked him up somewhere. I wasn't so sure. Rundel had apparently re-invented himself several times under different names, and I assumed he could do it again.

I was restless. I had tasted the adrenalin rush that trial lawyers thrive on, and it had not been bad. I thought about going back into practice, but then I remembered how tired I had been during the trial. I woke up some nights reliving the stress that had been my constant companion as I tried to save Logan's bacon. No, the practice of law was not for me.

Our lives on the key had reverted to normal. We fished, sunned, boated, drank, and whiled away the hours. Sometimes, we would remember Connie, and laugh about her. We never did get used to calling her Vivian, and no one ever mentioned that he or she felt betrayed by her subterfuge. If anything, Connie became a much admired memory, and, of course, the stories grew bigger and better, as they always do. Life was good on that lush island, surrounded by green water and peopled with my very best friends.

Chapter 31

On a bright August day, when the heat leeched the hydration out of my body, they came for me. I was fishing quietly, sipping a cold beer, watching the thunder heads build to the north over St. Pete Beach. It would soon be time to run south for home, and away from the lightening that always stalks ahead of the storms. The tide was low, and I could smell the mud flats near my fishing hole at the mouth of Tampa Bay; a melange of seaweed and shellfish and drying mud roasting in the sun. High overhead, a passenger jet was on final approach to Sarasota Bradenton airport, its turbines winding down as it glided toward the runway.

I thought about calling Logan to see if he wanted to have dinner with me at Moore's, but realized I had left my cell phone at home. Oh well, he'd probably be at Moore's anyway. Wednesday was the evening that the Longboat Key Literary Guild and Chowder Society met at Moore's bar for book talk, clam chowder and a bit of booze. It was a group of mostly elderly widows, put together by Dottie Johansen, and when they ran out of book talk, they gossiped about the island. When I had been away for a few days, I always made those Wednesday evening get-togethers, just to catch up on the island news.

I was watching, without much interest, a go-fast boat headed my way from the Gulf. It was coming straight for me, but there was plenty of sea room and I figured the pilot would veer off as he got closer. But he didn't. He was coming right at me at high speed, a bone in his teeth. I had left my engines on, idling softly on the flat water. As I watched the oncoming boat with rising trepidation, I saw a spit of fire leap from the side of the craft, and within a moment heard the crack of the rifle. I didn't know who they were, but I wasn't going to wait around to find out.

206

I jumped to the helm, and pushed the throttles all the way forward, heading north. My twin 150's would not outrun the big go-fast, but I had to get some sea room between us. I knew this water intimately, and I hoped whoever was driving my pursuer did not.

I headed for Passage Key, a small island that is a bird sanctuary, surrounded by very shallow water. I darted in close to the little spit of land, running full out. The go-fast boat slowed some as the sea floor rose to meet it. That gave me a couple of minutes. I rounded the end of Passage Key and headed across the open channel to Egmont Key, a much bigger island, with places to hide and a Coast Guard station on the north end. I thought I could not make it to the far end of the island before my pursuers overtook me.

The storm was moving fast now, headed for us. The air chilled slightly as it does when the storms push the air in front of them. I could see lightening in the clouds, bright orange bolts darting toward the surface. Thunder rolled over me, louder than my outboards. I didn't know if I was still being shot at, but I had hunkered down, making as small a target as I could.

I drove the boat in close to the island, between the beach and the large concrete formation that was once a gun emplacement, and was now about a hundred feet off the beach. The go-fast roared around the gun emplacement, planning to head me off as I came out of the small channel. I had counted on that. I turned sharply toward the beach, pulled back on the throttles, and ran straight for the shore, which was deserted on a Wednesday afternoon.

During the Spanish American war, the Army had built an outpost on the island, with large gun emplacements, buildings to house and feed the troops, and several miles of brick streets in the interior. The fort had been abandoned in the 1920's, and the subtropical flora began to cover the depredations of man. Egmont was now a state park, accessible only by boat. There were a few park rangers, all nearing retirement, who sporadically patrolled the island in all terrain vehicles. The non-native vegetation, Australian Pines, Mellaleuca and Brazilian Pepper trees, had been taking over the island for years. There was a move afoot among some of the more enlightened individuals in state government to rid the island of the interlopers and return it to its native condition. I knew the mile and a half long island well, and hoped I could hide out and work my way north to the Coast Guard station.

I cut the engines and jumped from the boat, as the go-fast made a wide arcing turn and headed back to where I had beached. I was running flat out, and was only aware that someone was shooting at me because of the sand kicked up by near misses. It only took seconds for me to disappear into the trees, but it seemed like forever.

I heard the go-fast idle down, and then voices over the muted sound of the engines. I could not tell how many there were, but I thought I had only seen three men in the boat. I found one of the brick roads, and headed north at a steady run. I knew I could keep up the pace until I reached the Coasties and safety. I was half-way to the Station when it happened.

Egmont Key is home to a multitude of gopher tortoises and assorted birds and other animals. The tortoises burrow into the ground, leaving gopher holes at the entrance to their homes. I found one of these, as I stepped off the brick road to avoid an Australian pine that had fallen directly in my lane of travel. I heard my ankle crack at the same time I felt the instantaneous pain that told me my running was finished for the day, if not forever.

I crawled into the brush beside the road, trying not to leave a trail that could be seen from the brick street. Soon, I heard voices, and three men came trotting down the road. One had a rifle carried at port arms, and each of the other two had what appeared to be nine millimeter semi-automatic pistols. One of the men, very fat, stopped not ten feet from me, leaning on the fallen tree, wheezing and motioning to his pals to keep going. I lay still, my face in the damp earth, scarcely breathing. I knew if they got to the Coast Guard station and didn't find me, they would start back along the road. I had no weapon and very few options. I probably could not even walk without help, and running was out of the question. I needed to get the fat guy's gun, somehow.

His back was to me, but I knew if I moved he'd wheel around with that nine pointed right at me. I couldn't stand without him hearing me. Movement toward him was out of the question. Maybe I could somehow lure him into the jungle like growth surrounding me. I had fought in jungles before, but I had always had an assault rifle to help. And other soldiers to back me up. Not now. I was alone, unarmed, and scared. I hadn't felt fear in a long time, but its bitter taste was no less acrid for the passage of so many years. I had to clear my mind, think, plan, and stay alive.

My ankle was throbbing, throwing welts of pain up my leg. It was either broken or badly sprained. I lay prone, with my arms in front of my body, as if reaching for the next handhold in the soft ground. There was nothing within reach that I could use as a weapon. The fat man's breathing was slowing, the audible wheezing less intense. I knew he would be moving on soon, and with him would go my best chance out of this mess.

Suddenly, the storm moving from the north was on us. The rain cascaded down like a jungle waterfall, loud and hard. Thunder boomed, close. The smell of ozone permeated the air. The fat man didn't move for a moment. I moved my good leg up under me, and bringing my arms back under my chest, began to push into a standing position. The pain in my right leg was exquisite. I stifled a moan, and as quietly and quickly as I could, stood with my weight on my left leg. I was now in full view, and dead, if the hunter turned his head. The noise of the storm covered the rustle of the underbrush as I stood. There was a palm tree branch lying atop a bush next to me, fallen from one of the trees that provided me some cover. It had a jagged end where it had broken from the tree during an earlier storm. I grabbed it by the end with the prickly fronds, cutting my hands. As I lifted the branch, the fat guy turned toward me, perhaps sensing danger.

A small tableau was, for a moment, imprinted on the wind; the fat man half-turned, I with the branch in front of me like a spear, the rain falling and a bolt of lightening, like a flash bulb, spearing the dark storm ravaged spot where two men were in a dance of death. I screamed, as the Army had taught me so long ago, supposedly disconcerting my enemy. At the same instant I took a step forward on my injured leg, and screamed again with the pain. My glands were working overtime, flooding my system with adrenalin, softening the pain. I thrust the branch in front of me, as the fat guy raised his pistol. The point caught him under the chin as he fired. A bullet tore at my left shoulder as blood spurted from the severed jugular of the fat man. My momentum took me forward, falling on top of the dying man, as he fell backward onto the red brick road. He gurgled something I didn't understand, and died.

My shoulder was burning. I reached around and found the exit wound. It was probably a clean shot that didn't do a lot of damage, but the shoulder was pouring blood. It was beginning to hurt more, as the adrenalin rush left me. My ankle would not hold my weight any longer. I knew that the sound of the shot, infinitely louder than the storm, would bring the fat man's friends and probably the Coast Guardsmen. I couldn't wait to find out who would get there first, and I was pretty sure the Coasties would not be armed.

I checked the nine millimeter. There was a full clip with a round in the spout. I was ready for business, but I didn't have the strength to pull the fat guy off the road. I sure didn't have the ability to get back to the boat before the hunters were onto me. I hobbled and hopped north toward the Coast Guard station. There was a bend in the road about a hundred feet ahead. I thought if I could get around that bend and into the brush beside the road, I'd see my pursuers before they were alerted by the body.

I was in agony. My shoulder was bleeding, and my left arm and hand were sticky with new blood. I didn't know if there was enough blood loss to take me out, and I wasn't sure how far I was going to get with my ankle. As I neared the curve, I heard the clop of shoe leather on the brick road. Someone was coming my way. I was exhausted, and wasn't going any further. The blood loss was taking its toll. I sat down in the road to await my fate, facing my enemy coming from the north, much as the Confederate soldier in the courthouse square in Bradenton.

There were two of them, huffing with exertion, coming my way at a fast clip. I raised my left knee and steadied the nine on it. They came into view, rounding the corner, skidding on the wet bricks as they saw me. The rifleman was raising his rifle, when I shot him through the heart. The other man dropped his nine, fell to his knees, raised his hands and sobbed. He knew he was dead. I had never killed a man who wasn't trying to kill me, and now was not the time to start.

"Lay down on your stomach," I shouted. "Use your foot and shove that pistol into the brush." He did as he was told, still sobbing and coughing and pleading, "Don't shoot."

I wasn't sure what to do now. I couldn't move far, and I surely couldn't walk this yahoo all the way to the Coast Guard station. It was still raining slightly, but the storm had passed on toward Anna Maria and Longboat.

Suddenly, I heard a rattling sound coming from the south. I turned in time to see a park ranger in an ATV slamming on his breaks as he saw us. "Holy shit!" he said, as I turned toward him, still pointing the pistol. He stopped right beside the dead fat guy with the palm branch still protruding from his throat. There was a lot of blood covering the bricks, and the ATV had made little tire tracks in it.

I dropped the pistol barrel and said, "Hold on, friend. I've got two dead here, and I'm hurt pretty bad. The guy on the ground was trying to kill me, and if I pass out, you and I are probably both dead. Call the Coasties and tell them to get here ASAP."

The Ranger lifted his radio to his mouth and said something I couldn't hear. "They're on the way," he said. "What the hell happened here?"

"Gotta save my strength. I'll tell you when the cavalry gets here." I was starting to fade. My gut wanted to throw out my lunch and my vision was blurring. "Ranger, take this pistol and keep both of us under guard until this is sorted out. That is the bad guy, but you can't take any chances." I gave the Ranger my pistol.

As I was passing into unconsciousness I heard the bad guy say, "Ranger, my name is Hale Rundel. I'm a businessman from Miami. That's the killer right there." I knew he was pointing at me.

Chapter 32

I slowly became aware of the beating of rotor blades. I was back in Viet Nam, riding a medevac from my last firefight. I had a bullet in my leg and another in my gut, but the medic had given me morphine, and I was floating on a soft cloud. Sweat was running into my eyes, and I lifted my hand to wipe it away. The hand wouldn't move.

Consciousness was returning, and I felt cold metal around both wrists. I opened my eyes and saw a young man in a Coast Guard flight suit bending over me with a stethoscope. "Lie still," he said, over the beat of the rotor. "We're on the way to Bay Front."

Bay Front Medical Center was the level I trauma center for this part of the Florida coast. I asked, "Not Saigon?"

"You're kidding, right?"

"Yeah. For a moment there, I thought I was on a medevac in Nam. What's going on?"

"We have you restrained until we can sort things out. The sheriff has your buddy."

"My buddy?"

"The other guy on Egmont."

I dozed off, gently rocked into slumber by the rhythm of the rotors.

When I awoke again, I was in a hospital room. Logan was standing beside my bed, looking down at me with a frown.

"Tell me it's not that bad," I said. "Do I need a lawyer?"

"Nah, but you'll need some crutches for awhile."

"Ankle busted?"

"All to hell, but the doc said you'd get full use of it back. Gonna take awhile."

212

I was aware that I was no longer restrained by handcuffs. "What happened?"

"The Coasties brought you here to Bay Front, and Bill Lester drove up to vouch for you. They operated on your ankle, sewed up your shoulder, and put you in this delightful room with me to watch over you."

"Where are the pretty nurses?"

"There ain't any. It was me or some ancient battle ax who thinks you're kinda cute."

"Geez. What about Rundel? Did you know he was on Egmont?"

"Yeah. Dead as a doornail."

"What?" I asked. "He was trying to con the ranger when I passed out."

"The only guy left alive was some moke Rundel picked up in Miami to steal a boat. Rundel had a bunch of palm fronds sticking out of his neck."

"I'll be damned."

"Yeah, the guy from Miami was telling the Coasties he was Rundel. Dumb ass didn't know there was a warrant out for Rundel. He tried to con the Ranger who found you, but he wasn't having any of that. He held you both at gunpoint until the Coasties got there. They put you on a stretcher on the back of the Ranger's ATV and took you to the beach so the chopper could pick you up."

"What happened to the guy from Miami?"

"There was a Marine Patrol boat nearby, and he came right over. He saw your boat and the go-fast, checked the registration, and found that the go-fast was stolen. Yours came back fine. They held the other guy for the sheriff and sent you here.

"I guess they weren't taking any chances, because you still had cuffs on when they got you here. They called Bill Lester after checking your driver's license, and Bill called me."

"What time is it?" I asked.

"Almost midnight."

"What day?"

"Wednesday. You've been out for about eight hours since the shooting."

"I missed the literary meeting." I said.

"That you did, but you've given the ladies enough to gossip about for weeks. They won't even miss you."

Epilogue

Two days later, Logan drove me home, across the Sunshine Skyway, Manatee Avenue and Longboat Pass bridges. Home to Longboat Key. Because my shoulder was still healing, I could not use crutches, and found myself plunked unceremoniously into a wheel chair. Logan wheeled me to the pool at my condo complex, and there I found a large group of friends, drinking, laughing, and holding a banner that said, "Welcome Home, Matt." The Key was coming back to life, moving on without Connie Sanborne, a little sadder for the experience, but still exuberant with the essential joy of life on a small island resting in the sun. Life was good.

Made in the USA
Coppell, TX
25 February 2020

16188605R00132